TERROR

FROM THE

CREVASSE

A NOVEL BY MICHAEL COLE

SEVERED PRESS
HOBART TASMANIA

TERROR FROM THE CREVASSE

Copyright © 2020 Michael Cole

WWW.SEVEREDPRESS.COM

ISBN: 978-1-922551-44-3

CHAPTER 1

Gentle swells wrinkled the lake as Todd Welling thrust the two oars into the water. His tackle box bumped against his seat as he rowed the twelve-foot aluminum boat out into the tranquil lake. Looking out into the water, he watched the rippling reflection of his night light off the lake's mirror-like surface. Watching the golden streaks against the seemingly black water, he gauged his distance from the lily pads.

This time of night, during the summer months, the fish tended to come in toward the shallows, while retreating to the deeper areas of the lake during the day. Then again, he had never tried this lake before. Todd would normally try his luck in the early morning hours, but his company retreat would mandate he attend seminars with his fellow Reiner Foods executives. Besides, the forecast called for torrential downpour all day tomorrow. Before that, it was supposed to be clear and sunny. Typical Michigan.

Todd was roughly forty feet from shore. Figuring he'd try casting along the pads, he anchored the boat. The metal barrel disappeared into the water, the rope going slack after only five feet.

"Damn," he said aloud to himself. When the resort owner told him the lake was shallow, he wasn't kidding. He had informed Todd of a few deep areas, but unless you were familiar with the lake, they'd be impossible to find in the dead of night. *Oh well. Let's give this a try.* He tied off the anchor and snatched his pole.

He opened his tackle box, rattling the contents as he grabbed a jitterbug lure. Listening to the prolonged call of a distant loon, he attached the lure to a swivel tied at the end of his line. He cast along the lily pads and began reeling it back in, stopping every few feet to allow his trophy to take the bait.

He felt his blood rush for a brief moment as he felt resistance from the lure. That excitement quickly dissipated, as the resistance was a dull pull rather than a struggle. *Weeds.* He groaned in frustration as he reeled back, bringing his *catch* into the boat. His fingers pricked against the hook as he pried the salad from his lure.

Todd cast into a different spot, only to have the same result. Two more casts followed, each one bringing in more vegetation. It was clear that this spot was no good for spinner bait, and even worse for crawler harnesses. He hauled in his anchor and adjusted the clamp-on light at the stern of his boat, pointing it toward the middle of the lake. The illumination was barely enough so he could see the decks along lining the opposite shoreline. Todd took his seat and gripped the oar handles, stroking the flat ends against the still water.

Todd kept his eye on the cabin lights as he rowed out. Being unfamiliar with this lake, he didn't want to get turned around in the dead of night. The interior lights were lit, as his fellow executives were enjoying a nightcap in the CEO's cabin. It would be a while before they would turn in for the night.

Looking over his shoulder, the light revealed greater detail in the opposite shore. He was halfway across the lake. Normally, this wouldn't be a typical spot for bass fishing, but then again, this lake was so shallow...

Todd moved for the anchor, tilting the boat to starboard. He let the line run over his hand as he lowered the weight, ready to catch it the moment it went slack. Only it didn't. The line went taut as the anchor touched down at the bottom of the lake.

Damn! Found that deep zone. Figuring he may as well try a couple of casts anyway, Todd snatched his pole back up. Drawing it back, he launched his lure seventy-five feet toward the shore. It sank for a moment, and he began reeling it in. There was no resistance outside of the natural weight of the jitterbug. A weed here and there, but nothing like the forest that was the previous spot.

Then suddenly, the line went tight, and the pole bent to nearly a full ninety degrees. Todd yanked back, fighting the intense tugging from the end of his line. That rush returned, this time to stay.

Todd stood to his feet as he fought the fish. The line pulled to the left, then to the right. He allowed the fish to wear itself out, reeling in each time it eased up. He leaned forward as the fish dove downward. The pole bent, its tip touching the water. Todd pulled back up and reeled it in. The light sparked a silvery reflection from the largemouth's scales as it came to the surface. It was at least sixteen inches. And still determined to fight.

As Todd moved to haul it in, it dove down again in a last desperate attempt to escape. Todd pulled back, redirecting the fish toward the boat. The line pulled against its jaw, bringing it upward...

...while it was still jetting to escape. Its flickering tail caused the bass to launch out of the water like a torpedo, right into Todd's torso. Caught by surprise, Todd staggered and fell backward over the seat. The fish flopped against the aluminum floor of the boat as Todd struggled to right himself. His back pressed against the stern, accidentally prying the clamp from its place. The boat interior suddenly went dark. At the same time, he heard a splash behind him.

"Shit!" Todd yelled. He whipped back, saw that the light had fallen over, then quickly reached over the transom toward the falling light. His fingers were just out of reach as the light sank. He ignored the largemouth's flopping as he watched the hundred-dollar piece of equipment illuminate the watery world beneath him. "Son-of-a-bitch," he said.

The light gradually faded, going possibly thirty feet down. Suddenly, it all went dark. Todd let out another frustrated moan, assuming the circuits got fried from the water. Then again, the light should have been water resistant. It didn't matter, because the damn thing was out of reach regardless.

Todd felt the fish flop against his foot, the fishing line still attached to its mouth. Prying the hook out without light was sure gonna be fun. He dug his cell phone out and switched it to flashlight mode. It shone a light onto the fish, which rested against his shoe, flapping its gills. The fish he was so happy to catch, he now felt a bitterness toward.

"Oh, you're DEFINITELY gonna be dinner for sure," he said. "It's what you get for losing my light. Little bastard."

****

Unknown to its owner, the lost light had continued its spiraling descent. Away it went, lighting the darkness within the lake's deepest secret. The crevasse was a mere twenty feet in length, and only four feet wide. The edges were a world of weeds, obscuring the anomaly from any view above. The throat of the tunnel was far larger, channeling down over two-hundred feet. It grew wider the deeper it went, the twisting beam of light illuminating the jagged granite exterior that separated the underground lake from the world above.

The golden beam of light turned a lime color as it mixed with the dark green glow of bioluminescent algae that coated the rocky walls. Like a star, it sparkled as it fell deeper into the cavern.

Crumbs of green residue floated about as the fish dug its jaw at the wall. The odor of ammonia within the thick coat of algae gave away the presence of the twelve-inch crabs burrowed in the rock. It wiggled its tail, generating enough force to dig its head further into the wall. Its closed jaw, encased with rigid scales, tug into the small crab tunnels like a drill.

After successfully widening the tunnels, the drill-head fish flapped its needle-nose-shaped jaws. It sensed the familiar taste of shell. Unfortunately, that shell was hollow, crunching easily into tiny flakes. The fish had only found the molted shell of the crab that had previously burrowed in this wall. The fish brushed its pectoral fins outward. Extending like folding fans, they pushed the fish away from the rocks.

Free from the granite tunnel it had burrowed into, its unblinking eyes scanned the underground world around it. They took in the various colors and shapes that defined the area. This area was rife with rock walls, as opposed to the vast openness of the rest of its world. There was an abundance of creatures that lived here, ranging from crabs to thirty-foot fish. Schools of shrimp, bright blue in color, swarmed between volcano-shaped vents that protruded from the seafloor. They fed on green algae around them, exposing the glowing blue fungus underneath.

An infant pike swam near, zigzagging near the school of shrimp. It chomped down on anything it could grasp. Then, it spotted the drill-head. Its need to feed dissipated, and it darted off into the vast world beyond a series of mountain-like rock formations. In maturity, it would've been the alpha predator of this world. But in youth, it was prey, as vulnerable to larger predators as a speck of calcium would be to the bottom-dwelling crabs.

The drill-head pressed forward, contemplating pursuit. It typically fed on crustaceans and bulkier, slower moving fish. It was capable of quick bursts of speed, but not long, drawn-out pursuits. It was a lazy feeder, and thus, it chose to remain here. There were always crabs to be found in the crevices and pores in the rock below, and even in the rock ceiling above.

Though, not here, for the most part, as the rock ceiling was formed differently than all other areas the fish ventured. It had a funneling shape, like the inside of the abandoned shell it recently crushed. Every day, there'd be a strange glow that pierced its world, a thin, golden radiance that could barely be seen. The drill-head had inspected the funnel before, detecting a narrow passage, too narrow for a creature its size to seamlessly pass through. Such an effort would certainly cause a few scales to be yanked from its flesh.

The fish felt vibration coming from the funnel. It was water distortion, caused by motion. Then, there was light. The fish thought that it was the golden radiance of daylight, only to realize that this light was nothing but a mere speck in comparison.

Though small, it was much brighter. Descending from above, it spiraled in circles, a motion not caused by fins, but by simple trajectory dictated by weight and water currents. The fish faced the light, propelling its ten-foot bulk toward the strange illumination. The object's natural spine swept the beam of light over its eyes, sparking a reactionary flinch from the creature.

Never had it seen anything so bright. The color, though much brighter, was similar to dim streams of sunlight that managed to break through the opening above. Other than that, such uniformities like night and day did not exist. The only light known to the fauna was the constant glow of algae, the blue glow from fungus that grew on the cavern floor, and the illuminations given off by other species. Often, lifeforms would use lights to signal for mates. The process to create life often resulted in death, as predators would pick up on these signals and home in on the unsuspecting seeker.

The fish studied the clamp. Beyond its freefall, it did not generate any distortion or odor. It did not appear to be living. However, its light was like a beacon, drawing the fish closer.

Other species of fish swam near, converging on the strange light like peasants around a Messiah figure. Each one was touched by the glow of its light. A panfish, five-feet in length, moved in to feed on it, only to be chased back by the drill-head. The fish darted back, circled around, then cautiously moved in again. The drill-head extended its jaws and lunged. If anything would feast on this thing, regardless of whether it was edible or not, it would be *it*. Once again, the panfish darted from reach. Other fish moved closer to the speck. Finally, the drill-head unleashed its fury. It zipped toward another small pike, then another drill-head, then finally lashed at all other fish in the gathering, all of which were smaller than itself. The peaceful assembly had quickly turned into a frenzy. Creatures zigzagged back and forth, fleeing the wrath of the ten-foot scavenger.

It snapped those needle-nose jaws at the panfish, which narrowly darted out of reach, and fled deep toward the seabed far below. The drill-head slowed into its natural leisurely pace. It was alone now. It took a minute to regain its energy before searching for the golden light. It pointed itself downward.

The object had nearly completed its descent, settling between two large mountain-shaped rock formations. Reflecting its light was a silvery body laying along the rocks. Scales. The drill-head moved closer. It saw fins. That panfish was making yet another attempt at stealing its prize.

This time, the drill-head would not stop until the perpetrator was dead. It was not about personal pride, nor acting on a grudge, as the fish had no such concept. It was simply survival of the fittest, and usually, the biggest fish in the area was considered the fittest.

It descended. It opened its jaws and zeroed in on the panfish's right pectoral. Yet, the enemy didn't move as it had before. It simply remained in place, jaw agape, unmoving except for a few twitches. It was as though the creature was lodged in place.

As with all the animal kingdom, the drill-head recognized signs of distress in other organisms. Not out of empathy, but as a means of detecting threats. And the panfish was in distress, its head and tail jerking as though it was clutched in the jaws of an immense predator.

Then came the tingling sensation of water displacement. From pores within the rock emerged wormlike appendages. Each of these arms were connected to a larger body, each one roughly the size of the panfish they seized. Though smaller, they had advantage in numbers, and a viciousness matched only by the thirty-foot alpha predators.

The drill-head immediately recognized the threat. They had taken over its former hunting grounds to the north, an area that was previously teeming with life. Now, it was a dark, fungus-ridden abyss, with thick slime secreted from pores in the creatures' mantles coating the rocks.

The fish jerked to the right, barely out of reach of those deadly tentacles. Immediately, it spotted slime coating the blue fungi, and bodies of several fish it recently chased now trapped in the clutches of twisting tentacles. Like an invading army, they had quietly crept into the area. There was motion all around the drill-head. Squids, using jet-propulsion, were flocking around it like birds.

The fish turned around, only to see the tentacles of another squid unveiling like a flower, ready to lash out and grab it. It turned again, only to nearly end up in the grasp of another creature doing the same.

There was nowhere to go but up.

The squids formed an enormous group, chasing their prey in unison, their movements as graceful as the tiny shrimp that fed on the algae.

Its energy was quickly waning. It could sense enemies closing in on all sides. As it entered the funnel above, the drill-head had a feeling of vulnerability. It had boxed itself in. Turning back would only result in it falling into the clutches of the flesh-eaters. Their jaws were like buzz-saws, designed to cut through the thickest armor scales.

Once again, there was nowhere to go but up—right through the crevasse.

The fish summoned all its remaining energy and blasted through the narrow passage like a missile. Scales went to war with the rock walls. It sensed pain, first from the ripping of scales, then the sting of water that touched its skin. Scales were not the only thing that broke. Its bulk, passing through the two-hundred feet of space at fifty-miles per hour, broke large segments of hollow rock from the narrowest areas.

In the span of a few rapid heartbeats, the fish emerged in the world above with an explosion of rock. And even then, it didn't stop. It continued straight on upward. After thirty feet, it came upon a new sensation, one completely unfamiliar to it. It was like the water had vanished, and for the first time, the fish felt the intense pull of gravity.

****

For the second time, Todd Welling fell backward, startled by the explosion of water. Not even a dozen yards from his boat, something breached. His frantic mind could only compare the sight to that of a humpback whale he saw on a trip to the North Atlantic.

And like the breaching whales, there was a body behind that curtain of water. Whatever it was, it was roughly the size of his boat. He dug for his phone, eager to shine his light on it. The bass he recently caught still flopped against the aluminum, the hooks having just been pried from its jaw. Its twisting motions were matched by the huge mass that collapsed back into the lake.

Todd gasped as a tsunami struck the boat. He ducked down. Water crested over the gunwale, soaking his clothes and equipment. The boat leaned, causing him to tense. His knuckles turned white, as did his face. The boat rocked back and forth until, finally, it settled.

The fisherman stood up and shone his light into the water. There were swells all around. It only took a few moments to track down the moving creature that nearly capsized him. His heart leapt into his throat. Memories of news reports from two years back flooded his mind. The whole state had heard of the incident in Rodney, Michigan, located in the lower peninsula. He was always skeptical of such things, even when photo and video evidence were made public. In the world of technology, even the cameras lied, almost more-so than politicians. Then came the talk about an underground lake where the beast had supposedly come from. Todd was no scientist, but he couldn't understand how such a thing could exist. It seemed far too unbelievable.

It only took a span of ten seconds to make him a believer. His light reflected the scales along its body. Its dorsal fin sliced the surface. Its body was like that of a crappie, only ten feet in length. Its head was different, and extremely angular and bony.

He started to remember the reports of the many people who were killed by the Carnobass in Rodney. For the first time in his life, he understood what it felt like to be on the bottom of the food chain. Terror struck. He couldn't stand the thought of dying like this. He looked around, again measuring his distance from the shorelines. He had no motor, and one of the oars had fallen off when the water struck the boat. In addition, he was still anchored to the deep zone.

Best to stay still. It was obvious he would never outrun the fish. Best to not move around and draw attention to himself. Perhaps it would not take interest in his boat, and simply swim away.

Before he could turn off the light, the fish stopped and rapidly did a one-eighty-degree turn. It was moving faster now, as though it was chasing something—or being chased.

Against his better judgement, Todd panned his light around. There were new swells, originating roughly twenty-feet out from the bow of his boat. Something else was moving along the surface. Whatever it was, it was going for the fish.

There was another splash. The fish did another sharp turn. Then another.

The light shook in Todd's grasp. There were several of these creatures. Like piranhas, they converged on the fish. They were EVERYWHERE! New splashes struck the boat. The fish tried to breach again, but the things were now on it. Leathery appendages wrapped around its bulk. Each of these arms was attached to a mantle, making Todd think of documentaries he had seen about Humboldt squids.

The fish wrestled in the grasp of two of the creatures, which latched themselves onto its body. It corkscrewed along the water's surface, snapping its jaws like scissors, but had no success in fighting them off. A series of tentacles found their way around its snout and pinned it shut like a crocodile's, while others found the tailfin.

The fish convulsed, but not in a way indicative of a struggle. Rather, it appeared involuntary, as though it was having a seizure. Its fins extended and fanned, as did its spinal dorsal fin.

Todd crouched low behind the gunwale, finally switching off his flashlight. The silver moonlight shining down from the atmosphere provided just enough illumination for him to get the gist of what was happening around him. The sounds of struggle stopped completely. He could see several swells rocking the boat as the things pulled the huge fish beneath the waves. One by one, the squid-creatures disappeared. At least, it looked like they did. Their skin was dark and it was night, making it hard to see them unless they were moving.

Several moments passed.

Todd's desire to reach the shore was hitting astronomical levels. He tried to wait, but couldn't compose himself any longer. He *needed* to get out of here. First, he needed to cut the rope anchoring him down. Slowly, he reached for the cleat where the rope was tied. He unfolded a pocketknife and gently ran the serrated edge over the yellow rope, being careful not to generate too many vibrations. Meanwhile, he watched the silvery reflection on the water. It was smooth. Perhaps those things returned through wherever they came from.

Where did they come from? Was there a crevice beneath this lake? Todd didn't know, nor was he eager to find out. Leave that to the scientists to figure out.

His knife worked against the rope. Strands frayed with each slicing motion until, finally, it fell away. Todd watched the water again. Nothing. Gently, being careful not to rock the boat, he moved into the center seat. He pulled the oar from its lock. The plan was to use it like a canoe paddle and steer himself to the nearest dock.

Its edge never got to touch the water before Todd heard a drumming sound. He looked down, seeing his fish spending its last moments of life attempting to flop into the water. Each thump generated a loud, metallic echo that traveled deep into the water below.

"No! No! No! No! No!" he muttered. He fell on his knees and tried to scoop up the fish, his frantic attempts succeeding only in creating new vibrations.

The water split apart in thick waves. Todd stood up on his knees and shrieked, gazing at the tentacles that uncoiled in front of him. They extended outward, exposing the creature's slimy mouth. Instead of a beak, similar to the Humboldts and giant squids of the ocean, this narrow mouth resembled a Venus fly trap, except lined with many rows of teeth. The jaws extended, making way for a long barb to protrude between them. It was like the proboscis of a mosquito, spraying yellow fluid from the tip.

There was no time to react. As soon as he saw the beast, it lunged at him. Its tentacles stretched, seized him by the arms, legs, torso, and neck. All at once, they pulled him toward the mouth, their efforts matching the strength of three bodybuilders. The force of the motion submerged the bow, allowing water to invade the vessel.

The proboscis pierced his shoulder. Todd tried to scream, but couldn't. It was as if all the air had been sucked out of him. His body twitched. He was alive, yet, not in control of his body. He could feel the slimy tentacles covering his face, followed by the sensation of lake water. Then, he blacked out.

As he disappeared beneath the waves, the boat was half submerged. The water quickly filled the center and rear compartments, and within moments, all evidence of Todd Welling's existence vanished beneath the waves.

CHAPTER 2

At first, Andy Cornett thought he had dreamt the strange battering sound that intruded his senses. Fifty-one years old and plagued with arthritis in his hips, he leaned out of bed with a groan. He grunted as a joint popped. Even only after being in bed for seventy-minutes, he was stiff as glass, and often felt as fragile. It seemed his body demanded he be in constant motion, or else it would descend into this state of taut joints. It sometimes felt as though his muscles were getting weaker, yet his bones were heavier.

He activated his reading light on the nightstand, then remained seated up in bed, glaring at his own shadow pasted against the wall. For the next moment, he listened. Maybe it was nothing after all. Just his imagination playing tricks on him. It had done so before. Then again, the very first time, it turned out to be real.

Those bastard college kids.

It was three years ago when he awoke to a similar noise. His truck was in the shop at the time and a friend from work was kind enough to drive him home for the night. Apparently, at two in the morning, a small gang of twenty-year-olds must have thought he was out of town for the night. He awoke to the sound of a hammer crashing against a padlock.

Shotgun in hand, he stepped outside to greet the bastards who believed they could help themselves to his wine cellar. All it took was the cocking sound of the pump action to scare them off. Andy lost nothing that night, except a padlock, and a little peace of mind.

He remained seated, his mind stuck in that annoying realm of indecisiveness. On the one hand, he wanted to lay back down and go back to sleep. On the other hand, he couldn't take his mind off the possibility that someone was trying to get into his wine cellar again. If only that sound would appear again, then at least he would know.

Finally, he did hear something, but not what he expected. It sounded almost like a tremendous splash down in the lake. It was summer, thus it wasn't uncommon for youngsters to screw around at night. But never *that* loud. Whoever made that splash had to be morbidly obese at best. That, or really close.

Andy pushed himself off of the bed and stepped into the living room, which faced the lake. He turned on the outside light and peered out. His house was right on the water, his front porch being a privately owned pier with a picnic table and four chairs. To the left was his boat garage, which stored his MasterCraft. He couldn't see the overhead doors from the windows, and the only reason he looked was because of the swells in the water right in front of them. There was no wind driving them and he didn't hear any boat motors on the lake. This late at night, with most people asleep, any boating activity would stick out like a sore thumb. However, there was nothing. No swimming, no fishing, nothing. Not even the orange glow of bonfires on any of the shore areas.

He checked his watch. It was five minutes after one. At this point, he figured it was nothing. Then again, he was up now. Might as well check.

Andy tied the drawstring on his pajama pants, which hung loose. Last thing he needed was for them to sag down below his buttocks while confronting a potential burglar. His white shirt was old and full of holes, but it would do. He debated taking his shotgun out with him. He was still groggy from barely over an hour's sleep, and hated the idea of handling a dangerous weapon with compromised senses. At least, in the initial incident three years prior, he had gone to bed early and gotten over four hours of sleep, making him more alert.

Eh, what the hell?

He pulled his shotgun from his bedroom closet, loaded eight shells, then stepped out the front door. He walked from the driveway over to the cellar, which was located adjacent to the garage. The padlock was untouched, the double doors showing no signs of damage. Being overprotective of his precious goods, Andy removed the padlock with his key, then shone his flashlight inside. Resting in place was his vast assortments of wine and whiskey, much of which he made himself. It was a great side business that brought in a decent supplementary income. Plus, it served as a hobby. Nothing better than a hobby that brought in cash, under the table or not.

A *thump* made him jump back. He shone his light around him, then heard it again, along with a splash. It was coming from the front of the house. He closed the cellar door and hurried around to the right. He climbed a tiny flight of stairs and was up on the pier. The water was lapping at the support beams. Andy pointed his light at the shoreline several feet to the right for comparison. There, the water was still. These swells were specific to this spot, meaning something was pushing them along.

Something splashed ten yards out. Probably just a fish. Andy didn't bother looking. At least, not the first time. There was another splash. Then another. He pointed his light.

It was only in his light for a brief moment. It was no bluegill or bass. In fact, he would have described it as an eel, raising its head out to inspect the space above water. It was leathery and had a dark color, maybe dark green. As soon as the light touched, it retreated.

Then came the thudding sound at the overhead doors on the waterline. Andy turned to look. The doors were shaking ever so slightly. There were more laps in the water, surrounding a shape that was pressed against the garage door. Andy stared, trying to figure out what he was looking at. It resembled the abdomen of a disgusting grass spider, except five feet long, with paper-thin fins protruding from the rear and sides.

Next, he saw movement from something much smaller and thinner. Protruding from its front were worms, the tips of which slithered along the doorway like snakes. Not worms. Tentacles, like those of an octopus. Now, Andy was again trying to determine if he was hallucinating or had drank the previous night. Common sense eliminated that possibility. It would take way more than two glasses of wine to make him see things like this.

More and more slithering objects latched themselves to the garage door. It was then that Andy realized there was a second creature. Like its brethren, it was attempting to lift the door. A third approached from behind them. The door mechanics groaned as the door was lifted upward.

Now, Andy was fully alert. He started to back up, shotgun tucked under his arm as he fumbled for his phone.

It was inside. He turned and grabbed the doorknob. It was locked. He had remembered to grab the cellar key but not the housekey. Priorities.

Metal screeched. The doors were lifting.

Andy started making his way to the steps at the edge of the pier, which led down to the side yard. By the time he cleared the picnic table, he noticed more movement in the water. There were more of these bodies. Five. Seven. Ten. Twelve. TWENTY! And counting, all converging on his garage.

He noticed the tentacles were trailing behind each body. They were moving *backwards*, jet propelled by water pumped through their mantles. They were literally squids in a freshwater lake, and for some reason, they wanted his garage.

Suddenly, he was longing for the simplicity of fending off college kids from his winery. He pumped his shotgun, then made his way to the steps. He only cleared the first two when his eyes caught the sight of lapping water on the shoreline. The water there was unmoving minutes ago. A slight adjustment of his flashlight illuminated the sight of two of the things crawling out of the water. Without the obscurity of the lake, Andy had a more direct view of their physiology. Like squids, they had a mantle, but the heads were different than what he had seen in books and on television. The head was almost a completely separate section of body, much like that of a spider. The tentacles were mostly attached to the head, the 'joints' located on the underside.

The image of a spider was prominent in his mind when the legs swung to the side and coiled into upside-down U-shapes. The beasts lifted themselves onto their legs, and like arachnids, started scurrying up onto the property. Right towards the stairway.

Now shrieking in terror, Andy backed up onto the pier. He pointed his shotgun and squeezed the trigger. In his grogginess, he had forgotten to pump it first. Until he did, he might as well have been carrying an expensive piece of pipe. He pumped the weapon, pointed it, then felt a wall of slimy black water encompass him. There was the tightness of leathery arms with no bony structure, curling around his elbows and waist. Only then did he realize the tips of those appendages contained hook-like claws that raked his clothing and skin.

The squid that ambushed him from the edge of the pier pulled him closer to that arachnoid head. There were no fangs—only a mouth with buzz-saw teeth. Between those teeth came a rigid spear. Andy shrieked again, then convulsed as the tip of that spear punctured his ribcage. It barely got further than an inch, which was all the creature needed to do its work.

His muscles contracted and his mouth foamed. The shotgun fell from his grasp. His mind became a haze of images. His body was no longer his own. He couldn't move. He couldn't even really think. He could only feel.

What he felt was tightness and a slimy sensation over his skin. The images continued to come and go. He then smelled metal and grease, then heard clattering sounds. Tools falling over. Fuel drums being moved aside. The walls were being cleared of the various belongings.

He was in his own shed.

There was the sensation of standing upright, even though he was still in water. That slimy sensation intensified. Then, all he felt were vibrations. That slimy substance hardened into a crystalline resin.

There he was, a prisoner in his own home, embalmed against the hull of his own boat, alongside a stranger he didn't even know was there.

CHAPTER 3

Golden sunrays penetrated the windshield and assaulted Gregory Goodman's eyes as he drove east on Circle Drive. As usual, the weather forecasters were wrong. They had called for torrential rain. As far as Gregory Goodman was aware, rainstorms didn't come with sunny skies. He wasn't complaining.

"At least something's going right this morning," he said to himself. He lowered the visor. Go figure, the sun was half-an-inch below its reach. He propped himself up slightly, positioning himself into the shade so he could see where he was driving. He spotted the blue street mahogany sign reading *Good Lake Resort.*

He steered his truck onto his driveway. Over a dozen vehicles were parked in marked spaces on the right side lined from a thin tree line near the entrance to a hill facing the lake.

On the left side was his private driveway, located behind his garage. His house was located at the edge of the hill, overlooking his eight cabin properties which lined the shore. It was a week where he was fully booked, something he rarely had. Luckily, these people either didn't read the *Yelp* reviews, or just didn't care. He didn't ask. However, he needed to work fast, or otherwise suffer the wrath of new bad reviews, which would be genuine ones this time. He stepped out of his pickup truck and carried his loot from the hardware store back to his garage.

There was much to do. First, he had to make sure to fix the plumbing that the occupants of Cabin Three complained about. Then he had to be sure to retrieve the key from Cabin Two and have it cleaned out by three-o'clock, when the new tenants were expected to arrive.

He hadn't even had his coffee yet. It was nine-o'clock now. He could spare a minute to get a mug going.

Julian tossed his tools and pipes in the garage and hurried to his house. He filled the Keurig with water and started it up. Simultaneous to the push of the button, his phone buzzed, as though activated by the electronic action. He looked at the number on the screen. *Consumer's Energy.* Of course it was.

Begrudgingly, he answered the call.

"Yeah?"

"Hello, this is Tabitha from Consumer's Energy. Am I speaking to Craig Goodman?"

"It's Greg."

"My apologies. I am calling to inform you of three overdue payments for your property on Archer Road. The property titled, uh..." He heard the flipping of papers, *"Butternut Lake Resorts."*

Greg took a breath. *Don't sound irritated...don't sound irritated. She just works there. Not her fault...*

"Looks like you have a total of four-thousand-two-twenty-one outstanding."

"Wait, what?!" His voice was like an erupting volcano.

"That's uh," Tabitha was sounding nervous, *"that's what your file indicates."*

"Your 'file' should indicate that I vacated that property two months back," Greg said. "I don't own it anymore."

"It does, sir, but these payments are for March, April, and May."

"March, April, and..." Greg gnawed on his lip as he processed the information. That crook Darryl Drake. He sold that guy the property for quarters on the dollar. The only reason he went with that offer was because the guy stated he would take on the missed payments.

Handshake deals. Greg Goodman of all people should've seen the writing on the wall. He had intervened in disputes resulting from such catastrophes. But desperation often led to poor judgement. He heard somebody once say, 'don't make decisions when you're drunk or emotional, because you're bound to make the wrong ones.' And now, Greg was feeling that sentiment to a tee. Drake had no legal obligation. Promises meant nothing if they weren't on a contract. Fact was, he was lied to straight in his face. The worst part was he should've seen it coming a mile off. That's where the desperation came in. That property was an open wound, bleeding his financials while not bringing in new blood. His 'reputation' had cost him that high-profile property that, two-years ago, brought in over a hundred grand in revenue.

"Alright, uh, I'll get to it as soon as I can," he replied.

"Failure to do so will generate interest in future bills."

"Yeah? Go ahead. Double the rate for that place," he said.

"I'm referring to your current properties on file."

Greg swallowed.

"I'll get to it as soon as I can," he said again. He saw the Keurig complete filling up his coffee mug. Fed up with the caller, he hung up and went for the mug—the one truly good thing going for him today. A small spoonful of sugar, then one of creamer, made the coffee light brown. Perfect.

He raised it to his lips, started to tilt, then felt the warmth of it just millimeters away from where it needed to be...

The doorbell rang.

Greg's jaw tightened. Probably that lady in Cabin Three, pestering him about the plumbing. *Lady, I literally just got back.*

He set the coffee cup down and stepped through the living room. Through the screen door was not the Cabin Three occupant, but the skinny eighteen-year old of the folks in Cabin One.

Greg forced a smile. *Gotta be friendly.*

"Hi."

"Hey," the kid said, his eyes droopy, his demeanor of someone who'd rather be anywhere else but here. "Uh, we have ants in the kitchen."

Greg shrugged. "Okay... that occasionally happens. We are on a lake in a rural area..."

"No, I mean they're everywhere. Mainly under the sink, and all over the garbage can. Some of them are carrying these little white things. I don't know if that means anything..."

Greg swallowed again.

White things—larva?! Oh, for CRYING OUT LOUD!

He managed to subdue the words, but not the expression in his eyes. Out of context, it looked as though he was about to go postal on the kid—a misrepresentation that was evident in his suddenly alert appearance. The kid took a step back, his eyes no longer droopy. Instead, they were analyzing the stability of the five-ten, hundred-eighty-three pound figure on the other side of the door. The greying goatee and mustache, which normally added charm to his appearance, now looked like something worn on a mob boss.

"Hang tight a sec, kid," Greg said. He hurried back into the utility room, then returned with a spray-bottle. "Spray the worst spots with this. I'll be over as soon as I can to get a look at the problem."

The kid took the spray-bottle, then shook it a bit. It was only a fourth of the way full, if that. He glared at Greg with questioning eyes.

"It's all I have on hand. I'll be over there as soon as I can," he said.

"Alright."

Greg felt that there was a question-mark at the end of that word, the way the kid said it. He started down the hill to Cabin One. Greg remained quiet, listening to the complaints from his parents as they battled the invasion inside, their curse words muffled by distance.

"This is one of those days," Greg said to himself. 'Domino days,' he referred to them as. They were days when the shit hit the fan and only got worse as they went along.

He returned to the kitchen, where his coffee was waiting to serve its purpose. He lifted it to his mouth, ready to down it.

Crash!

Greg jolted from the sound of something heavy crashing to the ground just outside the house. There were sounds of arguments, as well as the thumping of smaller items falling over.

"Now what?"

He put the mug down and hurried outside. At the bottom of the hill was the storage rack, where the kayaks rested on mounts. At least, they used to. They were in the sand now, surrounded by two men and women—the occupants of Cabin Four. They were bickering with each other on how to properly lift them up, with one of the women retorting that it was heavier than she expected. The other woman was seated on the ground, cursing up a storm, while on the brink of tears. She was holding her bruised foot which broke the fall for one of the kayaks.

"Everything alright down there?" Greg called. All four of them looked up at him.

"Yeah…uh, well, maybe no. We might've cracked one of your boats here…"

Greg's jaw tightened, suppressing a barbarian scream. Again, he faked a smile.

"I'll take a look at it. Nobody's hurt, right?"

"Nothing she won't recover from," one of the guys said.

Good enough for me. Greg turned and started for the door. If he could just get to his coffee before the next domino tipped over…

"Oh God! Oh my GOD!!!"

Greg spun at the scream of the hysterical woman running out of Cabin One. She was clawing at her hair, then her clothes. For a moment, it looked as though she was about to strip down in front of everybody.

Her husband trotted out behind her. His expression was one of amusement as he watched his wife go nuts over the ant infestation.

"For godsake! It's so gross!" she complained.

"What? The Queen? She's just lying there, big and fat! She's not gonna bite you!" the husband teased.

"Ugh!" the wife groaned. Her hair was like that of a wild mustang. The only thing more disorderly was her demeanor.

Greg realized it was a matter of time before her rage was directed at him. Interaction was inevitable. Best to speak first and at least acknowledge the issue.

"Give me just a sec, I'll be right down to take a look at it," he called down.

"I can't believe you keep these cabins in this condition!" the wife shouted at him.

"It's…" Greg stopped himself from retaliating. Yes, it was a lake property. These things occasionally happened. But customers weren't paying for excuses, and right now, he could not afford genuine bad reviews on top of the fake ones. "Bear with me. I'll be down there in just a minute. I just need to…"

"Excuse me?!"

Greg turned around and saw a truck had pulled up on the main lot. A man and a woman, both in their forties, approached.

"Uh, hi! Can I help you?"

"Good morning," the woman said. She took a second to stretch her back and arms, then to get the kinks out of her knees. By the looks of it, they had been riding in their truck for hours. Greg glanced past them at the vehicle, only to realize the bed was packed with belongings. "Cathy and Tim Perkins. We have a reservation for Cabin Two."

This can't be happening.

"Oh, hi! Good to meet you," Greg lied. "Um…" He glanced between them and the chaos taking place at the bottom of the hill. "You're early."

"Beg your pardon?" the man named Tim said.

"When you made the reservation, it was stated that check-in was at three p.m. I'm still waiting on the current occupants to vacate, and I have to clean and get the cabin ready."

Tim scratched his head. He thought back to March when he made the reservation by phone. His face soured as the memory returned to him.

"Oh, damn it."

Cathy gave Tim an annoyed look. "Nice one, genius."

"Hey! It's not my fault!" he defended himself.

"Yeah? We've got six hours to kill. What the hell are we gonna do for six hours? Spend it at the grocery store?" Greg felt like that question was directed at him as much as it was at Tim.

"There's golfing, trails to hike on, there's canoe rentals on the Cook River…"

"Where's that?" Cathy said.

"About forty-five minutes north."

"Ugh!"

It was obvious Cathy had no desire to be back on the road, and by the looks of it, she was not a golfer. Greg had to think fast. Yeah, it was their own fault for coming early, but as a businessman, he had to find some way to appease them before they could settle. If it wasn't for all the other nonsense going on, he could have their cabin cleaned up within an hour and have it ready for them early. But now he had pest and plumbing issues to deal with. The plumbing should be quick as long as nothing else came up. The ant situation, however, was undetermined.

Think! Think! Think!

He glanced up at their truck. There were at least three fishing poles protruding from the bed.

"Here's a solution! You see the dock for Cabin Two?" He pointed down the hill to the left, first at their cabin, then at the dock extending into the water in front of it. Tied to the posts was a twelve-foot aluminum boat assigned to that cabin. "If you guys enjoy fishing, this would be the ideal time to do it. I sell bait in my shop. Nightcrawlers, mainly, and a few spinners. I saw a neighbor out on the lake this time yesterday morning. He caught a thirty-six-inch pike!"

There was enthusiasm in the couple's eyes. They looked at each other, the wife shrugging.

"We really appreciate that," she said.

"Not a problem. Once I've got your cabin squared away, we can do the payment when you come back in."

"Sounds great," Tim said. They both went back to the truck and retrieved their fishing poles and tackle boxes. They came back, wearing ballcaps and life vests. "How much for the bait?"

"Three bucks a dozen," Greg replied.

"We'll take four," Tim replied. He pulled out some cash, then handed it over to Greg.

"Be right back." Greg hurried into his garage and went for the refrigerator in the back left corner, located at the end of a long wooden workbench. Upon opening it, he immediately felt warm air instead of cool air. "What the—" He pulled the machine back and checked the plug. It was in properly, but the fridge was hot. He quickly unplugged it and checked the back. He checked the freezer portion and saw no ice buildup. He plugged it back in. No motor sound. "Son of a prick!"

"Everything okay?"

The Perkins were approaching.

"Y-yep! Just give me a sec!" Greg grabbed the nearest tub of nightcrawlers and opened the lid. They didn't look great, but they would do. Only God knew how long that fridge was running warm. He grabbed the next tub. The worms in there were dead. As well as those in the next. And the next.

This was a domino day to define them all. Usually, it was a series of five or six mishaps that took place over the course of the day. Not in a fifteen-minute period!

The next tub seemed okay. Two were left. Greg said a silent prayer and checked them. They were sickly looking, soggy in appearance, but BARELY alive enough to serve their purpose. He stood up and bumped the fridge with his boot, punishing it for the crime of being broken.

He stepped outside, handed the worms to his customers, then walked them down to the dock. So far, they didn't check the tubs.

"Where's the best place to go?" Tim asked. Greg led them to the edge of the dock and looked out at the lake. Most people described the lake as peanut-shaped, and while Greg could see that comparison, he always thought of it more as the number eight, as the lake was comprised of two main oval bodies connected by a very narrow passage in the center. Originally, due to its segmented layout, the community wanted to call it Twin Lake. Problem with that was there were several 'Twin Lakes' already in existence in Michigan. Thus, the community settled on the stupid Peanut comparison. The east segment was only slightly smaller than the west, though equally as deep.

"It's a pretty shallow lake, really," Greg explained. "Really, you can try anywhere and you should find some pretty decent luck. There is a deep drop off somewhere in the middle of this section of the lake. Goes down about thirty feet, like a gorge. But everywhere else is seriously no more than twelve feet for the most part."

Tim and Cathy looked at the calm water. A gentle breeze passed over it, causing a few ripples to lap their way. There were eight properties on the other end of the lake. It was a small lake, though not the smallest they'd ever seen—roughly a six-hundred-and-fifty yards wide. But it was calm and quiet, which was exactly what they were looking for in a getaway.

"How busy are the residents on this lake?" Tim asked.

"Eh," Greg shrugged. "It might get a little busy today. We were supposed to get thunderstorms, but as you can see," he pointed up at the sunny sky, "that didn't happen. Plus, it's summer…and Saturday, so some of the homeowners might take advantage of the day. But overall, it doesn't get too crazy. People like to kayak, fish, hang out on pontoon boats. It's not a good lake for speedboating, so you won't have to worry about stuff like that."

"Sure about that?" Tim asked. He pointed at the dock labeled "Resort Owner's", which held an eighteen foot pontoon boat on one side and a sixteen-foot speedboat on the other.

"Oh, that," Greg said. He shrugged. "I used to have another property on a much bigger lake. Had to relocate the boat." Not wanting to invite questions as to why he lost that property, he pointed to the U-shaped bend at the west shoreline of the lake. There was one property there with a dock that extended fifteen feet out. "See the end of that dock there? Cast a line about thirty feet off of that. I saw someone pull an eighteen-inch bass the other day."

"Sounds good to me," Cathy said. She was already lowering herself into the boat. Tim followed her in and untied the mooring.

"Alright, sir. Thanks a bunch. See you later on."

"Not a problem. I'll try to get your cabin squared away as soon as I can, if I can get past all the other issues plaguing me right now."

"Excuse me?!"

Greg looked over his shoulder and saw Mrs. Brown from Cabin One, glaring at him and impatiently throwing her hands up into the air. He turned his gaze back to the Perkins.

"Case and point," he said under his breath. They smiled and started rowing out. Greg gave the lake a quick glance, absorbed the calming effect of its tranquility, then turned to meet the customer.

"There's ants EVERYWHERE!" Mrs. Brown exclaimed. The husband stepped out of the cabin, worn down from listening to her nonstop complaining.

"Oh, honey, he had other customers to tend to," he said. She shot him a glare.

Their eighteen-year old son stepped out with the spray bottle.

"It ran empty," he said.

Greg sighed, then stepped in and made a right turn into the kitchen. The sink cabinets were open, revealing a world of black specks moving about.

"Hoooly shit," Greg muttered. "Yeah, they are trying to form a nest."

"That's disgusting!" Mrs. Brown complained.

"I'll get on it asap," Greg assured. "I just need to make a quick run to the store."

"Weren't you just there?"

"Not for bug bombs and sprays," Greg said. "Bear with me, I'll get right on it." He didn't wait for a response. He started back up the concrete steps leading up the hill between Cabins Two and Three.

"You've got to be kidding me!" a woman shouted from inside Three.

"I had to go!" a man replied defensively.

"You couldn't have waited?!"

Greg didn't like what he was overhearing. Cabin Three—the one with the plumbing issues.

"Oh no. Oh, God, please," he muttered. He circled back and went around the front. A three-hundred pound man of forty stepped onto the front porch, then smiled nervously at Greg.

"Oh! Hi, Mr. Goodman!" Mr. Kendrick said.

There was the sound of a flush, then a disgusted groan from the wife. She stomped outside to berate her husband.

"Jesus, Don! It's so disgusting. Oh, the smell!" Mrs. Kendrick stopped when she saw Greg. It only took a few seconds for the odor to follow her out like a rolling fog.

Greg closed his eyes. There was no faking a smile this time.

Mr. Kendrick nervously ran a hand over his balding head, then smiled.

"Thought I'd test it…"

"Oh, God! There's one on my leg!" Mrs. Brown shrieked from Cabin One.

"Oh, relax. He's about to take care of the issue right now," they heard Mr. Brown say.

"I want new sheets! I want new mattresses! I'm not eating ANYTHING in there!" Mrs. Brown ranted.

"You're gonna take care of the plumbing first, right? Isn't it an issue of first come first serve?" Mr. Kendrick said.

"I'll…" …*Kill you*… "take care of it," Greg said.

"My bad, Mister. Shouldn't have eaten those bean burritos last night. Whew!"

SWEET MARY!

Greg felt beads of sweat taking form. His hands were quivering. He wanted to run away to some far-off land and never return. Too bad landing a job anywhere would not come easy, unless he was lucky to find an employer who didn't bother checking work history.

He was moments from exploding. He needed one good thing at the moment. ONE! And that good thing was the coffee he had waiting for him in the house. He hustled up the cement steps and made his way into the house.

There it was, right there on the counter. He reached, felt the ceramic handle of the mug.

"Hey! Excuse me?! Greg?"

He stared at his pale reflection in the window, then turned his gaze to the right. Joe Hall, the leader of the company retreat that occupied Cabins Five through Eight, was walking up to his house. Greg reminded himself to be nice. After all, this company, Reiner Foods Industry, added fifty bucks per cabin on their own accord to accommodate the short notice. Considering those four cabins were larger, therefore costing an extra hundred bucks a week each, Greg didn't mind showing a little extra gratitude. From what he gathered, the company had planned a retreat at a resort on Lake Huron, but pulled out at the last moment after a reported bed bug outbreak at that location. With all other resorts fully booked for the summer, Joe Hall suggested a quieter, more casual location for their retreat. And Greg Goodman's *Good Lake Resort* had reservations waiting to be filled.

Joe Hall wore jeans and a black t-shirt, as opposed to the suit and tie he arrived in. He was somewhere in his upper thirties, wore glasses, and had a polite demeanor.

Greg put the mug down and stepped outside to greet him.

"Mr. Hall. What can I do for you? Everything okay with the cabins?" *Please say yes.*

"Oh, yeah, the cabins are fine," Joe replied.

Oh, thank God. SOME good news for a change.

"It's just…I hope this doesn't sound weird, but I was wondering if you might have seen one of our associates," Joe said. "Todd Welling. Thirty-five years old fella, dark hair, wears white tennis shoes."

"He's the one who asked a hundred questions about the fishing, wasn't he?" Greg said.

"Yep! That's the fella!" Joe said with a chuckle.

"Unfortunately, I haven't seen him. Is he usually the type to disappear on you guys?"

"Not deliberately, though I can see him losing track of time if he's having too much fun fishing. But we have a seminar in forty-minutes, and he's nowhere to be seen."

Greg stepped to the edge of the hill then looked to the shoreline to the right of his personal dock. "Which cabin was he in?"

"Seven," Joe replied.

"The boat's not there. He's probably out on the lake." Greg glanced out into the lake. They had a fairly clear view of the west segment. "I don't see him. He might be out over on the east segment. I can't really see over that way from here."

"Odd. He went out last night. Nobody saw him come in, but then again, he deliberately went out late. Knowing him, he had some good luck and decided to head back out before our seminar."

"He's an early bird?"

Joe nodded. "We went on a trip last year, and we really had to tug his arm to keep with the schedule, which is laid back to begin with." He sighed. "I'll probably have to take a couple of the guys and go looking for him. He's dead meat when we find him."

Greg chuckled.

"You want to borrow an outboard motor? That way, you won't have to row and work up a sweat?"

Joe smiled. "Sir, I would greatly appreciate it." Greg stepped back into the garage, found the motor, made sure it was filled with gas, then gave it to Joe. "You need me to install it for you?"

"No, our training director, Ernie, is all about this kind of stuff. He can do it," Joe answered. Greg was happy to hear that, because he already had a hundred things to do at the moment.

"Alright. I have to run back into town…again."

As though on cue, Mrs. Brown shouted from the lakeshore. "There's one in my shoe!"

"Oh, babe, that's a fly," Mr. Brown said.

"Case and point," Greg said to Joe. "Gotta go to the hardware store and get my nuclear warhead to destroy the bug invasion. I shouldn't be long though. If you guys need anything from me, don't hesitate to knock on my door."

"Thank you, Greg," Joe said. He started down the hill and made a right for Cabin Eight, where he resided.

Greg scanned the lake with his eyes again. It was odd that someone would just disappear like that, but then again, he didn't know Todd Welling. As Joe described, he liked fishing more than the meetings. Perhaps he was the type who didn't give a damn and would rather take the chastisement than attend the meetings. These rentals weren't coming out of his pocket.

"Probably over on the east segment," Greg said to himself. There was more chatter from the occupants of Cabins One and Three. It was going to be a long day for sure.

First thing's first—coffee!

Greg burst through the kitchen door and went straight for the mug. He grabbed hold of it. No interruptions. He lifted it to his lips. No interruptions. He took a sip, then spat it out.

Cold.

He stared at the useless brown liquid with contempt.

A long, shitty day indeed. He poured it out, and rather than make a new mug, he grabbed his truck key and went out to the driveway. Rust flaked from the ten-year old Ford F150 as he climbed inside. The engine sputtered. The check engine light came on.

Greg stared at the light as though it deliberately appeared to mock him. For sixty-seconds, he suppressed a series of cuss words, then finally backed out of the driveway.

CHAPTER 4

It was a ten minute drive back into town, but ten minutes that Greg could be using to get his work done. He could envision Mrs. Brown's escalating grievances and the consequential demands she would make. She'd probably make him refund a hundred dollars out of their six-hundred weekly rental. Her husband seemed laid back enough. Perhaps he would have her calmed down before such a conversation would take place.

The ant spraying was a day at the beach compared to the work he would have to do in Cabin Three. He turned pale just from the thought of it. Hopefully, as bad as this was, maybe this would be the extent of the chaos the day would bring. Maybe, just maybe, it wouldn't get worse from here.

The first part of the trip was a few minutes down Guy Street, which contained nothing but wooded area and private residences. That road dead-ended at Zolciak, where Greg would take a left-hand turn into town.

There wasn't much to the town of Tonette. There were a couple of restaurants, a grocery store, police and fire station, a couple of gas stations, and a hardware store ten minutes further east. Greg didn't want to take that much time. Luckily, Pete's Orchard Grocery Market should have all the bug killer and disinfectant he would need. He would probably grab a few candles for Cabin Three. Now that he was thinking of it, he would probably grab a fresh bottle of shampoo. He would certainly use it once everything was done.

A quarter-mile from the edge of the business area was an intersection with Crabb Road, which was a long stretch of pavement that went southwest, connecting with the highway. Normally, Greg paid no mind to Crabb Road, as it was a two-way stop, yielding to drivers on

Zolciak. This time, however, Greg had no choice but to ease on the brakes.

The oversized semi-truck could not seem to make the turn without ending up in the ditch. It was a tanker truck, likely delivering gas to the Jerky Station. Clearly, this was this driver's first trip to Tonette, or else he would've known he'd have better luck making a turn further down at Pierce Road, about a mile further east.

Greg waited and watched as the driver backed up a few feet, tried again to make a right, but could not seem to make the angle. He straightened the truck out, then reversed back onto Crabb. At first, Greg thought the guy was being curious and letting him through before making further attempts. Greg had just tapped his foot to the accelerator when he realized the driver was making another go. Two seconds later, the truck was blocking the intersection again.

Greg threw his hands up. "Oh, for chrissake!" The truck inched forward, cut to the right, and once again, nearly ended up in the ditch. It backed up along Crabb. The window opened and the driver waved Greg along.

Finally!

He drove through and continued on to town, glimpsing back to his rearview mirror at the amusing sight at the driver attempting to make another turn. The idiot would be in that intersection all day unless he realized this road was not intended for Semis.

The buzzing of his smartphone interrupted his amusement. The number on the screen looked familiar, but he couldn't quite place it. In that case, it was either someone who had made a reservation, or one of his current tenants.

"This is Greg," he answered.

"Hey, this is Ken Allen, in Cabin Two. I'm ready to leave, but it looks like you're not here."

Greg closed his eyes. *Shit! The security deposit—and they paid in CASH!*

"Oh, shoot! Hang tight. I had to make a brief run into town. I thought you were still in the process of packing, so I figured I had time."

There was the voice of Ken's wife in the background. *"Is he coming back? I really want to get on the road."*

Ken replied to her, *"I'm talking to him right now! He said he'll be quick. Just hold on."*

"I have to work tomorrow. We've got a six-hour drive back. He KNEW we were leaving…"

"I'll be back in ten…make that fifteen minutes," Greg said. "Just bear with me." *That ought to be the new motto for my business.*

"Okay. We'll wait," Ken said. He hung up right after, clearly annoyed. Greg tossed his phone into the passenger seat.

"Okay, new policy going forward—NO cash payments," he said to himself. At least, he could refund security deposits electronically through credit or debit payments. In fact, that was the way it ought to be done, as an inspection usually needed to be made to make sure the tenants didn't cause any damage during their stay.

Finally, he saw the Jerky Station, a brick building with six gas pumps in the front lot. It was the first landmark to the business section of Tonette. Another block down, he saw the Fire Station. Across the road from it was the Sheriff's office.

Greg felt his blood boil. Perhaps it was just the stressful morning he was having—plus the fact that he didn't get his coffee. Today, he couldn't even bear the sight of the two-story building. There were three Interceptors in its lot. Either the Sheriff was letting the Deputies hang out in the station, or she was having issues with maintaining staff. Considering who it was in office, and the attitudes of his former co-workers, Greg suspected it to be the latter.

Half a block past it was the grocery store. Only one intersection stood in-between him and his supplies…

And the light turned yellow, right as he was within a hundred feet. Right out of range of gunning it and making the light. If there were no cars on the intersecting road, he would've gone for it, but he knew Michigan drivers. As soon as that green light came on, those accelerators were touching the mat.

Greg's hands strangled the steering wheel as if it was at fault. The traffic went through, and within ten seconds, the lanes were clear. The temptation to run the light tugged at Greg's soul, but like a good citizen, he remained in place. It seemed the light would never turn green. He glanced at the time on his screen. The normally ten-minute drive had taken sixteen, thanks to that idiot semi-truck driver.

He's probably still back there, trying to make that turn.

Finally, the light turned green, and like the Michigan driver he was, he blasted the truck right through. Time was ticking away. Already, he had three cabins with pissed off customers inside. With each passing moment, the likelihood of repeat business and good word of mouth was slipping away. Luckily, there weren't too many places taken up in the lot. He parked as close as he could, hopped out of the truck, and hurried inside.

****

Deputy Bill Hoskins stepped out of Pablo's Diner on the corner of Zolciak and Pierce, just in time to hear the screeching of tires. An old Ford was speeding into the lot and pulled up near the handicap spots.

"Someone's in a hurry."

Bill turned back and saw the Sheriff stepping out behind him, coffee in hand. She stepped beside the twenty-two-year old rookie and watched the driver of the truck sprint into the store.

"I guess he really needed some paper towels," Bill joked.

"More like toilet paper, the way he was moving," Sheriff Hannah Tyler replied. Her expression was a combination of amused and irritated, the latter emotion mainly due to the fact that the driver narrowly avoided collision with a parked vehicle as he cut through the lot. That feeling only intensified as she continued staring. It was hard to tell from here, but that truck looked to be parked at an angle, rather than fitting properly into its slot. If that was the case, he was partially blocking the handicap zone—which was a pet peeve of Hannah's.

Bill was heading back to the SUV when he noticed the Sheriff's expression. He glanced between her and the store, then read her mind.

"Is it something worth looking into?"

"I think so," Hannah replied. Cutting through the lot, that was one thing. But blocking a handicap spot, that was a douche move. It would be a personal pleasure to slap a parking ticket on the windshield of that truck should that be the case. She climbed into the driver's seat, waited for Bill to get in, then started the engine.

As she cut the wheel to drive onto the road, they noticed one of their patrollers catching a red light at the intersection. Through the driver's side window, Bill saw the ballcap worn by Officer Jake Bing. As he waited at the light, he turned his gaze slightly toward them. There was no sense of acknowledgement—something Bill tended to notice whenever the other Deputies were around the Sheriff. They were nice enough to him; *enough* being the key word. In the six-months he spent with the department, he noticed their attitudes harden whenever around him. It wasn't that they were jerks, or even generally unhappy people. In fact, he had seen Jake on the beat with Deputy Zach Cassidy, and interacting with residents. In those encounters, they seemed happy and pleasant to be around. Only when working around the Sheriff did they have that dull expression on their faces, and lately, it seemed to happen whenever they were around Bill as well.

He wondered if it was because Hannah had unofficially taken him in as her personal protégé. Were they jealous? Did they think Hannah was too hard on them? Bill didn't think so. Then again, he had seen a couple of Deputies transfer to other departments. Being the new guy, he didn't ask too many questions.

The light went green and Jake Bing drove off. Bill cocked his head to the left just enough to see Hannah's expression in his peripheral vision. Her sunglasses blocked her eyes, but he had ridden with her long enough to know the Deputy bothered her. There was a hint of a sigh as she steered onto the road and accelerated through the intersection.

There was clearly some beef between her and the Deputies, but as usual, Bill didn't have the stones to ask why.

Hannah took a right turn into the parking lot, then pulled up behind the Ford F150.

"Surprised this hunk of junk even held together after his little stunt," Hannah quipped. There were pieces of rust peeling off the bumper. The exhaust pipe was frayed, the rear passenger tire clearly low by a few pounds of pressure. Hannah didn't care about the mechanical details as much as she did about the placement of the vehicle.

Her suspicions were correct.

"Look at that," she said. She got out of the SUV and stepped along the passenger side. It was four inches past the blue line. She looked over at Bill. "We have a winner here. Hand me the ticket book so I can give him the prize."

"You got it," Bill replied.

****

Greg made his way into the lawncare aisle. The empty section in the shelves stood out like a sore thumb.

Be just my luck that THAT'S the spot for the item I need.

He stepped forward. All around the empty space were foggers, baits, and various weed killers. All stuff he could use, with the exception of the one thing he *really* needed.

A store employee walked by. Greg raised his hand. "Excuse me?"

"Yes?"

"Do you have any more of the Ortho home defense spray?"

The employee looked at the label on the shelf. "Oh, no. I'm sorry, we're out. I do believe we'll be getting it in stock soon."

Greg nodded, while fantasizing banging his head against the shelf.

"Any idea when?"

"Not sure exactly. Might be a truck coming in later today, but I'm not sure if this'll be on it."

Of course not. Greg forced a smile. Wasn't the employee's fault.

"Appreciate it." He waited for her to turn the corner before he mimicked a strangling motion. The only other spray was *Roots*, some kind of all natural spray. The stuff did practically nothing for killing bugs, but apparently it promoted the environment, which somehow got the damn stuff patented.

Greg had no other options. He loaded his shopping basket with bug bomb and the crap spray, as well as a few indoor and outdoor baits and traps. His mind messed with him, making him think his phone was vibrating, even though it wasn't. The gathering of supplies only took three minutes. Unfortunately, only one aisle was open, and the customer in front of him apparently needed to buy the whole left section of the building. There were two carts loaded to the brim with all kinds of product. To top it off, the customer buying all the crap made sloths look like pro-athletes. He grabbed one item at a time, slowly putting it on the conveyor belt, then slooooowly reached for the next.

Greg glanced around. Of course, the other staff were busy with other things, or simply pretended not to notice him so they could goof off. And there was no self-checkout section. 'It takes away jobs' he once heard the owner say. Well, fine, then have your staff do THEIR jobs.

It was all frustrating. Greg closed his eyes and inhaled.

The world isn't out to get you. Just relax. It'll all be fine. I promise, it won't get worse from here.

When he opened his eyes, he noticed movement outside the main window. There was a Police SUV. He recognized the silver color and green stripes of the Ford Police Explorer based SUV. That was not a Deputy vehicle, but the one driven by the Sheriff herself.

"Oh, great," he said under his breath. His mind started developing procedures to avoid encountering her on his way out. He couldn't even stand to look at the bitch. Just knowing she was here on the same lot as him made him want to throw a case of bug spray through the glass.

Maybe they're just goofing around. Just wait. Maybe she'll just drive off and...

He leaned forward, towering over the other customer's cart as he strived for a better view. The Sheriff was right behind his truck, jotting down his license plate!

"What the hell is *this?!*"

Greg dropped his basket of goods and marched for the door, brushing past the customer. As he reached the exit, he saw Hannah Tyler slap the ticket onto his windshield.

She looked the same as ever, sporting those aviator-style shades as though it made her a badass. Her blonde, curly hair was tied back into a ponytail. Acting to the false tough-girl look was the sleeve tattoo running down her left arm. Thunderstorms and lightning? Did she think that made her look electrifying?

He stepped outside with a vengeance.

"Hey?! What's the deal?!"

Hannah was halfway in her vehicle when she saw him. At first, she wore a cocky smile, which faded when she recognized his face. For a moment, she looked alarmed, the way she looked in her rookie year when he saw her ticket a vehicle which happened to belong to the district attorney.

Saving face, she straightened herself in her seat.

"Good morning."

"A smartass. Same as ever," Greg replied. He yanked the ticket from under his windshield wiper. "What's your issue?!"

Hannah shrugged her shoulders, trying to maintain the image of confidence. In reality, had she known it was him, she probably would've let it pass.

"Should have been more careful parking, Greg," she said. "Saw your little *Mad Max* stunt pulling into this lot. First of all, you almost hit that car behind us, and second of all, look down."

Greg glanced at his tire, then back at her. His face was almost purple now.

"It's a few inches over the line. I was on my way out," he said. His own words enraged him further, as he was self-aware enough to know how he sounded. For years, he had heard similar excuses from several receivers of speeding and parking tickets. However, this wasn't just some cop—this was Hannah Tyler. The fact that this town elected her as Sheriff made him sick.

There was a young Deputy in the SUV with her. Greg didn't recognize him, but there was the eagerness of a hot-blooded young officer eager to prove his worth. He stepped out of the vehicle and pointed a finger at Greg.

"Hey, sir, you're only gonna make this worse for yourself if you push it," he said.

"Bill…"

The buzz-cut rookie looked back at his superior, and was surprised to see her waving him back to his seat. 'I'll handle this,' she mouthed.

She looked back at Greg. "Thought you drove an Excursion."

"Had to get rid of it," Greg stated. He leaned in. "Couldn't afford the payments."

The jab worked. Hannah's shades failed to conceal the guilt in her eyes. Still, she refused to concede. Greg wanted to laugh, but managed to exhibit self-control in that regard. It was clear she was either appeasing her own ego, or saving face to not appear foolish in front of the new rookie.

"Sorry to hear that," she said. "But it's no excuse for partially blocking a handicap zone. You're not beyond the law, Greg. I have a job to do."

"Ohhhhh," Greg said, rubbing his boot over the blue line. "You're concerned about ethics! Except when it comes to promotion, right?"

Hannah didn't respond.

"Court date's on the ticket," she replied. "You know the drill. Either pay by phone, or plead your case to the judge." She closed the door, buckled in, then drove out of the lot.

Greg watched them drive away, then tossed the ticket onto the pavement in a fit of rage. The wind picked up and carried it away. Right then, he remembered that the courthouse phone number had changed since he left the department, and he didn't know the new one. The only way to find out was by looking on the ticket.

"Oh, shit!" He ran after the ticket, which dodged his grasp repeatedly. It even seemed to be toying with him, whipping around his feet like a scurrying insect, until finally, he pinned it with his foot. He grabbed it and held it up, then scowled at the mud stains that obscured the phone numbers.

He growled like an enraged beast, then tossed the ticket into his passenger seat. *Now*, his phone was buzzing. He looked at the number and realized it was Ken Allen again. He didn't bother answering. Instead, he hurried back into the store and stepped around the checkout aisles.

There was one piece of good news: the fat lady in front of him was finally finishing up. Now he could finally ring his stuff out and—

Greg glanced around at the floor, realizing his basket of items was nowhere to be found. He turned to look at the utility aisle, just in time to see one of the stockers placing his items back on the shelf.

His phone buzzed again. He looked at the screen. *1 Voicemail.*

The stocker started walking for the front, saw him standing there, smiled and held the basket out.

"Hello! Would you like a basket for your shopping?"

CHAPTER 5

The secretaries and account managers for Reiner Foods brought chairs and coolers to the campfire area in the yard in front of Cabin Eight. There was white ash and the crumbling remnants of burnt logs that warmed smores the previous evening.

Normally at this point, Joe would nonchalantly scan the crowd for blushing cheeks from the female secretaries. Usually, on these retreats, there'd be at least one spontaneous hookup…sometimes between people who were already married. The men and the women were separated into different cabins, but that wouldn't stop them from pairing up. These cabins were larger and had more bedrooms than the other half, allowing for most of the staff to have their own rooms. Privacy led to sneaky behavior. It was a combination of personal amusement mixed with concern for the productivity of his employees that prompted Joe to keep an eye out for signs of such activity.

This time, however, he barely even noticed his crew were setting up for the ten-o'clock outdoor seminar he had arranged. Todd Welling had not yet returned. Had he not known the guy had gone out onto the lake last night, it would've been easy to assume he departed that morning and simply lost track of time. Joe tried to convince himself that Todd simply had a successful trip and was just too eager to go out again. Had there been a live-basket, bucket, or stringer displaying any catch on the dock, Joe would've gone with that theory. But there wasn't.

Joe knew Todd well enough to know that he didn't like hauling fish back out for a second trip. He'd store them at the shore, and had the equipment to do so. Plus, he was a showoff. He'd be eager to display his catch to everyone, especially the secretaries, of whom he'd get a kick out of their disgusted reactions.

There was only one boat on the water right now. It held two people—the ones who attempted to check-in this morning. Not Todd's boat. He looked to the narrow passage that led to the east segment. The way the shore curved, it was impossible to gaze into that section of lake. Too many trees.

"Should we go on without him?"

Joe Hall turned around and saw Ernie Yeller, the training director, standing a few feet behind his right shoulder. The thirty-eight year old's brow was wrinkled with concern. His hair started going grey five years ago, much to the amusement of his staff, to which he replied it was because of the antics of the account managers. Joe expected a similar remark pertaining to Todd's disappearance.

"What do you think?" Joe asked.

"Hey, you're the boss. You're footing the bill," Ernie replied. It was how he always responded to such questions. Ernie enjoyed his role in the company, and he was very good at it, but he never saw himself as a high-level decision maker. His specialty was building relationships with clients and expanding sales territory—skills he now passed down to his account managers. One of his philosophies was that he didn't do anyone's job for them. That included the CEO.

Joe looked at the water and sighed. A decision had to be made. He glanced back at the employees. By the looks of it, they were taking their sweet time getting set up. Hell, some of them appeared as though they had just crawled out of bed. Others weren't even there yet. Joe had hit the hay around ten. As he drifted off, he could hear the antics of his employees seated around the fire pit. He remembered thinking that it didn't sound like they'd be heading in anytime soon.

Also, it was around that time Todd went out on the boat.

"He's probably in that next segment of lake," Joe said.

"Probably," Ernie said. "You want to go out and get him?"

Joe gave him another glance. Like himself, Ernie was dressed fairly casually in jeans and a buttoned t-shirt. Nothing that would be fouled up too badly by being on a boat. Plus, the resort owner was kind enough to lend them the motor.

"Yeah, let's go take a look. As you said, I'm footing the bill. The idiot has more than enough time during this retreat to cast a line. I literally need a couple of hours each day." He felt himself growing irritated as the words came out, as though he was just realizing these facts. "Yeah!" This time, he spoke with zest. He turned toward the crowd of employees. "Hey, everyone, keep setting up. This seminar will be postponed a tad, while Ernie and I go lasso Todd and drag his ass back here."

"He's *still* out there?" one of the account managers said.

"Seems to be the case," Joe replied. Ernie grabbed the outboard motor from the cabin and began installing it to the boat.

"You think he's okay?" one of the secretaries asked. Joe could sense concern brewing within the group.

"Oh, yes. He's fine, I promise. Todd's just being…Todd." A few employees chuckled. "Just continue setting up. Make sure somebody props up the white board. Everything is gonna go as planned. No worries."

A few minutes later, Ernie waved over at Joe. "All set and ready to go!" Todd immediately headed for the dock, briefly glancing back at the others.

"Keep out of trouble. We'll be right back." He took a seat at the front of the boat. Ernie sat at the stern with the motor. He yanked the ripcord, which sparked life into the engine. After unlooping the mooring line, he twisted the handle to first gear, pushing them out into the lake. Joe waited until they were a few dozen feet away from the shore. "I'm gonna kill that guy."

"Who knows? Maybe we're in for a fish fry!" Ernie joked.

"We better be," Joe replied. "Next company retreat might be at a winter campground. See how these knuckleheads like that."

"Yeah—I might conveniently get a stomach bug around that time," Ernie said.

****

Cathy tossed a line out, landing the crawler harness precisely where Greg had recommended. So far, she found nothing but weeds. She understood fishing—she'd done it most of her life. It took patience, regardless if it was done for sport or recreation. It wasn't the lack of bites that bothered her; it was the continuous snagging of weeds. They had a way of tricking her into thinking she had a bite, which doubled the frustration.

What tripled the frustration was Tim's constant shifting in his seat. Each movement caused the boat to wobble. He wasn't having much luck either, and was clearly acting out of boredom and stiffness from the long and early ride. He threw another cast toward the center of the lake. He waited a moment, reeled in the slack, then waited. So far, nothing.

He leaned back and extended his left leg. The boat rocked again. Cathy spun back to look at him.

"You auditioning for *West Side Story* over there?!"

Tim was taken aback by her irritation.

"Sorry. I'm stiff. Usually, the unloading process helps me walk it off."

"Whose fault is that, dummy?" Cathy replied. As soon as she faced away from him, Tim proceeded to mock her with various childish expressions. She pulled on her rod, struggling to free her lure from the evil clutches of the weeds. Suddenly, the line went slack. When Cathy started reeling it in, she immediately noticed the weightlessness. She had lost her lure. "Oh, come on!"

Tim chuckled. She turned and stared at him, which was successful in shutting him up for a few short moments.

"You're in a mood today," he said.

"Living with you tends to have that effect," she said. Tim pretended to be offended with an exaggerated gasp.

"I'm hurt," he said.

"Good."

"Really hurt."

"Excellent."

"I might as well throw myself overboard."

"Water's right there." Cathy pointed down over the gunwale. Tim scoffed.

"Damn!"

She looked back at him. "What?!"

"What do you mean, 'what'?!" he exclaimed. Cathy stuck her tongue out at him, much like she did when they met in their freshman year of college. He was studying business, and she was studying marketing. Both programs required them to take the dreaded biology-course. It was there where they met, though they didn't actually interact until two-thirds of the way into the semester. They had to do a lab which required them to identify mitochondria by injecting some kind of solution onto the cells that neither of them could remember.

Even if Tim had been a science major, he wouldn't have learned anything from that class anyway, as his attention was mainly fixed on Cathy's legs the entire time. Unless it was ice cold, she often wore shorts, eager to show off the musculature earned from four years of high school cheerleading. Her blond hair was much longer then. Now, it barely hung underneath her ears. Not a terrible look, but Tim preferred it longer. She wore jeans most of the time now, even in the summer. Though she never said it out loud, Tim knew it was because her exercise routine was cut by over a third. In addition, their diets weren't the greatest. Back in their teens and early twenties, the burgers and French fries were no match for their athletic metabolisms. Once they entered their thirties, their bodies started slowing down. Combined with a less-active lifestyle, the muscular tones gradually disappeared. That wasn't the worst part; the realization that losing the weight was harder than it used to be was.

Tim's midsection was gradually starting to expand as well. Not obese by any means, but it was a sign that middle age was around the corner. He didn't pay much mind to it, as he was a take-each-day-as-it-is guy. Age came with life, and being married, he didn't feel he needed to pump iron to impress the ladies anymore. And he still thought Cathy was hot...maybe not her increasingly sour attitude, but her looks were just fine. He'd seem MUCH heavier women younger than her. So she was ten pounds heavier than her prime days. Big deal. He just wished she thought the same.

"You didn't answer me," he quipped. She stuck her tongue out at him again. He smirked. "I love it when you do that."

Cathy scoffed. "What?"

"You heard me."

"Yeah, I did. You're weird."

"Hey. *You're* the one who married me."

"Well, you *did* get me drunk before you popped the question," she replied. "Plus, you had just bought me *Kid Rock* tickets. I would've said yes to Danny DeVito at that point."

"Hey, don't knock Danny!" Tim said. He watched her attempt to tie a new lure onto her line. She kept glancing over her shoulder toward the cabins. The look of disdain was still there. He watched her chest puff out. That deep inhalation was like the gust of wind that came before the tsunami.

"I can't believe you made me wake up at four in the morning, and we can't even get into our cabin." She opened a bottle of water and started to drink.

Tim leaned back and rolled his eyes. *Ohhhh boy. Heeere we go.*

"It's not my fault."

Cathy spat her water out then looked at him with wide eyes.

"Excuse me?!"

Tim reeled in his line, hoping a fish would bite and naturally draw attention away from his mishap. Instead, he caught weeds. Unlike Cathy's, his lure was able to escape the snag intact.

He cleared his throat, then smiled. "You're pretty."

"Ugh!" Cathy turned away. Would he ever learn that trick hadn't worked since their second date? "We've got meats in the cooler. Coffee creamer. And milk. The ice will probably melt by the time we're able to load it into the fridge. It's bound to go bad."

"It will not go bad," Tim said. He threw another cast out, only to catch another weed. "Jesus! Is the kelp forest in this lake?" He pulled back, bending the pole to the max. Either the weed would come free, or he was going to lose the lure. He felt a release. The fact that there was weight at the end of his line ensured him that he kept his lure. "Finally."

He reeled it back to the boat.

"I thought that guy said the fishing would be great," Cathy said. Tim shook his head. She was in one of those states of irritation that made her want to lash out at anything and everything.

"Babe, bass love weeded areas." He could see the vegetation dragging behind his lure just a couple of feet under the water. "Who knows? At this rate, we might just deforest the whole lake." He pulled the three-foot string of weeds out of the water, then reached to untangle it from the crawler harness. "If you want, we can—what the hell?"

"What?" Cathy asked.

Tim held his hand away from the weeds. There was a thick coating of slime all over the stem and the leaves. It was thicker and heavier than water, and warm. Its color was a clear green. Whatever it was, it clung to the weeds like glue, as well as his hand.

Cathy finally glanced over, thinking Tim was just being inept, as usual. She squinted when she saw the weird substance on his hand.

"Make a friend with that plant, did you?" she joked.

Tim snickered. "Okay, Mrs. Bipolar. Where'd the sense of humor come from?"

"Anytime I see you having some sort of misfortune, it just kind of brightens my day," she said, smiling.

"That why you always say no to sex?" Tim asked. He groaned as more of the goop fell onto his lap.

Cathy burst out with laughter. "Why would you need me when you've got your pal there?"

Tim tried shaking the fishing line, hoping the weeds would come off on their own. His wish was not granted, forcing him to dig his fingers through the slime in order to reach the hook. "Ugh!" he muttered, his face rippling with disgust. He twisted in his seat to get a better position. The goop and the weeds completely blocked out the metal hooks, forcing him to feel around to locate them. After five seconds, he successfully found one—rather, its tip. "Mother of ass!"

Tim jolted in his seat, knocking over the tub of worms. Sickly invertebrates, brownish purple in color, slowly writhed on the metal floor.

"Having trouble over there?" Cathy asked.

"Laugh all you want." Tim started peeling the weeds apart, splattering thick droplets of the goop onto the boat.

"Way to make a mess," Cathy said.

"Not like it's on your side of the boat," he retorted. He looked down at the worms, which were now completely coated in the stuff. "See? I'm a nice guy. They were thirsty, and thanks to me, they have something to drink. Or eat…not sure if this stuff is liquid, or what." After a minute of untangling, the hooks were finally free. Tim tossed the vegetation back into the water, then ran his hand over the surface. "Son of a bitch."

"What's the matter?" Cathy asked.

"I don't know what this shit is, but it won't freaking come off," he said. He lifted his hand then tried shaking the goo off, with little success. He straightened his posture, then started raking his hand on the edge of the boat. It peeled away like jelly, with the inner layers having turned pasty white. Tim ran the back of his hand over the gunwale, then glared at the residue. A lot of it had turned pasty white all of a sudden. Not only that, but it appeared to be crusting.

"More issues?" Cathy said.

"Uh, I don't know," Tim said. He looked at the thin remainder that covered his left hand. "It's almost like it's crusting."

Cathy snorted. She tried to control her laughter, but failed. She covered her mouth and shook with each giggle.

"You're gross," Tim said.

"Sorry," Cathy said. *Eh, that's a lie.* As she previously stated, there was a little evil side of her that enjoyed Tim's misfortunes. Knowing this, he leaned forward and reached out at her face.

"Woo-hoo-hoo!" he babbled, his fingers inches from her face.

"Get away from me, sicko!" Cathy exclaimed, leaning back. The boat rocked as she leaned back against the rim of the bow. "Ow!"

"Oops. You alright?" Tim asked.

"I hope the next plant oozes all over your face," she remarked, pulling herself back onto the seat. Tim spent another minute wiping his hand on his pantleg.

"Whatever this stuff is, I don't think it's from the weeds," he said. He looked at his hand. It felt dry, but otherwise alright. The stuff was off, and that was all he cared about.

He didn't pay it another thought. He was no ecology expert. It was probably just some crap that built up in the bottom of the lake. Maybe Cathy was right; maybe it was secretion from the weeds.

Cathy tossed out another cast. No bites. Only weeds. She shook her head in frustration.

"Why don't we try a different spot?"

"Whatever you say, your highness," Tim replied. He yanked the motor cord and started the engine. "Which way?"

Cathy followed the shoreline with her eyes. There were several properties along the northside, all of which were surprisingly quiet for what she would expect on a Saturday. Each property had a dock with a pontoon or aluminum boat moored to it. Yet, nobody seemed to be around.

Perhaps when you live on a lake, thus get to see it every single day, it loses its mystique. She shrugged, feeling it was a reasonable thought. She continued looking at the shoreline, then finally selected a spot to the northeast.

"Let's try over there near the bend," she said. Tim cupped a hand over his eyes to block the sun as he looked.

"By that house with the boat garage?"

"Sure! Why not?"

Tim shrugged. "I wish I was so rich I could afford to have a garage on the water." He secured his fishing line, pulled up the anchor, and engaged the throttle. He steered the boat along the bend, coming within a dozen yards or so of the private docks.

Cathy did a double take on one of the docks in the center. It was vacant, but yet, had signs of use. There was an overturned folding chair at its edge, and a fishing pole leaning against a post, unattended.

Did the owner just say the hell with it and call it a night?

She shrugged, then checked her phone. It was a little past ten now. As much as she enjoyed fishing, she just wanted to be in the cabin right now. Maybe get a suntan on the beach…as long as nobody was looking.

Figuring she might as well rebait her line, she reached for her tub of worms. Then she remembered the one that Tim spilled then refused to clean up. Might as well grab one of those. She leaned over the center seat to reach for them. Her hand stopped a few inches short.

Cathy stared.

Some of the worms were submerged in a puddle of that sappy substance Tim brought in. She saw it when it came out of the water; it was somewhat green, but mostly clear. But now, it looked as though it was turning a shade of white. The worms underneath were unmoving, as though frozen in stasis.

"Something wrong?" Tim asked. Cathy almost jumped at the sound of his voice.

"No!" She didn't intend for it to come out as a shout. Regardless, Tim held a hand up, signaling 'peace!'

She looked once more at the anomaly, then returned to her seat, not interested in touching whatever that stuff was. She opened a new tub of worms and baited her hook.

CHAPTER 6

It had gotten to the point where Greg was watching the sky to make sure space aliens weren't descending on him. When he finally got to the checkout counter, for the second time, his debit card chip failed to work. It took four attempts before he finally got out of there.

To top it off, the store alarm blared in his ear.

"Warning. Please return to the checkout counter. Apparently, you have an unpaid item in your bag." And go figure—the staff actually wanted to check his receipt and items. Every other time that faulty alarm went off, they never seemed to give a damn. But THIS TIME, however…

By the time he finally got in his truck, Greg felt like he was at the end of a countdown. Each tick got louder in his mind. He had told everyone he'd be back in less than a half hour, and here he was at the forty-minute mark.

Right off the bat, he struck a pothole getting out of the driveway. His reactionary "fuck!" made the sound of impact sound like the drop of a pebble in comparison. It wouldn't be the last time the exclamation would escape his vocals.

He arrived at the intersection of Zolciak and Crabb—where the damn semi-truck driver was halfway through, still trying to make that turn. There was no getting around. The ENTIRE intersection was blocked. By the looks of it, the truck was not going anywhere.

By that point, Greg had enough. He got out, motioned for the driver to step out, and completed the turn for him.

"Hey! What's going on?!" he said. His voice came out like that of a store manager on the verge of lecturing staff for slacking. It took everything for him not to have explicative vocabulary in every other word. The driver was a fairly young guy, maybe mid-twenties, and glassy-eyed. Greg's combativeness quelled a bit when he saw the glassy eyes and the neat blue shirt. The guy had actually bothered to change clothes. Definitely a first-year driver. First-year, tired, and nervous.

The driver stepped out and pointed at the engine.

"The wheel won't cut," he said. "It only goes so far and stops. Gets worse with each attempt," he said.

Greg softened his hard expression. "Sounds like you have a power steering issue."

"I don't know," the driver said.

Definitely first year. The way these truck companies hired these days, they put their recruits through minimal training—just enough to put themselves and everyone else in danger. He had seen the results of this during his time with the county. Compared to the numerous accidents and the mangled bodies he pulled out of crushed vehicles, a power steering issue was a day at the beach.

"Here, let me take a look," Greg said. The driver showed no qualms. He stepped out of the way and let Greg climb up into the vehicle.

At eighteen, he had gotten his CDL, and twenty years later, despite only having driven one year of that, he still recalled most of his training. He put the truck in reverse, then slowly backed out of the intersection. He tugged hard at the steering wheel, which was so stiff, he could barely nudge it. Unfortunately, it became clear that the truck had a power steering leak. If anything, he was lucky it didn't happen to him while he was on the highway.

Well, I guess I'm not the only one having a shitty day.

Greg climbed out of the truck. "Yeah, I hate to break it to you, kid, but your truck has issues. You'll have to get a repair guy out here. You could put power steering fluid in it, but it'll only get you so far before it drains again. You've got a leak somewhere in there." He tapped on the engine.

"Great," the driver said. He looked to the sky and groaned. "I knew today was going to suck."

Greg snickered. "You're telling me, bud." He tapped him on the shoulder, then got back into his pickup. By then, his phone was vibrating again. "For the love of God, just hold your horses!"

The entire way back, he listened to the rattle in his truck that definitely was not there before. Probably a muffler issue, which made sense because the truck was loud. The whole exhaust was probably rusting out from underneath him. More repairs, meaning more money being yanked from his pocket.

The wind came through his open window and sent the yellow ticket lapping over the passenger seat. It looped in a perfect circle, then flattened out, pen marks taunting him with the likely fine he was facing.

Money, money, money. If only he was as good at making it as he was spending it.

The truck held together long enough for him to get home. At least he was home, and not stuck on the side of the road waiting for pickup that might take all day to get there. That sense of comfort vanished with the sound of a bickering family down by Cabin One. The Brown family, particularly the wife, was still having a meltdown over the ant situation.

You'd think she was in a mental asylum.

He grabbed the door handle and started to let himself out when he noticed Ken Allen and his wife standing outside his house door. They had their arms crossed, staring at him as though he had violated their honor.

"You know what? To hell with perspective—I'd RATHER switch places with that trucker kid," Greg said to himself. He got out of the truck and switched to 'customer-service mode'. "Alright. Let me get you your security deposit. Sorry about the delay. We're having a little crisis in two of our cabins." He hurried to the door and let himself in.

"Yeah, I know. I've had to smell AND listen to it," Ken Allen said. His voice conveyed his impatience. He was eager to leave. Good. Greg was ready for them to leave as well. No point in inviting them to return next year; that ship had already sailed.

Greg handed Allen his hundred dollar deposit. "Thanks for staying," was enough for a goodbye. Ken Allen and his wife were out the door without a word. Greg took a breath, looked at his cold coffee, then through the window at the cabins.

Maybe NOW I can get a quick cup in.

He loaded up the Keurig and started it up. As it brewed, he watched the lake and the cabins in front of it. The Browns were gathered at the picnic table, with the wife pacing back and forth, scratching her arms and legs nonstop. Their eighteen-year old son was at a tree by the left, sorting through twigs, prodding them at the dirt as though to test their stability. The Kendricks were on the dock, watching the water, and avoiding their own stink. Further to the east, it appeared that the Reiner employees who occupied cabins Five through Eight were gathering around the firepit.

At least they weren't causing him any grief.

The Keurig completed its task, filling the room with a marvelous aroma that almost took the mental anguish away. Greg took the coffee, took a long inhale, then stirred in the creamer.

"Finally." He lifted the mug to his lips.

An ear-shattering scream filled the air. Greg jolted and spun toward the window. Hot coffee splattered his chin and hand.

"Yeow! Son of a—"

There was more shouting from below. Cabin One again. The eighteen-year old was running out of the cabin, clawing at his arms. Greg let his mug drop into the sink as he dashed outside. He went down the hill and arrived at the Cabin. The parents were gathered near their son, swatting his face and arms with towels they had drying on the line. They ripped his shirt off, revealing a few red welts.

"What's going on?!" Greg said. Mrs. Brown spun to face him, her face red with anger.

"Look at this! The ants were trying to eat him!"

Greg snorted. He had no regrets for this one. It was clear from the get-go that they wouldn't be returning customers. He stepped by her and leaned over the kid.

"I'm fine!" he muttered. Greg winced at the sight of the welts. Most of them were on his arms, though a few had made their way to his back.

"They went after you with a purpose," Greg said.

"Yeah, they were trying to eat me."

Greg closed his eyes. *You're definitely your mother's son.*

"Uh, no, I don't think so."

"What do you call *that*?!" Mrs. Brown said, pointing at the bites.

"They were all over him when he came out," Mr. Brown said. Greg raised his eyebrows.

"You went in there, and they *jumped* you?" he asked.

"No," the kid said. "I saw the Queen under the kitchen sink. I thought I could nudge her out with some sticks. Then suddenly, the regular ants raced up the stick, up my arms, and were trying to eat me."

Greg paused for a moment, allowing his mind to silently speak the various insults he had in store for them.

"It's no surprise they went after you," Greg explained. "Ants are a hive mind with no regard for their individual well-being. You went after their Queen. They don't take that bullshit. Mess with an ant Queen, or a beehive Queen, and you're in for a rude awakening. She'll send signals that she's in distress, and all the workers will rush to her defense. And that's what they did here."

"So, you're JUSTIFYING it?!" Mrs. Brown exclaimed. Greg looked at the sky again.

You know what, God? Send those space aliens down.

He could sense she was angry for angry's sake by this point. One thing he had learned in the department was that there was no sense in arguing with a person in that state of mind. All he could do was fix the problem and hope they wouldn't attempt to sue him.

"Be right back." He started up the hill to get his supplies. As he did, he felt the wet spots of his shirt pressing against him. He had spilled coffee all over his clothes.

He stopped for a moment and looked out to the lake. He could see the Perkins motoring along the north side of the lake. By the looks of it, they were content fishing for a while. Hopefully so, because he had a lot of work to do before he could get to prepping their cabin.

First thing's first—gotta change.

CHAPTER 7

The east segment of the lake was not as perfectly rounded as the west. It widened from the center, then hooked a bit to the south. Joe Hall counted twelve properties surrounding this section of the lake. Each one had its own dock and some sort of boat. As of yet, there was nobody on the water they could see—including Todd Welling.

Ernie leaned back against the transom, his left hand clutching the prop. He guided the boat into the center of the lake. He watched the waves rolling past them. He could see a forest of weeds in shallower areas. What caught his attention was the water itself. It almost appeared cloudy, like a bowl of thick soup. It had been a year since he had been on a lake like this. Perhaps it was normal, though he didn't think so. Nobody complained about it as far as he knew. When Joe Hall researched this area for their retreat, he discovered several photographs of people catching pike and largemouth, as well as photos posted by the owner on the resort website of people swimming. Then again, cloudy water wouldn't make for good publicity. Who knows? Those photographs might not have even been taken here for all Ernie knew.

Joe was seated at the front with his phone in hand. Still no answer from Todd. He considered yelling his name, but was afraid of gathering attention from the locals.

"Maybe take us around to the crook to the right," he suggested. "Maybe he's fishing back there."

"That's pretty much all that's left for us to look," Ernie replied. "Maybe we should consider asking around."

Joe wasn't sure he was at that point, yet. The thought of asking around the shoreline, 'hey, have you seen our friend?' seemed a bit embarrassing. Plus, there didn't appear to be many people out. There was some chatter coming from the northeast edge of the lake. A group of twenty-somethings were out on their dock, getting ready to go out. Secured to their dock was a pontoon boat, which was being loaded up with camera equipment and fishing supplies. Though they had the rods, bait, and nets, it didn't appear like it was a recreational trip.

Joe kept an eye on them as Ernie steered them to the east. Making a video, perhaps? YouTubers, by the looks of it. They certainly didn't look like a professional, trained crew of experienced cameramen. Professional or not, he certainly did not want to be caught on camera searching for his missing associate. Being the CEO of a growing company, such footage could easily be twisted by competitors should the footage appear online.

Reiner Foods CEO caught searching for drunken associates.

"No," he finally answered Ernie. The training manager was not entirely pleased with that response, but Joe was the boss. He guided the boat to the right and pointed it into the crook at the edge. It was a small cove extending three hundred feet to the south. There were two properties on each side. There were residents on the left doing what appeared to be maintenance on their dock.

No boats. No Todd.

"Damn it! Where the hell is he?" Joe said.

"I'm telling you, Joe. We should ask around."

"He probably went off into town," Joe muttered.

"With whose car? I checked this morning. His truck was in the lot," Ernie replied.

"Good point. And the boat's still missing from the dock," Joe said. He glanced between the homeowner in the cove, then back at the six or seven YouTubers behind him. "Alright, fine. Let's ask this guy up here if he's seen anyone."

Ernie put the boat into second gear and sped toward the cove, slowing down as they came within a couple hundred feet of the dock. At fifty feet, he killed the motor and switched to the oars.

The homeowner looked up and saw Joe waving at him. There was a look on his face mirroring his thoughts of 'who the hell are these guys?'

"Can I help you?" he asked. As the businessmen approached, they saw a bunch of tools on the dock by his knees.

"Hi," Joe said, somewhat nervously. "Sorry to bother you. We're trying to find a friend. I was just curious if you've seen any unfamiliar faces fishing over this way in a twelve-foot aluminum boat?"

The man's expression softened somewhat. Clearly, these people weren't agitators, like the noisy group across the lake.

"Nope. I'm afraid not. Aside from you guys and those nitwits back there, the only person I've seen out on this lake is my neighbor, Jack."

He pointed across the cove. Joe looked at the empty dock, then back at the lake.

I didn't see anyone out there...

The resident noticed Joe's expression. "You alright there?"

Joe wasn't sure how to address it, since there clearly weren't any places for any boaters to sneak off to. Joe wasn't a fool, but like all humans, he had his share of dumb moments. Once, he spent a half-hour looking for his phone...while holding it in his hand the entire time. He remembered how his mind was fixated on something he needed to look up on the internet, and he needed his phone to access it. He had gone back and forth through his house, looking under papers, inside file cabinets, and even the pantry. Even more embarrassing, he sent a text during that time. The use of the technology was so automatic, that his brain didn't even register the fact he was using it.

Memories like that made him nervous whenever he couldn't locate something. He worried he was the fool that couldn't find something that was right in front of his face. Maybe Todd was in the west segment. Maybe it had a cove similar to this one. Joe didn't recall seeing one, but then again, he didn't look too hard over there. Maybe it was on the far corner and he just didn't notice it.

"Uh, no, I'm good," Joe said. "Sorry to bother you, Mister..."

"Just call me Hank. And no, you're not bothering me. Unless you're the one who tore up my live-basket."

"Beg your pardon?" Ernie said. He rowed the boat around the other side of the dock and saw the metal basket torn apart. In addition, there was all kinds of strange slime all over it, which seemed to have hardened into some kind of paste.

"I had two bass in here last night, and I was gonna clean them this morning," Hank said.

"Maybe a turtle," Joe suggested.

"I thought that for a moment too," Hank replied. "Though, I've never seen one actually tear off the lid. It's almost as though it knew how to reach in and get my bass. And do not get me started on what this crap is." He took a screwdriver and flaked some of the dried substance off the dock.

"Odd," Joe said. "You've never had this before?"

"No. Not at all. I don't even know what it is." Hank stood up. "It almost seems like a chemical compound of some sort."

Ernie looked at the water again. The cloudiness stuck out like a sore thumb. Hank noticed it too.

"You guys staying over by that cabin resort over there?"

"That's right," Joe said.

"You never know who comes into town. I'm worried someone might've spilled something in this lake. Whatever this is, I don't think it's natural. Lakes don't dirty up like this unless it's introduced to something foreign. You see anyone over there acting weird?"

"No. We only arrived yesterday," Joe replied. "The people in the other cabins seem normal enough."

Hank shot a glare at the group of twenty-somethings. "I hope those asshats didn't do anything stupid for clicks."

Joe shrugged. This conversation had already gone on longer than he intended. Not that Hank was unpleasant to be around, but he had a seminar to start, and he was eager to check the west segment again. Hank had mentioned catching two bass recently. Obviously, the fishing in this lake was decent. Maybe Todd was out here, and they simply missed him.

"Alright, Hank. We oughta be going. Thanks for your help."

"Not a problem. Hope you find your friend."

Joe and Ernie waved as the latter turned the boat around and started the motor. They steered to the north and hooked to the left back toward the west segment.

"Catch anything?!" someone shouted. They looked to the crowd by the pontoon boat. Standing at the edge of the dock was a young man with long, shaggy hair. Joe didn't know who he was, nor did he care to, but a secret part of him envied the guy's effect on the ladies. There were at least three women in bikinis standing around the guy, rubbing his shoulders, back, and waist. Either he had the charm or the money, or both.

Joe didn't want to waste time with conversation with these guys. However, he didn't want to be rude either—especially considering one of the cameras was pointed at him.

"No. No luck!" he called back, pretending to be upbeat.

"Stick around if you wanna see me catch a forty-inch pike!" the guy stated. "I'm about to start a livestream."

Yep, definitely a YouTuber.

"No thanks. But good luck!" Joe said.

Ernie chuckled. "What a shame. He could've made you a star."

Joe chuckled. "Yeah, I'm sure I don't need his help."

Ernie glanced back, his eyes fixed on the hour-glass figures on the dock wearing thin bikinis.

I might have to make a YouTube channel of my own, someday.

He smiled at the fantasy as he continued to steer the boat toward the narrow point between the lake segments.

****

Tim Perkins disengaged the motor as they closed within forty yards of the property with the floating garage. The shore curved to the south, forming the narrow passageway between the two lake segments. The depth here was roughly the same as their previous spot. The trees along the bend cast a lengthy shadow over this spot. Perhaps the fish flocked here to escape the sunlight.

Cathy had her hook baited and ready to go.

"I better catch something, or you're dead meat," she said.

Tim scoffed. "*I'm* dead meat? You're deciding to be mad at me again for getting you up early."

"Yep!" Cathy replied, her tone somewhat upbeat. Tim wasn't sure if she was genuinely pissed or just messing with him. He suspected the latter; it wouldn't be the first time she did that. Unfortunately, it worked. He was on edge now, eager to please, and afraid of setting her off. This would lead to her teasing him for being a wuss.

Cathy cast out a line as Tim set the anchor. She watched it splash down a few meters from shore, then waited. After a minute, she tugged back a little, hoping the little bounce would get a fish's attention. After a minute, she repeated the action. No bites.

Soon, there was drag. Her heart thumped. It didn't appear to be a weed. Yet, the lack of actual pullback killed the excitement. A fish would be trying to run by now. No, she was simply dragging dead weight. Probably weeds. She couldn't think of what else it could be. The more she reeled it in, the worse the drag got. Slowly, but truly, she brought her lure closer to the boat.

Tim chuckled, watching her strain.

"Having trouble there, are ya?" he said. She sneered at him.

"I'm not impressed with this lake so far," she replied.

Tim shrugged. "I'm not either. You see how cloudy it is?"

Cathy stopped briefly to look. She didn't notice it before, but now she couldn't unsee it. The water looked...strange. *Thick* was the only word she could think of to describe it.

She cocked the reel a few more times, then lifted her lure over the side of the boat.

"Oh God!" she muttered. Tim looked up from his fishing line to see that his wife had brought in a string of the strange jelly-like goop. There wasn't even a weed attached to it. She had simply cast into a random spot and brought the stuff in. Cathy looked over at him. "What the hell is this stuff?"

"I don't know," Tim said. He glanced down at the floor, where the goop preserved the spilled worms. Beside the partially dried puddles were the worms that had avoided the substance. They were dead and dried out in the sun, unlike their brethren who rested preserved in the strange substance, even though it seemed to dry like paint over them.

He then became very aware that the skin on his left palm was very stiff. The tiny remainder of the stuff that had gotten on him had dried out. Whatever it was, it seemed to maintain this jelly-like form while in the water, but dried when exposed to air.

"I don't think this is normal," he said.

"No shit," Cathy said. She made a disgusted face at the strand of slime on her line. She tried flinging it off, but was only successful in severing a few droplets. Whatever it was, it was hanging on like glue. Cathy hated the idea of severing the line, but there was no way in hell she was going to touch this stuff.

"Maybe we should ask someone about this lake," she said.

"Hmm. Not a bad thought. Let's head in and talk to Greg," Tim suggested.

"Hell no. Not Greg," Cathy said.

"Why not?"

"You think he'll give us an honest answer. The guy's not gonna risk harming his business by telling everyone that this lake is full of…" she looked at her line, "whatever this crap is." She leaned over the side and gazed down at the water. She could see the forest of weeds ten feet below. The water was like a massive cloud, stringing all of the vegetation together. "Good God! Tim! Look at this! You can see it in the water. It's everywhere!"

Tim took a peek. The weeds reflected the sun's golden rays, illuminating the stringy texture of the slimy substance. As Cathy pointed out, it was everywhere, strung along the lakebed like an enormous spiderweb.

He squinted. There was something else there between the weeds. At first, he assumed it was just thick globs of the substance, or maybe submerged lily pads. They were roughly the same color. Still, he couldn't take his eyes off of them. When he noticed one, he noticed more. Once he saw them, he couldn't unsee them.

They were fish. Large fish, including large pike and walleye. They swayed gently with the weeds, as though a light breeze was passing under the water. Tim couldn't take his eyes off of them. The sight once again brought to mind the image of a spiderweb, and these fish were trapped in it like flies. The further he looked, the more detail he saw. Caught in certain strands of slime was residue which, at first, he thought was just natural debris from the lake. Then he noticed distinct shapes, like fins and jaws. Some of the fish had been viciously torn apart.

The others writhed in their trap, hopelessly trying to escape the inevitable fate that claimed the others. They weren't dead, as Tim initially assumed.

No, this was not normal. Neither Tim or Cathy considered themselves expert fishermen, but they had done it enough to know what healthy lake water should look like. This was not healthy. How was this not in the news? Even in a small town like this, such pollution ought to spark some kind of internet outrage. Tim couldn't imagine the locals were okay with their lake being like this.

"You know what?" Cathy said.

"What?" Tim said.

"I'm no longer pissed at you for getting us here early," she said. Tim looked over at her. "You didn't make the payment yet, right?"

"No."

"Good. We're going home," she said. "I'm not paying six-hundred bucks for a week at 'Swamp-ville.'"

Tim was relieved to hear her say that.

"Yeah, I was thinking the same thing," he said. "What about the hundred-dollar down payment?"

"Let the idiot keep it," Cathy said. "We haven't been here an hour yet, and already I'm at the point where I'd PAY a hundred dollars not to be here. I just wanted a week of peace and quiet, with my only obligations being swimming and sunbathing whenever I felt like it. This water is disgusting. I feel sick just being here."

Her point was made loud and clear. Tim nodded, then secured their fishing rods. Next, it was time to haul up the anchor. The boat rocked with his movements. Cathy made another disgusted groan. She couldn't believe they had driven all that way for *this*. She felt more than disgusted; a part of her felt scared. She didn't know what this strange substance was, and it bothered her. She looked to the west. She could see the dock with the unattended fishing rod. Why hadn't that person come out yet?

Cathy looked to the floating garage. The overhead door was halfway open, the white paint marred with strange incisions. Why was it like that? Why was the outside deck in disarray?

Why was the water rippling outside the garage?

Her eyes went to the weeds below her. Like trees bending to hurricane-force winds, they swayed in her direction. A shape passed over them, its dark green pigmentation exposed by the sunlight. It was no bigger than her husband in size, yet it glided effortlessly. Definitely an organism of the depths.

The forward half of the shape broke apart into eight coiling 'snakes'. Like cobras, they lashed at her at once.

The anchor hit the metal floor by Tim's right foot with a blunt *thud*. Right away, he grabbed the ripcord for the motor.

"Alright, let's get the hell out of here."

With the yank of the cord came a tremendous splash from behind him. He heard Cathy shriek, a sound which lasted a split-second before it was consumed by that of another splash. Tim spun back and saw her feet before they plunged beneath the water.

"Cathy?!"

He lunged for the bow, inadvertently causing the boat to sway to the right. Beneath the lapping water, Tim caught a brief glimpse of his wife's blue jeans and red lifejacket as she was yanked from view.

There was no opportunity to dive in after her. There wasn't even time to process what had just happened. The water erupted right under his nose. He saw green, leathery flesh, and a mouth lined with razor teeth. Tim shrieked and fell backward, barely out of reach of the claw-tipped tentacles. One appeared after the next, all clinging to the port bow. The boat teetered to the left.

Tim's mind descended into a whirlwind of panic. Such terror didn't allow for thought of his wife's well-being, or even comprehension of what it was that was happening. All he knew in this moment was pure survival instinct. Evolutionarily speaking, he was no different than a chipmunk evading the talons of a hawk.

He grabbed the motor prop and twisted it to third gear. The propeller sliced the water, pushing the boat forward. Tim steered to the right. The boat, still in the creature's grasp, teetered further to the left as it dragged it along. There was a sound of scraping metal, followed by a splash. Relieved of the creature's weight, the boat shot forward.

Tim was still on his back, his legs propped over the seat. He steered blindly, while struggling to stand himself up without losing any speed. He let go of the prop and clawed at the seat. The motor straightened for a moment, then started pulling to the left. After five seconds, he righted himself, just in time to see the aluminum boat passing right in front of him.

****

"Holy crap! Ernie, lookout!" Joe shouted. The training manager tried steering them to the left, but it was too late. He had seen the boat's odd trajectory, but didn't anticipate it to suddenly steer back in their direction. Its bow struck the starboard quarter.

The boat's occupant was flung across its twelve-foot length. Joe and Ernie heard the *clang* of his forehead striking the gunwale.

The breach in their vessel was obvious, due to the water rushing in. The other boat wasn't much better. Its bow was folded inward, forming metal arrows along the edges. Still, it was in better shape than theirs, which would be under water in a minute or two.

Joe and Ernie each took an oar and paddled toward the boat that struck them. In those few moments, they felt their own boat get heavier and heavier. Ernie, who stood at the rear, felt the water rise to his shins.

After they closed the gap, Joe quickly stepped over to the other boat. Its occupant was barely conscious, his face covered in blood. There was a gash in his forehead that appeared to cut all the way down to the bone. Ernie stepped over just as the water reached the top of the seat. The motor wasn't there any longer, having broken off in the crash. Making matters worse, this boat was flooding as well, though more slowly than the other, whose stern had almost completely submerged.

****

"Good God!" Greg Goodman was on his hands and knees in Cabin One's kitchen. The ants really did make a stronghold in here. The previous occupants had mentioned seeing a few, but from what they had mentioned, it was just a few scouts. These bastards had literally just moved in and decided to take the place for themselves.

"Not today," he said. He twisted the nozzle of his spray bottle of Roots Home Defense and opened fire on the ones crawling over the kitchen floor. The wet little dots continued to scurry about. Cursing under his breath, he continued dousing them. Some finally started to die, though more likely due to drowning rather than chemical exposure. He would need his vacuum cleaner to clean out all of their carcasses. To add to his duties, he would have to disinfect this entire cabin.

Lovely. How could this day get any worse?

He heard a distant sound of impact, followed immediately by reactionary shouting from outside.

"Holy shit!"

"You see that?!"

"Whoa!"

There was the sound of running feet as people congregated along the shore. Greg dropped his supplies and hurried out the door, immediately seeing people pointing out into the lake. Some of them were covering their mouths in shock. Then, he saw the two boats. One was on the verge of sinking, with its occupants climbing aboard the other.

"What the hell?!" he muttered. Those were *his* boats. What was going on? He sprinted up the hill to his garage, found the keys to his speedboat, then ran down to his private dock.

"I think they crashed," Mr. Kendrick exclaimed. Greg paid him no mind as he boarded his speedboat. He started the engine, backed it out, then throttled toward the scene.

The bow of the vacant twelve-footer was up at a forty-five degree angle, and the other appeared to be weighed down at the front. He could see Joe Hall and one of his employees waving at him. They appeared to be pressing a handkerchief against Tim Perkins' forehead.

"Over here!" Joe shouted.

Yes, I'm not blind. Greg brought his boat to a stop alongside theirs. The forward section was completely filled with water. The two men hauled Tim aboard. He was sprawled out on the deck, mumbling some kind of gibberish.

"What the hell happened?!" Greg said.

"I don't know. He was driving around like an idiot, and suddenly he came right at us," Joe said. He noticed Greg looking down at Tim, then back at the boats, and out at the surrounding water. "Greg! This guy's bleeding badly. We gotta get him to shore. No offense, but what's the holdup?"

"He was with his wife," Greg replied. "I don't see her anywhere."

"Oh shit," Joe muttered. They all gazed out at the lake.

"She was wearing a life vest...but I don't see her anywhere," Greg said. He glanced down at Tim Perkins. Joe's handkerchief was completely soaked in blood. Time was not a luxury; Tim's vitals were fading rapidly.

Greg made one final attempt to locate Cathy. With her red lifejacket, she should've stuck out like a sore thumb. Instead, all he saw was a glassy lake. Cursing under his breath, he steered the boat back to shore, then dug his phone from his pocket.

"9-1-1. What's your emergency?"

CHAPTER 8

Sheriff Hannah Tyler crossed the briefing lobby on the way to her office. As she did, she glanced briefly at the two-dozen mailboxes for the Deputies. Five of them were empty. In a week, that number would increase to six.

She entered her office and took a seat. On her office desk sat a resignation letter. The officer was transferring south to Bay County. In his letter, he did not mince words about his reason for leaving—something Hannah expected. In fact, she was surprised he hadn't transferred sooner. He had made his feelings well-known when Hannah first became Sheriff, more specifically, during her campaign for Sheriff.

Hannah only read the first half, then skimmed the rest for the necessary details pertaining to the end of his employment. She jotted down the date and stuffed the letter into a yellow folder, where it would likely reside for several years, before ending up in the shredder.

So, I played a bit dirty, she thought. Her justification did little to put her at ease. Her actions had consequences that she should have anticipated. She didn't mean for it to go as far as it did. Her parents had always taught her to win at all costs, to let *nobody* hold her back. Her mother owned a restaurant in Mason County, where her father taught MMA after retiring from the Sheriff's Department. She tried not to pay attention to the rumors surrounding his reasons for why he took an early retirement, or why he was he was fined two-thousand dollars for violations during cage-fighting competitions. Then there were the accusations of false information spread about the only other restaurant in town by her mother. Whether they were true or not, it hurt the business, and drove more customers to the only other restaurant within twenty-five miles.

Her family had the win-at-all-costs mentality. Everyone else were nothing more than obstacles in the way to success. "The world isn't fair," they said. "There are winners and there are losers. Big dogs like to eat."

On her desk was a photo of her father, taken three years before his death in 2015. He was a man who looked as though he was carved in stone. That hard stare he wore on his face was identical to most memories she had of him. Though he died six years ago, she still felt like he was watching over her shoulder, coaching her on how to succeed.

Beside his photo was a frame of a second-place medal when she used to run four-hundred meter dashes. His reaction was for her to try harder next time. It didn't matter that she beat eight other people; it only mattered that one beat her. There was no "congratulations" or "good try, kiddo." Just a sense of disappointment.

"There are winners and there are losers. Big dogs like to eat." It was a phrase ingrained into her mindset. She wondered what Dad thought of when his cancer diagnosis took a turn for the worst. Did he feel like a loser for not beating it? What about Mom? With their busy schedules, they only spoke by phone once every couple of weeks, and the conversations were very routine. "How's work?" "You seeing anybody?" "You won't believe what idiots we had at the restaurant the other day." More often than not, Hannah found herself trying to get out of those phone conversations because of the phony relationship they displayed.

Phony. That seemed to be the word that defined Hannah Tyler. Her Deputies knew it. Fire and EMS knew it. The County Clerk's office knew it, and the Tonette town board knew it, though they kept it to themselves. As long as law and order was maintained, it was considered bad taste for office officials to publicly bash a county Sheriff.

The town seemed mostly unaware. Most people didn't vote for local offices anyway. According to the data, only eleven percent of the county even voted. Only State and Federal Offices got the masses to show up to the polls. Most people in Tonette didn't even know the name of the Township Director. When it came to the new Sheriff, they assumed she won the election fair and square with a superior work record and business plan going forward. But her peers knew the truth, and they resented her for her tactics.

It wasn't fair and square, but she won all the same. She wanted the position bad enough—at least, she thought she did. Big dogs wanted to eat, and with Hannah's upbringing, she had a big appetite. Had to reach the top of that ladder, no matter the cost.

Hannah achieved her goal. She was both the youngest and the first female Sheriff to be elected to office. She should've been over the moon with joy every single day. Except, she felt lower than ever. Only when she had the responsibility of that goal did she truly start to question her parents' mindset.

Yeah, most of the town paid no mind to her tactics, and with some effort, she could pretend to be ignorant of the morale of her Deputies. Sooner or later, she would get some new hires, which would help level out the attitudes toward her. But there was one person's judgement she couldn't ignore: herself.

Hannah knew she was a phony. She didn't really *earn* the position. No matter how she justified it, there was no escaping that truth. Every time she lied to herself, it was like adding purchases to a credit card balance. Each lie piled on the other, like mounting debt. And seeing Greg Goodman today felt like a debt collector reminding her that the payment was due, no matter how hard she tried to bury it.

She heard the lobby door open. Bill Hoskin gave her a wave as he passed by her office. In his hand were two traffic tickets. Before the door slammed shut, two other officers stepped in. It was Deputy Jake Bing and Zach Cassidy. The two must've met up since she saw Bing patrolling on Zolciak Road. Cassidy was in the middle of telling a story regarding his girlfriend's brother. Whatever it was, Bing was rolling his eyes. Hannah knew little about it, but it sounded like the subject of their conversation was a troublemaker.

Zach Cassidy was known as a go-getter the entire time Hannah knew him. He was often the first one arriving at a scene and one of the last to leave. He had a lean figure, reminiscent of being on the diving team. All-in-all, he was a model Deputy, up until Hannah was appointed to the position. His attitude quickly went from model employee to 'fuck this place'—a sentiment shared by much of the department.

As far as she knew, most of these guys still spoke from time-to-time with Greg Goodman. She wished she'd considered that when she refused to cancel his ticket. Undoubtedly, it would come up in a future conversation. They would look at it as kicking somebody while they're down. Worse, actually, considering she was the *reason* he was down in the first place.

She listened to their chatter as they marched down the hallway. It was almost ten-thirty. Close to the time they routinely went to the vending machines. She could hear them greet Bill Hoskin as they passed by.

"Hey Rookie! What you got there? Finally pull somebody over by yourself?" Zach always sounded like he was munching on something when he spoke. Probably because he was, most of the time. All that swimming burnt energy. He was practically a vehicle in constant need of gas. Jake Bing, while also part of the diving team, wasn't quite as committed, thus had an average build. He'd probably be leaner if it wasn't for the steady diet of spaghetti.

She heard Bill chuckle. He always did that around the guys. He was impressionable and nervous, despite his attempts to seem confident. Hannah couldn't judge him for it, really. She was the same way when she first started.

"Yeah. Caught one going seventy over on Myles, and caught the other on the way back," he replied. "Punk ass kid driving his dad's Porsche."

"Did he give you lip?" Jake asked.

"His dad did," Bill replied.

"Don't forget the stakeout spot over on Springer Road. People love cutting through that zone at eighty miles an hour," Zach replied.

Hannah noticed how he spoke slightly louder than before, as though he intended for her to overhear. *Yeah, we're training this kid better than you ever could.* Maybe she was looking too far into it. Then again, they had frequently been taking subtle shots at her since she took office. Nothing too blatant that she could outright penalize them for. Besides, it wasn't just them, but *most* of the department.

At this rate, it would only get better by attrition.

"Dispatch to Unit One."

"Yeah, go ahead," Hannah said.

"We've got a report of a boat accident on Peanut Lake. EMS has been notified and is en route. One serious injury. One person reported missing."

"Oh, damn!" Zach's voice echoed.

"Hey kid, you wanna ride with us?"

"Uh, sure," Bill replied.

Hannah stood up from her desk, her radio still held to her lips. "Dispatch, did they confirm this missing person was on one of the boats?"

"Affirmative, Sheriff."

Oh, that's not sounding good.

"Copy that. What's the address?"

"5810 Circle Drive. Good Lake Resort." Hannah stepped out into the hall.

"Bill, you're gonna ride with me. Zach, Jake, your timing is perfect. You're probably gonna have to change into your diving gear. There might possibly be a deceased person in that lake."

"Whatever you say, Sheriff," Jake replied. He tapped Bill on the shoulder before walking off to the locker room. "Don't muddle up the crime scene till we get there."

"Think that's what it is? A crime? Or just an accident?" Zach asked.

"Probably an accident...with some tequila involved. Don't know how you can crash two boats together in broad daylight like that."

Hannah waited until the two Deputies disappeared around the corner.

"Come on, Bill. You're driving."

"Okay. Where's this lake at? I don't believe I've been there," he said.

"It's easy. I'll guide you along the way. Just take Zolciak to the intersection at Guy, then make a right, and it's a straight shot for about five minutes, with a left hand turn at Rolfe. Follow the bend for about a minute, which'll take you to Circle Drive. We'll find the resort from there."

She couldn't blame him for not knowing. She had to think of it for a second before she remembered. There were over two-dozen small lakes in the vicinity, some of which were so small, they were practically ponds. Most were home to residential areas, with only local cabin resorts, and those typically attracted people who wanted peace and quiet. Since she first hired in the police department, the vast majority of fatalities involved vehicular accidents, and incidents with livestock, and a small handful of homicides, spread out over the course of her ten years there.

Luckily, as unfortunate as the case was, it sounded pretty cut and dry. Boat accident, possibly involving alcohol as Jake mentioned. Nothing more than that. The worst part would be locating the body. Other than that, it would probably be a simple report, and a few unfortunate phone calls to make.

Bill pulled a car key from his pocket. "Ready to go when you are."

"Hey, I was waiting on you," Hannah replied. They went out to the lot together and boarded Car Three. He turned on the flashers, then sped out of the lot.

CHAPTER 9

Ryan Hodges wasn't always a man of ego. He had grown up a skinny, timid person, always backing down from the jocks and intellectuals. More than once, he lost a girlfriend to another, more confident man. Considered himself unfit for the modern age. He wasn't good with electronics; until six months ago, he still owned a flip-phone. This led to people jokingly referring to him as old-timer, even though he was only twenty-six. Ryan wasn't the kind of guy who took solace in the virtual world. He enjoyed the outdoors, particularly fishing. On weekends during the high school year, his parents would have to force him to come in from the creek and complete his schoolwork. He passed, barely.

College wasn't much better. He had a few ideas of what he wanted to do, but couldn't stand the extra courses he had to take in order to obtain the degree. Geometry? What does geometry have to do with being a park ranger? He figured it was just another way for the college to squeeze money out of him. He never made it past the first semester. He hated college, and the easy-to-offend culture that surrounded it. Every other week, there was some sort of gathering taking place. Professors would give social and political lectures that had nothing to do with their courses.

So, Ryan dropped out. Instead, he took a few online business courses, figuring he could start up a bait and tackle shop. Doing so took longer than his naïve younger self anticipated, as he needed to raise money to get inventory, a down payment on a facility, and advertising. That last part was the real kicker. Some commercials cost thousands of dollars.

Gosh, that's the kind of money I want to make! Not spend!

A few cheap routes got him nowhere. Still, through working odd jobs and saving, he put up the money for a shop not too far from a public lake. A few locals started shopping there right away, but it wasn't enough to break even. He realized starting this kind of business in the UP might not have been the best idea. The populations were low up there. In some areas, a person could drive a few miles without finding any private residences.

Not wanting to give up on his ambition, he needed to come up with something fast. That was when he met an old high school buddy, David Mitchell. Buddy might not have been the right term—agitator seemed more appropriate. David was a stereotypical high school jock who was always in the gym, playing football, popular with the ladies—including Ryan's high school sweetheart. More than once, Ryan was the butt of various jokes. "Can't keep a girl pleased." "Ryan's the best thing for a chick. She's gotta experience the wuss first, then she'll *really* appreciate the real man when he comes by."

It was by happenstance that Ryan and David crossed paths again. A mutual friend from high school, Mandy Bassinger, sent out invitations to a party she was hosting at a lake. It was at the last minute that Ryan learned that David Mitchell would be there as well, a revelation that almost made him cancel. When he saw the former jock, he expected to see a Mr. Olympia wannabe, flexing for the babes while sweet-talking them. Instead, the man he saw had lost about fifteen pounds, and was limping on his left side. He wasn't sickly in appearance, but definitely did not hold the super-confident masculine traits Ryan remembered him for.

Ryan assumed life only got better for David once he got into college. Far from it. At age twenty, David was involved in an automobile accident. It was winter. Freezing water had caked the roads of Marquette. David had the green light and was going through the intersection when he was t-boned on the driver's side. The trucker that hit him had tried to stop, but had no traction on the ice. David woke up two days later. Facing paralysis from the waist down, he underwent numerous surgeries. The Doctors performed their miracles, and after being confined to a wheelchair for six months, David was able to walk again, albeit with the use of a cane.

The experience had humbled him. Though not a pushover, he had a much gentler quality than previously. He even took up conversation with Ryan. To both their amazement, the two kept in touch, once David and the girls at the party convinced Ryan to set up a *Facebook* account.

There was more to that party than brats, beer, and social media. Wherever Ryan went, he brought his fishing rods with him. They practically resided in the back of his truck. While everyone else was swimming, smoking weed, and eating, Ryan took the opportunity to go out on the dock. He garnered laughs at first until he hooked a seventeen-inch largemouth. The leaps and bounds that the fish made during its fight drew the attention of everybody.

This led to a curious observer asking a few questions about fishing. How to do it? What kind of bait? How do you know if the fish grabs the hook? High as a kite, the partygoers assembled at the dock as though attending a seminar. Smartphones recorded the session, as well as the catching of a thirty-two-inch walleye.

The video was posted onto *Facebook*, with Ryan being tagged by Mandy. In the comments section, somebody wrote that Ryan should start a *YouTube* series. He took it as a joke when he read it on his computer. Joke or not, it sparked curiosity.

He downloaded the video, opened a *YouTube* account, and uploaded the video. During the next few days, he almost forgot about it, as he was caught up in store managing duties and casual fishing. Then, that following weekend, he decided to open *Facebook*, only to see dozens of notifications. People were posting on the video Mandy had tagged him in, as well as posting to his page directly. There were also a few notifications in *Messenger*. Every single one was pertaining to the video.

"Holy crap, Ryan. You've become an overnight sensation," Mandy had posted.

Ryan opened his *YouTube* account and saw that the video had ten thousand views. In addition, his account had three-hundred-and-fifty subscribers. He didn't know what that meant at first, which led to a couple of days of research. For a seasoned *YouTuber,* those numbers meant nothing. But, for someone who uploaded a video on a whim, he was practically an internet celebrity. It didn't take long for the ideas to roll in. What if he used this to promote his store?

Ryan decided to take a risk. He purchased recording equipment, microphones, and downloaded editing software. He spent the next few days filming himself fishing, while giving how-to lectures. He made a half dozen videos, the first of which garnered almost the same number of views as the initial one. The next two uploads, however, made only half that. Then the next ones made only a third. The subscribers, which had increased to four-hundred-and-fifty, had leveled off. Soon, though, it turned to four-forty-nine. Then four-forty-eight.

He knew what he wasn't doing right: he didn't know squat about editing. He didn't know how to line up appropriate shots. His videos were long and uncut, while the original upload was short and to the point. To make matters worse, he could never get the fish in frame when he hooked it. He was always tugging at something off camera, which led to a few comments accusing him of faking it.

A month later, Mandy set up another party. It was mainly comprised of the same people, all of which were now fascinated with Ryan's 'celebrity' status. That was when the ego began to rise. It was slow at first, but it would soon skyrocket, along with his subscriber base. Little did Ryan know that here at the party, his luck would change for the better. David Mitchell was a video-editing major in college, and had just gotten back from a video shoot in Wisconsin. Since a potential career in sports was no longer an option, he decided to put his brain to work. He enjoyed filmmaking and was fascinated with the editing process, so why not pursue a career in it?

It was the exact expertise that Ryan was lacking. He arranged for them to meet privately to discuss his proposition. David was hesitant at first; he didn't have *YouTube* in mind when he decided to pursue filmmaking. With consideration, however, he began to reshape his thoughts. The world was changing fast. *Hollywood* and even small independent studios across the country were failing. Streaming was the way to go, nowadays. He even had a couple of mentors suggest to him that doing-it-yourself is the way to work.

With no other work lined up, he decided to take a chance. Ryan had the charisma to be in front of the camera, and he already had some momentum going. With better editing, lighting, and camera positioning, they might possibly make something out of the *Ryan Hodges* channel.

Ryan was impatient at first. Proper editing meant more time between video uploads. It took a while before David could convince him that spamming the audience with constant, low-effort videos would soon drive an audience away. When the viewer count, comment numbers, likes, and subscribers started going up, Ryan's protests subsided.

Within two weeks, he hit a thousand subscribers. Ten days later, two thousand. An additional forty-five days and twenty uploads took him to ten-thousand subscribers. It would only get better from there. David helped set up an online store for his shop, as well as teach him how to get his stuff on *Amazon* and other online retailers. Sales went up immediately, as did Ryan's ego. He never considered it to be compensating for his formerly timid persona and the abuse it brought him in his teens. He lived in the here and now.

Needing to enhance his onscreen image, Ryan started hitting the gym every morning right before filming. Within a month, he was sporting sleeveless vests, even as late fall was making way for winter.

With additional resources at their disposal, the team took the show to various locations across the state, and eventually across state lines. To add viewership, Ryan hosted instructional videos on filleting and cooking fish, with David handling all of the behind-the-scenes tasks.

Then, they discovered a new trick, one that helped them make a bounding leap from seventy-thousand subscribers to a hundred in just a couple of weeks. Featuring hot girls in the videos, and more importantly, the thumbnails. It was a cheap, but effective method. Luckily, he knew exactly who to hire. Mandy Bassinger and her friends looked good in their swim outfits, and they all had a fascination with Ryan and his channel. Better yet, they were eager to get involved. Get paid essentially to model, and not worry about creepy corporate executives and producers? They signed contracts the same day they were approached. With their involvement, the subscriber and view counts climbed. With over a hundred thousand subscribers came sponsors and shoutouts from fellow *YouTube* stars.

Ryan Hodges had done it. He had turned his fishing passion into a career. His store was doing well, despite him being late to ship purchases due to his commitments to the channel. His high-school bully was now his employee. Better yet, the girls were no longer flocking to David Mitchell, but instead to Ryan Hodges. His gym workouts continued. Within a year, he had gained twenty-five pounds of muscle. His steady diet of fish helped pack on the protein.

Soon, Ryan was going to conventions, meeting with other independent sport show hosts, and getting offers from larger, more mainstream sponsors.

With every achievement, he wanted more. He was having too much fun with this channel. He was constantly researching successful series, whether it was book series, movies and TV shows, and other *YouTube* series. The last thing he wanted to do was risk getting stale. What he learned with studying trends from these other series was that they always returned to basics whenever they started losing viewers.

"Return to what drew people in from the beginning," was the conclusion.

Ryan had not lost any subscribers and viewers, but he did worry about potential burnout. The last several months contained several high-effort videos, each wackier than the last. It eventually led to a trip to the Florida Keys where they shot videos of spearfishing and fishing for blue shark.

Now, perhaps it was a good opportunity to slow down, relax, and return to basics. His uncle had a property in Tonette, Michigan on a private lake. Peanut Lake, it was called. He had fished there frequently in his youth, and remembered all the hotspots where the bass and pike often fed. Knowing his uncle, he'd let them fish for free. It would be a cost-effective way of shooting, while likely not losing any viewers for the short term. He could catch his breath, do something simple, and use his spare time to come up with the next ambitious series of videos.

The whole crew had assembled at the dock. They had heard the crash and could see the speedboat rushing from the resort area on the west segment. Because of the bend in the shoreline, and the trees protruding from it, they couldn't quite see what was going on. Judging by the frantic chatter in the distance, it wasn't anything good.

After a while, they could hear ambulance sirens gradually approach. Their presence was confirmed by the bright red flashers that streamed across the glassy lake.

"Damn," Ryan muttered to himself. The boat was ready, the cameras set up, the girls dressed up—if he could call it that. He was ready to start rolling. But with all the confusion currently taking place, he was at a standstill. He didn't have the bad taste to film the first responders. He wasn't THAT hard pressed for views. However, he had a livestream scheduled, and he didn't want EMS and the Sheriff's Department in the background. His show was about fishing, after all.

"You still wanna go out on the water?" Mandy asked.

"Hang on, I'm thinking," Ryan replied. He sounded frustrated, though not at her. Her hand touched his bare shoulder. Another hand touched his waist. It was Katy's. She stepped to his left, swirling her strawberry blond hair back.

"What a shame. I was looking forward to making you all look bad."

"Yeah? Who are you trying to impress?" Mandy retorted.

Katy smiled. "Before you worry about *who* you're impressing, you oughta make sure you have something to impress them *with*." Mandy's eyes widened, as she noticed Katy eyeing her figure. It was definitely a gesture toward her C-cup size. Katy certainly had superiority in that department. For whatever reason, the gods had blessed the bitch with breasts that would certainly tempt a *quid pro quo* situation in Los Angeles.

David Mitchell watched from the back of the dock. The pain in his hip throbbed along with his ego. He never got used to what he was seeing. Three years ago, all he had to do was talk sweet to any of these girls, and they'd melt like butter. Now, they were passing him by for the blade of grass that was Ryan Hodges. Except, he wasn't a blade of grass anymore. Though he wasn't as muscular as David used to be, his physique was far superior than what David could even hope to achieve. Working out came at a price of pain nowadays. Usually, he would have to settle for a half-hour on the elliptical. Even that hurt sometimes, especially in the winter. How the mighty had fallen.

He had conflicting emotions about working on this show. On the one hand, it was nice to be a part of a successful *YouTube* program. He did the math and learned that less than a percent of all *YouTubers* did well enough to make a living at it. He was part of a rare statistic and it felt good. What didn't feel good was watching the girls constantly vie for Ryan's attention. It wasn't simply an alpha male jealousy…though that played a small role as well. Rather, it was a symptom of Ryan taking all the credit for the show's success. Yeah, he started it. Yeah, he had the charisma. Yeah, he was the director…technically. But it was David who had the technical knowledge, who did the majority of the scheduling, worked long hours cutting and editing, as well as estimating costs for future episodes. On set each day, he was the one lining up the shots, while hardly appearing on camera himself.

The job paid well, so he couldn't complain. However, the vast majority of feedback always went to Ryan. Again, it made sense, since he was the face of the show, but it was still annoying. The guy's show wouldn't be half as successful without David's expertise. The long hours working probably played into David's growing resentment. What did Ryan do, really? Every day, his day comprised of showing up on set, fishing, explaining what he was doing. Sometimes there'd be script writing, but usually, most of what he said was adlibbed. He knew everything there was about the craft, and had developed a natural charm. Other than that, he would research locations online, which was more fun than work, because he would get excited about fishing in areas he never got to experience before. His life had essentially become a vacation.

"Ryan?" he called out. There was no response. The guy was too enthralled by the verbal sparring of the hot girls. "Hey, Ryan?!" This time, he turned around.

"What's up, David?"

"I suggest we delay the livestream by about an hour or two."

"Delay? But we've made several posts online letting people know it'd be at eleven," Ryan said.

"I know, but you really want sirens and flashing lights in your background? I can already see the comment section: *Dude, what's going on over there? Why is there an ambulance? Are those sirens I hear?*" David walked halfway up the dock, where he could see the flashers on west segment. It was too far away to tell, but it appeared EMTs dressed in white shirts were gathering around somebody at the beach. Something was going on for sure, and it was hard to know how long it would take. And the livestream was due to commence in fifteen minutes.

"Would people really care that much?" Katy asked. David couldn't help but notice she couldn't keep her hands off Ryan's waist. At least Mandy didn't make her wishes so obvious. Neither did Natalie, who, while extroverted, tended to be a little more reserved. She wore a thin jacket over her bathing suit, not intending to overtly show herself off until the camera was rolling. And there was plenty to show off.

"I don't know," Natalie said. "You've gotten plenty of comments from people who look forward to these livestreams, Ryan."

David sighed. Of course she would defer to Ryan's judgement. Then again, how could he blame her? He placed himself in her shoes...or sandals. *Would I listen to my employer, who had given me a moderate level of internet fame, or the skinny, crippled camera guy?*

They could hear more sirens echoing from the distance. Ryan glanced out at the water, then sighed. Surely, the mics were going to pick up on all the chatter taking place.

"Damn it."

"Ryan, I have the solution," David said. Ryan looked back at him.

"I'm listening."

"Let's shoot a video right now and upload it. Tell the audience we'll move the time to twelve-thirty. That should likely provide enough time for the paramedics and Deputies to do what they need to do, and not interrupt our show. I'll get on our *Facebook, Twitter,* and *Instagram* pages and inform everyone of the update as well."

"What do we do in the meantime?" Katy said.

David shrugged. "I don't know. Have an early lunch, perhaps?"

Ryan smiled. "OR...we head over to Archer Lake and shoot some footage there. If we leave now, we can probably get enough footage for a quick five-minute episode, and be back in time for the livestream."

Mixed emotions clashed in David's mind. On the one hand, at least Ryan was open to delaying the livestream. On the other hand, however, now he would have MORE work to do in the editing department, while Ryan spent his evening doing whatever. There wasn't time to argue. More videos meant more ad revenue.

"Alright. Give me a sec."

David grabbed a camera and tripod, then set up a small canopy to block the sunlight. He didn't have to worry about this video looking too pretty, being that it was simply a sixty-second announcement. He already had the intro music on file, so the editing process would be as brief as the video itself. Hell, it could be accomplished on the laptop.

"Alright, I'm ready to go whenever you are," he announced. Ryan took a few steps forward, putting himself perfectly in frame, with David guiding through hand directions. The girls huddled by him then smiled at the camera as though doing a modeling shoot. David counted down with his fingers, then gave a thumbs-up. *Action.*

Ryan snapped into his upbeat persona, pointing a finger at the camera, while sporting his perfect white teeth in a wide smile.

"Hey, everyone! It's Ryan here, your favorite angler, showing you how to nab the big one wherever you are in the country! This is an announcement concerning our eleven-o'clock livestream. I regret to inform you we have to delay it about ninety minutes. There appears to be a situation on the water. Nothing too major, but if you look over to my left, you might see some flashing lights. We're not sure exactly what's happening, but it seems there was a boating accident of some kind. I'm not sure if you can see on camera, but there is a boat half-submerged in the water. Definitely appears that two boats might have collided. You can hear the sirens in the background, so there's clearly more first responders on the way. So, what we're going to do is delay the livestream to twelve-thirty. I apologize for the delay, especially for it being at the last minute, but I just think it's best we stay clear of the water in case there's any follow-up investigation to the incident. Please tune-in at twelve-thirty. I promise, we'll have a fun time out on the water. See you then."

"Good." David shut off the camera. Seeing that he already had it, he would probably use it for rolling footage on Archer Lake.

Ryan clapped his hands. "Okay! If we move fast, we can get over to Archer Lake in six or seven minutes. Ladies, grab your stuff, and let's get in the truck. I'll drive, that way David can do what he needs to do."

"So nice of you to volunteer," David joked. His fake smile vanished as he spun around to run into the house to get his laptop. Pain soared through his body like lightning. That damn hip of his. It was always tormenting him, a constant reminder of his fragile state.

"You okay?"

David looked over his shoulder and saw Natalie approaching. The others either didn't notice he was hunched over, or didn't care.

"I'm good," he replied. "Stupid car accident keeps beating me up, even though it's been a couple of years."

"I can get the laptop for you," she said.

"No, no, no," David said, standing up straight. "I'm fine. I'll meet you over at the van."

"You sure?"

"Yes, Nat, I'm sure."

"Okay."

He watched her jog off for the driveway, brown hair waving gracefully behind her. Like Mandy and Katy, they used to flirt all the time back when he was a jock. Since starting the channel, most interactions they'd had had been business related. Either they were attracted to confidence, or muscular physiques. David had lost both.

Still, it would be a cold day in hell before he would let people do favors for him. He endured the pain and hustled into the house. He grabbed the laptop then boarded the van. While everyone else was bantering with each other and vying for Ryan's attention (and likely affection), he was working.

Story of my life.

Ryan steered them out of the driveway onto Circle Drive. They followed it around to the north until they reached Rolfe Street. Within ten seconds of making the turn, they saw flashing red and blue lights on the approach. Ryan pulled over to the side. He watched the Sheriff's SUV speed past him and make a sharp turn onto Circle Drive, sending gravel spraying across the road.

"Jeez. Must be serious."

CHAPTER 10

"Car Four en-route to Peanut Lake," Jake Bing announced over the radio.

"Dispatch copies. Ten-fifty-three."

Hannah Tyler listened to the radio chatter while Bill drove around the bend until it intersected with Circle Drive.

"Left or right?" he asked her.

"Take a right," she replied. He made the turn, then after thirty seconds, he saw the sign for *Good Lake Resort.* They immediately saw HVA and Fire Rescue after steering onto the driveway. Bill parked a couple of meters beside it and hopped out of his seat.

The officers passed the owner's house then looked down the hill, where they saw the paramedics putting the victim on a stretcher and pushing him up the hill.

"Come on." Hannah sprinted down the hill to meet them, then grabbed hold of one corner of the stretcher and helped to pull the patient up the tedious path.

"Appreciate it, Sheriff," one of the paramedics said.

"No problem." Hannah looked at the patient, seeing his head tightly wrapped in bandages, and his neck secured in a brace. "How serious is it?"

"He hit his head hard. Said nothing but gibberish this whole time. We gotta get him to the ER right away. There might be a potential brain bleed." Hannah and Bill helped to lift the stretcher into the ambulance. Before the paramedic shut the door, she pointed down the hill at the firefighters and civilians. "There's a few witnesses down there. The Lieutenant's got this gentleman's info. Hopefully that'll help."

"Appreciate it." Hannah pushed one of the doors shut then stepped away as the ambulance backed up then raced onto Circle Drive, blaring its sirens the whole way. She hustled down the hill. She could see the Fire Lieutenant's big bald head, glistening sweat which reflected sunlight like a mirror. He saw her and waved her over.

Hannah almost stopped. The guy he was speaking to looked familiar. Too familiar. So familiar that she recognized the very outfit he was wearing…because she had seen him just over an hour ago.

"Oh, you've got to be kidding me," she muttered. She glanced back at the house and the resort logo. *Good Lake Resort. Good—Goodman.* She remembered his various interactions with staff when he worked for the department, and how he'd humorously refer to his last name in corny ways like—Good Lake Resort. *Damn, I didn't put two-and-two together.*

"Uh, Sheriff? Is that…?"

"Yes," she replied. "Don't bring it up. Focus on the situation at hand." Bill didn't say anything further. The apprehension she felt was conveyed in her tone of voice.

"You *sure* you saw her in a lifejacket?"

Greg was fed up with answering this question for the third time. Lieutenant Gordon was only doing his job, and he was always a thorough guy. Maybe too thorough. Or maybe Greg simply didn't have the patience he used to.

"I watched her put it on when they got on the boat," he replied.

"Could she have taken it off in the meantime?"

"I don't know. I was just trying to get her out of my hair so I could get their cabin set up."

Joe Hall stepped forward from the crowd. "As you saw, the husband was wearing his. So…"

"Fact is, if she was wearing her lifejacket, we'd know it," Gordon said. He turned to face the water. "Hell, we'd probably be able to see her from here."

"That's what scares me," Greg replied. He could hear footsteps hitting the concrete stairs. He turned around, then groaned at the sight of Sheriff Hannah Tyler and her Deputy. "Oh, you've got to be kidding me!"

A few condescending responses formed in Hannah's mind, but she settled with, "Greg, this is a serious matter. I'm not gonna gripe about previous misgivings."

"Yeah, you'd rather forget that wouldn't you? What are you doing here anyway?"

"I *am* the Sheriff, last time I checked," Hannah replied.

"Trust me, I know," Greg said. "I meant, why aren't you in the office with your feet up? I'm shocked none of the guys are here. Or are you having personnel issues?"

Hannah ignored the rapid-fire remarks.

"Gordon, what happened? I saw the patient. Anyone else injured?"

"Nothing but a few bumps and bruises," Gordon replied, pointing at Joe and Ernie. "But Greg reported there was a woman in the boat with the victim. She's never turned up."

"Oh Jesus," Hannah said. "Was she wearing a lifejacket?"

Greg rolled his eyes. "For the millionth time, yes." He paced back to the shore and back. Did these idiots think he was responsible for his clients' actions? With the exception of kids, there was no policy about people wearing lifejackets on boats. People sometimes enjoyed swimming in the deeper areas of the lake.

"If she took it off, wouldn't it be floating somewhere out there?"

"It's over six-hundred yards across the lake, Hannah. If it drifted over there, it'd be easy to miss from here. Not to mention it could've drifted to the west segment. Either way, if she drowned, you're gonna need divers. Didn't Dispatch alert you to the fact that there's a missing person?"

"They did," Hannah said.

"So, where's the divers?"

"They're on their way," Hannah replied. She looked over at Joe Hall. "You were involved in the accident?"

"Yes, Sheriff."

"Explain to me what happened."

Joe and Ernie glanced at each other, then back at her. They knew what they were about to say would not make sense. Then again, this whole morning didn't make sense. Todd Welling was still missing, and he couldn't help but find it odd that there was hardly any activity on the other side of the lake. It was as though all of those houses on the north were vacant. On a Saturday, of all days.

Here it goes.

"Ernie and I took a boat out to look for one of our group members who we thought was out fishing."

"You thought?" Hannah said.

"Did you not find him?" Greg asked. In the madness, he had completely forgotten Todd Welling had taken his boat out.

"No," Joe answered. Nervous chatter erupted from the Reiner Foods associates behind him.

"He's gone?" one of them said.

"His truck's still in the driveway," another said.

"He's not here, though!"

Hannah raised her hands in an attempt to calm the crowd. "Everybody! Shhh! Calm down. Let's not get worked up."

"Last we saw him was last night!" somebody shouted.

Hannah briefly shut her eyes to help herself focus. She had not even gotten the witness testimony of the accident yet, and already the situation was escalating beyond her control. A drowning following a boat accident, while tragic, was a relatively easy case. But now there was a *second* missing person? For sure a missing boat.

Handle each problem one at a time.

"Sir, finish your story, please."

Joe cleared his throat. "We checked the east segment. Nobody was on the lake. Nobody. We came back, intending to double check the far side on the west. Suddenly, we see this twelve-footer come racing at full speed across the lake in a semi-circle. At first, he looked like he was gonna cut in front of us. Then he started hooking left and, before we could react, smashed into us."

Hannah raised an eyebrow.

"He was just…speeding?"

"Yes," Ernie said. "I don't know why. Maybe he didn't know how to handle an outboard motor. All I know was that he was trying to operate that thing as though it was a jet ski."

"Where'd he start from?" Greg asked.

"When we first noticed him? I think he was somewhere along the north bend," Joe answered.

Hannah shook her head. "None of this makes sense. Clear day like this? And he just happens to ram into your boat? Was he not looking where he was going?"

Joe shrugged. "I don't know, Sheriff."

Hannah looked over at Greg. "He was your customer? Have you noticed anything strange about him before he went on the boat?"

"He and his wife arrived early," Greg said. "I let them use the boat to fish while I got their cabin prepped. The guy seemed a tad clumsy, but not overtly weird. But, as I said, I only interacted with them for a few minutes."

Bill Hoskin stepped toward the water. In his mind, he tried to envision what Joe Hall explained.

"I guess the next question is *why*," he said. "Why was he driving the boat the way he did? Was he just an idiot?"

"I've seen plenty of them, kid," Greg said. "Though, I'd expect something like this on Archer Lake. Not here."

"Is it normally this quiet here?" Bill asked.

Greg watched the tranquil water, and the houses opposite him. "Quiet-ER. But not this quiet. What are you getting at, kid?"

Bill turned to face him and the Sheriff. "What if he was fleeing something?"

Greg leaned forward. "Pardon me?"

"We already acknowledge that nothing makes logical sense. There's one factor we haven't considered. Uh…" He began stumbling over his words, as though rethinking what he was about to say. "How, uh, how deep is this lake?"

"Shallow, except for a small ridge near the center here. Other than that, it's barely twelve feet deep. Not even that in most parts."

"And the ridge?"

"Maybe thirty. What are you getting at?"

"Well, considering the path the guy took…perhaps we should consider the possibility he was fleeing from something."

Depths, ridges, fleeing. The word 'something' implied organism. This kid was referring to the incident in Clare County three years back. Greg stared at him, then at Hannah.

"Seriously? Is this the kind of Deputy you hired?"

Even she didn't know what to say. "Bill, you're jumping to absurd conclusions awfully quick."

"What conclusions?" Gordon asked.

"He's referring to the appearance of the Carnobass in Rodney," Greg said. Immediately, several of the spectators started moving away from the shoreline.

"It's possible!" Bill said defensively.

"Deputy, if a Carnobass was in this lake, we'd know it," Greg explained. "Considering the reported size of that thing, there's no way it'd lurk in these waters without making its presence obvious at some point. It's too shallow. Every movement it made would cause disruption in the water."

"It managed to remain hidden in the other lake for a couple of days before it was discovered," Bill said.

"No shit, kid. Ridgeway Lake is way deeper, and covers a scope of over two miles," Greg said. "It's much easier for a large fish to remain hidden there. Not a shallow spot like this. Also, judging from the reported analysis on that thing, I can assure you that my boat motors WOULD NOT outrun that thing. Mr. Perkins would've been a goner the moment the thing saw him. AND if it was chasing Mr. Perkins, why would it stop right after the crash?"

His words helped to settle down the crowd.

"Could there be other species of fish?" Ernie asked.

"I'm sure there are, but the factors are still the same. It wouldn't be easy for a giant fish to remain hidden in this lake for long. Even if it was half the size of the Carnobass. And don't forget everyone, Rodney is over two hundred miles away. Almost three, actually. I highly doubt that supposed underground lake runs all the way up here."

Hannah stepped toward the crowd. "Alright, everybody. This isn't a press conference. Please, let us do our jobs. I assure you, everything's fine." Slowly, and somewhat reluctantly, the crowd dispersed. People returned to their cabins...with the exception of the Kendricks, who relaxed outside to avoid the aftermath of those late night burritos.

A police Interceptor arrived at the top of the hill. Zach Cassidy and Jake Bing walked down the steps, holding air tanks and flippers. Behind them was Deputy Ross Yang, who was as happy as his companions to see his old buddy Greg Goodman.

"Greg! How the hell are ya?" he said.

"Oh man!" Greg said, exaggerating a disgusted voice. He looked at Jake and Zach. "You guys must've really lost your minds if you have this knucklehead driving you around!"

The four of them laughed.

"He agreed to buy us pizza on the way back," Jake replied.

"Yeah? All done with the protein bars, are ya?" Greg said.

"Eh," Zach shrugged, "Saturday's our cheat day."

"You sound like a married couple dieting together," Greg remarked. "How about you, Yang? How's life treating you? No more high-speed chases, right?"

Yang chuckled. *Oh, the drive-like-an-Asian joke.* What he found funnier than the joke itself was the Sheriff's facial reaction. It was an obvious dig at her, rather than at him.

"Well, I've learned that the right side of the road is where I'm supposed to be," he quipped. *There, Hannah. Not all of us are easily offended white knights.*

Jake noticed the Sheriff standing a few yards behind Greg. He lowered his head and covered his mouth, pretending to cough.

"Oh, man. I bet this is awkward for you," he said to Greg.

"You don't know the half of it," Greg replied. "How many vacancies are there?"

"About to be five," Zach replied.

"Jesus. After one freaking year," Greg said.

"Maybe I should run against her next term," Jake remarked.

"You *sure* you want to do that?" Greg replied. Though it was only a joke, Jake still dreaded the thought.

"No. Not after what she did to you."

"Hey! Guys!" Hannah called out. "You can chitchat on your own time. We need to get out in the water."

"Yeeeees, Sheriff," Jake replied, obnoxiously. Greg looked up at their lot, then back at Hannah.

"With what boat?" he said.

Jake stopped, then chuckled. Greg was about to get even more pissed at the Sheriff.

"We don't have one." He looked at Hannah as he said it, then walked past her to the dock, where he proceeded to check his gear.

"Yeah? How were you planning to search the water? Just waddle in from shore and just, swim wherever? Like a damn penguin?" Greg said.

Hannah took a deep breath. "We were hoping you'd let us requisition one of your boats."

"Minus the 'we' part," Yang muttered.

"Oh boy," Zach said. They could feel the heat radiating from Greg's wrinkled brow. His eyes looked possessed, burning flames through the Sheriff.

"You know, I used to think New Coke was the dumbest thing on this earth," he said.

"Goddamnit, Greg, is this necessary?" Hannah said. "We have a missing person out there, and we need to get moving."

"I noticed that 'we' again," Greg replied. "You talk like I'm still a cop. I'm not. I have you to thank for that."

"Can we rehash this another time?" Hannah said.

"That's rich. First you slander me. Then, this morning, you ticket me. Now, you suddenly need my help."

Jake, Greg, and Ross perked up at once.

"She wrote him up?! This is getting better and better!" Jake said.

"Stow it," Hannah said. The Deputies pretended to focus on their gear. Their efforts at appearing inconspicuous failed. Hannah sighed, then waved Greg over. "Can we talk over there?" she asked, cocking her head toward the private dock.

"Don't wanna look bad in front of Gordon, huh? Can't be the Deputies. They're already aware of your bullshit," Greg replied. He proceeded to walk with her to the dock. "Except maybe him," he added, gesturing at Bill.

Bill Hoskin's heart was pounding. It wasn't his first exposure to unpleasant altercations, but it was the first time he saw the Sheriff nervous. There was clearly a history between those two. Bad breakup, maybe? Regardless, this guy Greg had absolutely no respect for Hannah's authority.

On top of that, his fellow Deputies looked rather amused. He wasn't surprised; it was clear none of them liked Hannah, though until now, it was never clear why. After seeing their interactions with Greg, and learning he was once a Deputy, his guess was they were simply backing up their buddy.

Hannah and Greg were on the far dock, a little over a hundred feet away. Bill took the opportunity to approach the three Deputies, who watched from Cabin Two's dock.

"Having fun yet, kid?" Zach said.

"No. I'm with the Sheriff. We have a missing person out here, and that douchebag wants to play games," Bill retorted. All at once, the three officers turned to look at him. And all at once, their smiles disappeared, and suddenly Bill was pierced by three stern gazes.

"Watch it, Rookie," Jake said. "That 'douchebag' was one of the best Deputies in our department."

"Believe me, kid, he's right to be pissed off," Ross added.

Bill suddenly felt ganged up on, then felt stupid for feeling so. He picked this battle, after all.

"What's their beef? She cheat on him or something?"

The three Deputies broke into laughter.

"Oh, man. Those two, together?! Imagine that," Ross said.

"Just add a laugh track in the background. That about sums it up," Zach replied. "No, kid. They weren't a thing. When Sheriff Mysinger was getting ready to retire…which was a little before your time, Greg Goodman and Hannah Tyler were both in the running for the position."

"Oh! So, he's mad because she beat him?" Bill asked.

"There's a little more to it than that," Jake said.

"By the looks of it, people were favoring Greg. He had a better message, more experience, and an actual business plan. Hannah, well, 'I'm the first girl to run for office here' was her platform, essentially. BUT…" He glanced back to make sure he wasn't overheard by Greg or Hannah. "She decided to use a different tactic."

"She pulled the accusations trick," Jake said. "She accused him of racial profiling, then she accused him of making all kinds of homophobic remarks. Sure enough, she managed to locate somebody he pissed off with a couple of speeding tickets, and had him make up all kinds of lies about Greg."

"Huh?" Bill exclaimed. It couldn't be. Hannah seemed professional enough. Not as perfect as the instructors he met in the academy, but not *that* bad. "How do we know they're not true?"

"How do we know they *are* true?" Ross said. "See, Bill, you're falling for the guilty-until-proven-innocent tactic. Not to mention the fact that this all came out a month before election."

"Besides, we can assure you, Greg Goodman was one of our best cops," Jake added. "He's no racist or homophobe. Or xenophobe. Or sexist. Or misogynist. Or a gynecologist. Or a dentist. Or a…"

"Yes, yes, I get the point," Bill said. "So, did he quit the force because of that?"

"Mainly because of the backlash that followed. Nobody believed him when he refuted the accusations. Guilty-until-proven-innocent. Even after the election, the Sheriff's Office received a lot of bad media for employing such a 'toxic' person. Unfortunately, Sheriff Mysinger had the backbone of a jellyfish. He was on the brink of retirement, and, more importantly, was in the process of setting up his own little private security company. Didn't want the bad press, so he cut Greg loose. He's practically been blacklisted at this point. Nobody will hire him. Worse, it's been hurting his businesses."

"He used to have another property on Archer Lake. That one was more high-profile than this. But word got around. People believe he's a sexist, racist, whatever-ist piece of shit. So, business practically free-fell. Now all he has is this place," Ross said.

Bill said nothing else. His view of Sheriff Tyler had been completely shaken. No wonder several Deputies had transferred in the last year. He found a bench and sat down, then stared at the lake while listening to the unpleasant conversation in the distance. Now, he was in Greg Goodman's corner.

"…and don't even get me started on the mounting debt I have because of the shit you pulled," Greg said.

"Greg, I didn't intend for it to go the way it did," Hannah replied.

"Bullshit, lady! You had every intention! What, you expect me to think you 'accidentally' stumbled across that prick Amad Hamdan, or whatever his name was?"

"Jesus, Greg, I—" Hannah paused. She was about to curse at him, but had barely enough self-control to hold back. What right did she have to be mad? She brought this all on herself.

"And now you have the audacity to ask me for help. Unbelievable."

"It's not as simple as that. I didn't know *you* were the resort owner. I figured I'd get help from whoever owned this place."

"Why don't you have police boats?" Greg said.

"I managed to get a couple for the bigger lakes," Hannah replied. "But not for areas like this."

Greg would have fallen for that lie had he not seen the budget in Mysinger's last months of office. He had managed to secure a deal on two boats for Archer Lake, and here Hannah was, taking credit for it. And by the look on her face, she knew she was caught.

"Okay, Greg, maybe we ought to have a discussion about this, but it doesn't change the circumstances of why I'm here. There's a missing person in this lake. Maybe two. This has turned into a very busy day. I HAVE to get my guys in the water. If you help, I'll get that ticket out of the system for you. And I'll have the department send you a check for three hundred dollars, for services and fuel."

Greg crossed his arms. It was a bribe, for sure. However, it worked. He was in need of money—a need that would probably increase once this news hit the internet. He would probably be looking at selling this property in the next year. What he would do after that, he wasn't sure yet. But in the short term, three-hundred bucks, and the elimination of a hundred-dollar fine meant a lot.

"Fine," he said. "Let me fuel the pontoon. Have your people on board in three minutes."

"Thank you," Hannah said, visibly relieved. Greg didn't care. He walked past her and hurried up the hill, stopping halfway after hearing Mrs. Kendrick burst out of Cabin Three with a vengeance.

"Goddamnit, Harold! Did you pour the coffee grains down the sink?"

"Uh…"

"Oh! My! God! Now the sink's clogged! Damn it, Harold. I tried pouring last night's vegetable juice and the expired milk down the sink. Now it's forming an unholy mixture! I didn't think you could possibly stink the place up any worse!"

Greg pointed a finger pistol to his temple and mimicked a gunshot, then continued to his garage.

CHAPTER 11

It was 11:15 when the group boarded Greg's pontoon boat. Greg stood at the helm, while Hannah remained at the starboard transom. It was the furthest distance she could maintain between them. She wished she could've talked Greg into simply lending the boat to them, but understood the type of control freak he was. He didn't like people messing with his equipment, not even in a situation like this. Plus, as a witness to the event, she needed him to guide the divers along the lake and determine where Cathy Perkins might be.

Jake Bing felt ridiculous for having a rebreather. At least it served a decent purpose. Though the lake was very shallow, it would've been a hindrance for he and Zach to constantly be coming up for air as they searched the lake floor. However, the flippers weren't doing him much good. Every time he moved, he got caught up in some weeds. Judging how thick they were in some spots, it made sense why Cathy might not have floated to the top. She could've easily gotten tangled up in the weeds and drowned—unless she wore a lifejacket of course.

It wasn't the time for speculation. Fact is, she was nowhere to be found. In fact, there was nothing to be found except Greg's sunken twelve-footer. It balanced on its right side, the bow pointed up, like a sunken treasure ship.

Up on the boat, Greg stood alongside Lt. Gordon, Ross Yang, and Bill Hoskin. The rookie was constantly looking back and forth, nervous about the water. His nervous energy was transferring over to Gordon. The Fire Lieutenant wasn't a timid guy, but he wasn't fond of water. Normally, a shallow lake such as this would not have bothered him so much, but Bill's remark about the 2018 incident in Clare County sparked nervous energy. He had almost forgotten about the whole ordeal.

Though, it seemed unlikely another such lake would exist right underneath this little thing. It made more sense that it would be under Lake Archer. And why do these lakes always connect to larger lakes? So many questions to a topic he didn't understand in the first place. With that thought in mind, he focused on what Greg pointed out: a large fish would be easy to locate in a lake like this. So far, the lake was quiet. Maybe a little too quiet.

Until Jake burst from the water.

"Phew!" he spat, yanking the rebreather from his mouth. "There's nothing down there, except Greg's boats."

"You sure?" Hannah replied.

"Sheriff, this dive is a breeze, compared to most I've done. This is so shallow I actually have the aid of sunlight. A woman, no matter what she wore, would stand out like a sore thumb."

Zach Cassidy emerged behind him. He pulled off his goggles and climbed aboard the pontoon boat. Sticking to his arms and legs were several weed strands.

"Brought you all some salad," he said. He sat on the floor and attempted to peel them off. They were coated in a slimy substance that almost seemed to act as a glue.

"Yeah, you can keep that," Bill remarked.

"That doesn't look healthy," Gordon added. "Greg? You see that often?"

Greg was equally as bewildered. "No. I haven't."

"Probably just some kind of protein buildup," Zach said. Though he knew it was unusual, it wasn't boggling his mind. His focus was on locating the missing person. "Well, as Jake might've already said, there's no body down there. Mr. Goodman, do you have any suggestions as to where we ought to look next?"

Greg looked to the lake's center. "Joe said he witnessed the Perkins speed along from the other end of the lake, near the private docks. That's Andy Cornett's property right there along the bend." He mimicked a trajectory with his finger, following it along the bend to their current location. "He said they went in a semi-circle then hooked left. We're standing over the crash site, so I would suggest we check over there."

"Works for me," Zach said. Greg brought in the anchor, then throttled for the new destination. For several seconds, there was silence, except for groaning sounds made by Zach as he peeled the residue off his legs. Even he was wondering what it was, despite the theory he made a few seconds prior.

"Some idiot probably spilled something in this lake," he remarked. "Greg? You ever have issues with your tenants dumping stuff in the water?"

"Not that I've seen. I'm on the water frequently, and I've never noticed anything like that," Greg replied. "Not until today, of course."

"No complaints when people go swimming?"

"No. Nothing," Greg said. "Yesterday, there were people swimming everywhere. There were people out fishing. No problems whatsoever. Then again, on my property, there are no weeds until you get about thirty feet or so from shore. People don't generally go out too far because of it."

"I see." Zach flicked a wad of goop from his knee. "Probably nothing. Just protein buildup."

Within two minutes, they were roughly a hundred feet from the shoreline. Greg dropped the anchor and killed the engine.

"If she's here, it shouldn't be too hard to locate her," Greg said.

"Knowing these guys?" Ross joked.

"Hey, we're not the ones who spent a half hour trying to scoop a quarter out from under the vending machine," Zach said.

"At least I would've made sure it was actually a quarter instead of a nickel before committing," Jake added. The band of cops broke into laughter.

"That sounds like Ross Yang," Greg said.

"Hey! Didn't you pull the fire alarm when you were assigned at the community college?"

"I try to forget about that," Greg said.

Gordon chuckled. "What happened?"

"I was a rookie. I wasn't quite used to third shift yet. Had to respond to a fire panel alarm. Went to the actual lever instead. I tried to unlock it, which set off the *actual* building alarm. Had to make a dozen phone calls after that, to let the administration and Fire Department know it was a false alarm." He winced at the memory. "Not the biggest highlight of my career." *Beats getting a false accusation, though.*

"Can we cut the chit-chat, gentlemen?" Hannah said. "Don't forget why we're out here."

"Yeah, because someone forgot to put on a lifejacket," Ross said.

"Part of me almost hopes we don't find her over here," Bill said. All eyes turned toward him.

"Excuse me?" Hannah said.

"Think of it. They crashed over there. Why would she have fallen overboard over here?" Bill explained.

Greg nodded. "Well, Sheriff, at least you're capable of hiring people with brains." He let a moment pass for the remark to burrow its way into her brain. "That said, he's right. If you do find her down there, it's probably the first step to a long investigation. You'll wanna get an autopsy done to make sure there wasn't any foul play or..."

"I know how the procedure goes," Hannah said. She turned her gaze to the two divers, who stood by the ladder. Clearly, they were hoping to witness a verbal sparring match. "You guys waiting for a snack, or something?"

Jake stuffed the rebreather into his face, then plunged into the water. Zach quickly followed. Immediately, they swam in opposite directions, their tanks cutting along the surface like dorsal fins as they swam above the weeds.

Jake Bing went to the west. There was a little bit of shade from the canopy, but it was still well lit by the sunlight. The weeds had a natural bright-yellow pigmentation. Like a forest of pine trees, they swayed back and forth from the distortion caused by his stroking.

He expected to see fish swimming about. Instead, in the six feet of water above the weeds, he was the only lifeform creating motion. Perhaps he scared all the fish away, or maybe they just preferred to stay in the deeper area. He didn't think too much of it. He was looking for a possible body, not fish.

However, there was nothing obvious. The weeds were thick, but not so thick to fully obscure a grown woman. It was a bit frustrating, considering this should've been a relatively easy search.

One thing he did notice, however, was the thick slime strung within the weeds. It was the same kind of stuff that Zach found by the boats, only this was WAY thicker. So thick, that it was taking on the color of the weeds themselves.

What the hell?

Now he knew why he didn't see any fish swimming about; they were caught up in this mess! They were everywhere, appearing dead at first glance. Then he noticed flapping gills. The majority were still alive.

Jake was looking at a world of fish, struggling to free themselves from this glue-like substance. He had never seen anything like this before. It suddenly made sense why Mrs. Perkins might've drowned. Forget being tangled in the weeds, she could've easily gotten strung up in this mess, just as these fish had.

He broke the surface and started swimming back to the boat.

"Guys, I think we have a bigger problem than that missing person," he said.

Greg and Hannah approached the starboard rail.

"What's the matter?" Hannah said.

"The lake floor, it's COMPLETELY covered in that slime shit," Jake said. "I've made enough dives to know it's not normal. We might have to get the EPA over here."

"You really think so?" Greg said.

"Dude! Just look down," Jake exclaimed. Greg looked straight down into the water. He had to pay close attention, but he could see the thick strands of goop, and the fish fighting to free themselves from it.

Gordon and Ross were looking as well.

"What in the name of…" the Deputy muttered.

"I don't get it," Greg said. "I had a couple of customers fish over here yesterday afternoon. They didn't see any of this stuff when pulling up their anchors. Being so thick, there's no way they would've avoided it. I even saw Andy Cornett fishing along that way. The guy reeled in a forty-inch pike."

"It's here now. Don't know what else to tell you," Jake said.

"A sudden appearance of underwater slime…right around the time of two disappearances…" Greg mumbled to himself. Somehow, it was connected. In his peripheral vision, he noticed Bill glancing at the water. Not even a half-hour earlier, he was chastising the kid for his seemingly absurd hypothesis regarding a crevasse in the lake. Now, he was thinking differently. Bizarre slime in the water was one thing. But two people disappearing, including Todd Welling, who never returned with his boat…

"Sheriff?"

"What?" Hannah said.

"You guys have any underwater drones?"

"No. Why?"

"Perhaps we should consider getting out of the water," Greg replied. Hannah scoffed.

"You serious?"

"Something's not right," Greg said. "All this stuff just appeared out of nowhere. I'm telling you. It WASN'T here yesterday."

"I'm all for getting back on land," Bill said.

"Don't you think we're overreacting just a little?" Ross said. "It's quite a stretch to go from weird slime to closing the lake entirely."

"Thirty minutes ago, it was a simple enough matter to claim the accident was just that, an accident. But Todd Welling hasn't shown up yet. The boat he took is still missing, as is his fishing gear. He's not answering his phone. And there's the question as to why we haven't found Cathy Perkins by the crash site. Something's off. I'm telling you, this slime was not here before. Something caused it, and it happened fast. Something that doesn't belong here."

Gordon started turning pale. "You discredited the idea that something could be in this lake. What changed?"

"It's called 'evidence,' Lieutenant," Greg replied. "I was thinking twenty-something foot fish. But I failed to consider what other surprises an underground lake could provide."

"Don't you think we oughta recon the deep zone before making such a conclusion?" Hannah said.

"That's where the drone will come in handy," Greg said. "Right now, I suggest you get your divers aboard."

Hannah realized she was put on the spot. Everyone was watching her, awaiting her next instruction. If she halted the search, and subsequently allowed Cathy Perkins' body to swell up under the water, and Greg's theory turned out to be wrong—word would certainly get around. It would definitely be used against her in the next election.

Was that Greg's plan? Was this his revenge? Would he really stoop this low?

"Jake, go get Zach. Tell him to come back," she said.

"You got it, Sheriff," Jake said. He chomped on his rebreather and plunged back into the lake. Greg hurried to the anchor. It was a strain to hoist it onto the boat. There was definitely more weight than normal, and definitely not from weeds.

Thrashing fins splattered water across the deck, surprising Greg to the point he nearly dropped the anchor. A thick glob of goop hung from the chunk of galvanized metal. Like a stringer, it contained several fish and uprooted weeds.

No, this would not have been missed by anyone who was out fishing yesterday. With that thought came the question…

Greg stared across the empty lake. By now, there should've been at least a half-dozen boats on the water. He always would see his neighbors across the lake, fishing off the dock, if not on the water.

Where is everybody?

Zach Cassidy had swum out over fifty-yards from the pontoon boat. Like his partner, he found a world consumed by this bizarre spiderweb of slime. It was like the surface of an alien planet, one that was undergoing some kind of mass extinction event.

There was not a square foot of lakebed that wasn't completely covered in the substance. He could see fish bobbing their gills, their bodies completely glued to the forest. Zach turned to the left and swam deeper into the center of the lake. The bottom gradually sloped, the weeds still covered in the bizarre substance.

There was something else…something that reflected the sun's rays. Zach descended. The thing was grey in color. Its front narrowed until it was an arrow-like point. The back was straight, the sides smooth. An aluminum boat.

He couldn't have swum all the way to the crash site. That was several hundred yards to the south. Unless…

He saw the number 7 painted in bright yellow across the bow panel. He swam a bit deeper. His heart thumped. Lying across the lake bottom were fishing poles, oars, and an open tackle box.

A tightening of a grab along his left shoulder caused Zach to spin back. He threw his arms out defensively, accidently striking Jake across the face. The Deputy waved his hands. *What the hell are you doing?!*

Zach pointed down at the sunken boat. Jake stared for a moment. Only Greg Goodman's resort had numbered boats…and one was missing, along with one of the company members. Before he could signal them to swim up, Zach swam deeper to investigate.

Wait!

Jake wished they had diving helmets instead of basic rebreathers, that way they could communicate through radio. Unfortunately, there was no way to verbally explain the new plan until they broke the surface. Jake swam after his diving partner, who was already down by the vessel, searching for bodies.

Though they still had visibility, it was considerably darker here than the shallower regions. They weren't too far from the deep zone. Judging by what they discovered here so far, Jake didn't want to wander too close. He took a moment to see if they could locate any bodies. There were none, and that scared Jake more than anything else.

Time to surface.

He turned to Zach and pointed his thumb to the surface. Zach was twisting and turning, while thrashing his arms like a madman. He had wandered back too far and was waist deep in the weeds, and subsequently, the slime. Immediately, it was all over him, hugging his diving suit like glitter. Zach tugged against it, unable to break its grip. There was a rippling effect with every movement. Each tug pulled at the entire weed forest, wrenching every strand of vegetation for hundreds of feet.

Jake got close to him and tried to pull some of the goop from his waist and elbows. Instead, he only succeeded in getting it stuck to his gloves. There was brief panic when he failed to pull free. With no other option, he removed the gloves, then paddled his flippers to elevate himself over the weeds. Using hand signals, he conveyed that he would return momentarily to help, then shot for the surface.

Greg started the engine then cut the wheel to port. While he made the turn, he couldn't help but stare at Andy Cornett's property. No way would that guy leave his floating garage door half-shut like that. And the markings...

Andy was very protective of his property. No way in hell would he allow for such grooves to be made in his expensive garage. And what the hell was up with the deck? And was the front window broken?

"Hey!"

It was Jake. Greg swung the boat around and brought it near him. There was no sign of Zach.

"What's going on?" Hannah asked.

"Greg, we found your missing boat," Jake said.

"WHAT?!" Greg said, followed by Ross and Gordon. "You're shitting me."

Hannah felt a cold shiver creep up her spine. "Did you find..."

Jake shook his head. "Not yet, but there's fishing gear down there." Hannah was convinced now.

"Alright, get in the boat now. Where's Zach?!"

"He's hung up. Got caught in the slime stuff. I need to help him break free. Greg? You have a knife I could borrow?" Greg opened a small storage compartment under the dashboard and dug out a folding knife. Jake replaced his rebreather, took the knife, then dove.

Greg suddenly wished he brought along some personal firearms. This lake, a place of relaxation and peace, now sparked intense anxiety. He watched the water settle, then watched the murky weeds sway back and forth.

"What's that?" Bill said. He was pointing back at Andy Cornett's property. Greg shrugged his shoulders.

"I don't see any—" He spoke too soon. It was a blink-and-you-miss-it moment. Something moved under the door in a rolling motion, resembling the portraits of ancient sea serpents. Rings expanded far from the point of origin, dissipating by the time they reached the pontoon boat.

"Probably just a fish," Gordon said.

Nervous ticks were battering Greg's eyelids and hands. He shook his head.

"I don't think so."

CHAPTER 12

Within their hive, the drones waited. They were quick adapters, having traveled from zone to zone in their underground world. It only took a few short hours to acclimate to the cooler temperatures of the surface world. It took several more hours for them to adapt to the strange illumination from above. It was more intense than the colors of their natural world, but nothing they couldn't adapt to. Already, they had successfully hunted in this new environment, and learned that the golden presence would not harm them, save for a mild strain to the eyes. But the drones had other senses beyond the limited capability of sight.

The sense of smell was useless, as this new world was full of unfamiliar odors. It was a struggle to know which came from prey, which came from the plant life, or which came from the results of human littering. It was all new. But one sense never failed the hundreds of generations of hunters: vibration. When they weren't actively seeking prey, they set traps. Sometimes it would take minutes, other times weeks, but the traps ALWAYS captured prey.

Like pings on a sonar screen, they felt the tugging of their saliva strands. The traps were quick to snag the puny fish that lurked in this environment, but they only provided meager sustenance. What was struggling now was much larger; much more sufficient for their goal of propagating the species.

All at once, the creatures stirred. Like an assembly line of troops, they filed out through the exit of their new habitat, hesitated slightly as the sun struck their eyes, then proceeded to follow the signals to the point of origin.

****

By the time Jake returned to Zach's location, he was completely entangled in the thick web. Jake had known him long enough to understand the body language of his head cocking back and forth, and the repetitive tugging of his right arm, which was snared up to his elbow in the stuff. He was pissed off and simultaneously on the verge of panic.

Hold still, you dumb idiot.

Jake hovered above his friend, being careful not to get himself trapped in the mess. Zach looked up, saw Jake holding the knife, then read into the sign language.

He answered with a thumbs-up. *About time! Now cut me free, you dufus!*

Jake went right to work. He unfolded the knife and ran the serrated edge over a thick strand of the goop. The stuff vibrated and rippled, only separating after several strokes of the knife. Even then, only a little progress was made. Very quickly, it was evident that this stuff would not cut easily. He would probably have more luck pulling it apart.

He paused momentarily to get a look at the space behind Zack. The weeds, and subsequently the slime, was all around him. Unfortunately, there was no way he could pull him out without getting himself snagged as well.

Zach looked up at him, his wide eyes visible through the goggles.

What's the holdup, dude?

Jake started working on the strand near Zach's right elbow. If he could free the guy's arm, then maybe he could uproot the weeds, thus destroying the foundation of the silk. Zach's arm snapped back, the elbow crashing into Jake's face. He rolled backward, flapping his arms to keep above the weeds. He corrected his posture, ready to smack Zach on the back of his head. That's when he realized his fellow Deputy was writhing frantically. He was looking to the north, while pulling desperately against his snare. Zach wasn't the type to panic easily.

Jake watched as the web rippled. But it wasn't rippling with Zach's movements. Whatever causing this was much bigger.

A shape took form like a green cloud. Jake's chest ached, as though his heart was swelling. Bill was right, it was a carnivorous fish, just like the creature from the crevasse in Rodney, Michigan. And now, it was coming for them.

As though pushed apart from the wind, that 'cloud' quickly broke apart into smaller forms, each converging on the trapped Deputy. Each one was roughly as large as a man. Appendages stretched from their rounded heads.

Now, Zach was screaming, his voice lost in a series of air bubbles. He pulled against the web as though trying to hoist an anchor. Web— they had thought of it as such in a metaphorical manner, but it was no longer metaphorical. These things had laid this trap here intentionally.

Jake made a split-second decision. There was no hope for Zach. All he could think about now was his own survival.

Zach looked back and saw his friend shooting for the surface. He reached up, his scream again drowned out by the water. Like a swarm of hornets, the creatures descended on him. Slimy tentacles constricted the human, easily overpowering him.

The Deputy writhed, his arms pinned against his body. He watched the flesh peel back on the creature's head, revealing its buzz-saw-like jaw, which opened wide. A needle-like barb emerged from the back of its throat. By the time Zach noticed its pointy tip, it plunged into his abdomen. Next came a rigidness, not caused by the constriction. All control over his body was lost, and after a few seconds, his mind was lost with it.

Jake looked down once, much to his regret. There were several of those things swimming in a circle. It was a cyclone of squids, and in the eye of that cyclone, one of them was pulling Zach free of the snare. The others were now ascending.

He stroked his arms and kicked his feet. The surface was almost there. So close. Just another meter or so.

There was the sensation of rushing water, followed by the sight of dark green leathery flesh in his peripheral vision. He slashed blindly with the knife, while still paddling for the surface. Slimy tentacles closed over his right leg.

Jake screamed, spitting his rebreather from his mouth. He grabbed for the surface as though it contained a ledge to some solid ground. Instead, all he found was air.

As though mimicking his motions, the tentacles lashed at the Deputy, the clawed tips raking his diving suit, and slicing the flesh underneath. One of the creatures closed in, exposing its jaws and the proboscis in-between them.

"Something's wrong. He's in trouble!" Hannah said. They watched as Jake thrashed, his head not quite able to breach the surface. It was as though he was swimming, yet held in place by some unseen force.

Greg throttled the pontoon boat toward him, cutting the engine as they came within a couple of meters. Ross and Bill leaned over the edge and reached for Jake's hands.

"Come on, buddy," Ross groaned. "Just a little—HOLY SHIT!"

Following an explosion of water, Jake was hefted over the surface. His mouth was wide open, spurting a mixture of lake water, blood, and foam. Five-foot long tentacles slashed the air like whips, while two of them constricted the Deputy like boas.

The group scuttled to the starboard side, caught off guard by the horrific sight.

"Good God! What is that?!" Gordon said.

"For chrissake, Hannah! Shoot it!" Greg shouted. It took a moment for Hannah to overcome the numbing grip of fear. She drew her Glock 19 and pointed it down at the squid's body. There were two segments, much like a spider's head and thorax. It seemed a simple enough matter to assume the smaller, more rounded segment was the head.

A squeeze of the trigger sent a bullet plunging through the green flesh, spurting dark liquid. The creature whipped toward her, then vanished beneath the surface, taking a motionless Jake Bing with it.

"Where is it?" Ross said. The two Deputies had their weapons drawn and aimed at the water. Ross covered the stern, while Bill covered the starboard side. The lake was lapping all around them, swaying their boat side to side.

"There's movement all over the place," Hannah said.

"Where's Jake? Zach?" Bill said.

"They're gone," Greg replied, his voice gravelly. Eyeballing the southern shoreline, he engaged the throttle. It was clear the Deputies were beyond saving at this point.

"Wait, what are you doing?" Hannah said.

"Getting us out of here."

"But Jake and—"

"They're gone," Greg replied. "As will we be unless we get to shore."

The words barely escaped his lips when the tentacles broke the surface. Their jagged hooks struck the bow rail, hoisting the five-foot body aboard. Greg jumped back right as two more arms lunged for him.

Ross and Hannah pointed their weapons and unleashed their fury, popping a dozen holes into its face. Black blood spilled over the console, partially washed away by the splash of its corpse hitting the water.

Bill turned pale, his weapon wavering in his grip. "Did you kill it?"

Hannah loaded a fresh magazine and approached the bow. Her ears were ringing from the intense *cracks* of gunfire, which added to the stress-induced headache. The thing was floating, surrounded by a cloud of its blood.

"It's dead," she replied.

Gordon leaned over the side and dry heaved. He ran an arm along his sweaty forehead. He stared at his reflection as he regained control over his nerves.

"Now, please, get us out—"

Several arms sprang from the water and embraced the lieutenant. Hooks pierced his flesh and pulled him over the side. The officers turned in time to see his feet fling over the railing and disappear beneath the lake.

Immediately, another squid creature emerged. Then another. And another. Suddenly, the water was alive with tentacled arachnids fighting to board the pontoon boat.

"Mother of Mary, they're everywhere," Bill muttered. Arms slithered up along the gunwale like giant worms.

Gunshots pierced the air, ringing the eardrums of everyone aboard. Bullets struck flesh, spilling black fluid over the deck. Squid bodies climbed onto the railing, only to fall backward. Empty magazines ejected and bounced along the deck, followed by the *click* of a replacement slamming home.

The squids were everywhere. At this moment, Greg and the officers were living the iconic battle of the *Nautilus* and the army of giant squids. Unfortunately, they didn't have the luxury of advanced submarines to win the day. They were on a simple luxury boat, which was violently rocking back and forth as the beasts converged.

Greg took the controls. Looking at his property line across the lake, it was clear he would not be able to make the distance. They needed to go to the nearest shoreline. He cut the wheel to port and pushed the throttle to its max. There was a spraying of green ribbons and black blood as the propellers cut through one of the creatures.

The boat shook as the bow struck another, driving it backward. Walls of water embraced the deck, soaking Greg's jeans and shirt. He pointed the boat at Andy Cornett's deck and gunned the throttle. A few hundred feet felt like miles. Still, it was better than crossing six-hundred yards to his private deck.

Hannah unloaded another magazine into the water, each shot resulting in a new cloud of black spurting beneath the surface. The stern of the boat dipped, drawing their attention to the three sets of tentacles hauling their masses aboard. These creatures had no sense of self-preservation. They were willing to attack the vessel at all costs, despite six or seven of their members being killed.

Ross loaded a fresh magazine into his Glock, then turned to aim at the intruders. He hesitated a moment, giving them a chance for their ugly heads to emerge. He heard a splash to his left and immediately felt the spray of water strike his shoulder. The next sensation was warm and slimy.

He spun back and forth, screaming hysterically, waving his gun about. All sense of training and discipline vanished completely. Shots fired into the overhead, then out to the side. Hannah jolted to her right as a round grazed her upper shoulder.

"No! No! Help!" Ross shouted. The gun fell from his hand and bounced along the deck.

Bill reached for him, only to be knocked backward by a lashing tentacle. Ross was lifted into the air, then yanked back and forth. He was wrapped in the clutches of two squids, both of which were eager to puncture him with their proboscis.

Greg looked back just in time to witness the flesh peel back, and the razor jaws separate. The stinger was bone-white, dripping with fluid at the tip. Ross convulsed at it pierced his shoulder, his movements quickly becoming jagged as the venom did its work. Then he was gone, along with his captors, who plunged into the water.

More tentacles took their place, folding over the guardrail. The creatures on the stern had lifted themselves aboard and were reaching at the officers, who backtracked near the helm. More arms reached over the portside. Soon, the boat was covered in arachnid things dripping slime.

Greg didn't waste time selecting his trajectory. He simply drove the boat right into the pier. Wooden planks uprooted and snapped. The guardrail folded inward and broke apart. Greg turned and helped Bill and Hannah over the front guardrail, where they leapt onto the pier. Greg planted his foot over the bar and made his leap, only to be suddenly yanked back. His shirt collar tightened over his throat, making his eyes bulge. He heard a ripping of fabric, and suddenly, he was free. He got back up, made the jump, then glanced back, seeing a portion of his shirt dangling from the tentacles' claws.

The creatures invaded the boat, their tentacles spacing out to their sides evenly. Like spiders, they scurried over the deck and onto the pier.

"Go! Go!" Greg shouted. Bill and Hannah hurried around the side and down the steps. Greg started to follow, pausing only after hearing a metallic thud at his feet. On the deck was a Remington 12-guage. Andy's. There were hints of dried slime around it; a conclusion to his fate, if the broken window and half-open garage wasn't self-explanatory already.

He snatched up the weapon, then followed the others, only to find them stopped dead in their tracks.

Several creatures were scurrying from the shoreline, dripping with water and slime. Like ants, they converged on the fresh meat standing in the grass.

"Go around the back," Greg said. "There's a road back there." They dashed around the back of the house, found the driveway, only to stop again. Two more of the creatures were already there to greet them, poised to strike.

Greg pointed the shotgun at the two squids between him and the cellar, then fired. Their heads exploded in a gooey display of mangled flesh and blood. Greg glanced back and forth, seeing a few creatures coming from the adjacent property on the west. These things were literally EVERYWHERE! They had completely invaded the north shore, likely during the course of the night. Judging by the broken windows, they caught the neighbors in their sleep, and hauled them into the water.

"Holy shit!" Bill shouted. He fired off several shots at the advancing things. Panic overtook him, and he raced for the driveway, emptying his mag into a creature which scurried to meet him.

"Bill, wait!" Hannah screamed. The beast did not care about the projectiles fatally plunging into its soft body. It leapt at the human, tentacles extended. Bill yelled as he was wrestled to the grass, then thrashed back and forth as it unveiled its jaw.

Hannah shot the creature through the head, spilling blood over the Deputy. He sucked in a breath, felt a brief sense of relief, then pushed the slimy corpse off his body. He stood up, only to see more creatures scurrying over the roof. One was already poised at the corner. That sense of relief was gone in an instant.

Like a grasshopper, the squid sprang. Two-hundred pounds of flesh drove Bill back to the ground. Like a javelin, its spear entered his belly. Bill grunted, his eyes wide. His face turned purple. His fingers coiled and his mouth frothed.

"Bill!" Hannah screamed. She took aim at the creature, but was yanked to the side by Greg. They ran to the east corner, only to be intercepted by another gathering of beasts.

The entire property had been encircled. All avenues of escape were cut off. Their window of opportunity was closing fast. Outrunning these things was futile. God only knew how many were waiting in the woods.

Hannah was on her last magazine, and Greg only had eight shells at most. Shooting their way out *Rambo*-style would only delay the inevitable. His eyes searched for a way out, ultimately locking on the cellar door. It was closed, but the padlock was open. Why? He didn't think that far ahead. The remaining options were simple: hide in there, or get torn apart out here.

He fired a shot at another creature standing between them, popping its head like a pinata. It reeled backward, its tentacles coiling from reflex actions.

Greg pulled the cellar door open, paused to make sure nothing was waiting for them in there, then waved at Hannah.

"In there!"

They dove inside and slammed the door shut behind them. Bolted along the door were two metal latches, with an additional one on each side of the frame. Propped along the wall was a six-by-four slab of wood. Greg slipped it between the latches, then jumped back as a beast struck the opposite side.

They could hear grass and bushes rustling, and the disgusting slimy sounds made by the movement of boneless limbs. Then, there was the sound of a body being dragged through the grass. The door shook again, then stopped. The board was holding.

It wasn't much of a comfort. They were trapped, with no way out, in a dungeon surrounded by monsters.

CHAPTER 13

Rubber skidded against gravel, bringing the van to an abrupt stop. The engine had barely been switched off when the driver's side door opened.

"Come on! Let's go, please," Ryan Hodges said. He waved his hands toward the lake as the rest of the crew dismounted. He checked his watch. 11:57. "Come on, we're gonna start this thing right on time if we're lucky!"

"Hey man, you're the one who got carried away at Archer," David Mitchell replied. He grabbed the laptop and camera, double-checked the internet connection, then hustled down for the dock.

"Don't forget the tripod," Ryan said. He was already at the pontoon, checking his face in a mirror like a bridesmaid. All three girls were down there with him, getting their fishing rods ready.

David groaned and turned back. He scooped the tripod under his elbow then hustled down the small hill. His hip and back was on fire at this point. He had been standing for the past hour nonstop at Lake Archer, and now, he would get to do it all over again here for the livestream.

The lake was clear. There was not a single boat on it. The only signs of life were a gathering by the resort. Something was going on, though they could not quite make out what. There was a lot of commotion, and though they couldn't make out what was being said, David felt a sense of apprehension.

"Good! No flashing lights. Nobody on the water. We're set to go!" Ryan said.

"Hang on," David replied.

"For what?" Ryan said.

"Well, we don't know what's happening. Maybe we should delay the livestream until tomorrow."

"You serious?" Ryan said.

"Give me a break," Katy said. "I'm ready to show y'all up."

"Yeah? Like you did this morning?" Mandy said. Katy stuck her tongue out at her. Mandy posed, just as she did when she hooked a twenty-eight-inch walleye a half-hour prior.

"If Ryan's good for going on the lake, then I'm down with it," Natalie said. Her compliance stung the most. David always thought her to be the most rational one. Or maybe, he thought of her too much, which hurt more to watch her stray closer to Ryan.

David sighed. Maybe he was reading too far into it. Either way, he was outvoted.

"Dude! What are you doing?" Ryan said. He was pointing at his watch. David set up the tripod, connected the camera to his laptop, and made sure he was connected to the channel. He held out his hand, signaling for the girls to pass him the cord to the other two cameras. At a click of the mouse, he would be able to switch the feed to give the viewer different perspectives.

"Alright, we're gonna be live in fifteen seconds," he announced. Ryan rolled his shoulders, did a few pushups against the gunwale to obtain a quick pump, then stood at the center deck. He watched the cameraman count down with his fingers, then snapped to action.

"What's going on, everybody?! Thank you so much for joining us on this beautiful day. Once again, I apologize for the delay, but we're here now, ready to take you out on a tour of Peanut Lake. This really brings back memories of fishing with my uncle when I was a kid. Now, I get to take on the role of mentor, and share new experiences with all of you. Looks like we have a lot of people tuning in. Uh…" He leaned up slightly, waiting for David to write the number of viewers on a notepad. "Three-hundred-and-fifty-two people so far. More will tune in within the next ten minutes or so. Meanwhile, I say we get started. What do you say, ladies?"

"Show them how it's done, Ryan," Mandy said.

David cringed. So corny.

Ryan undid the mooring, then started the engine. "Our voyage begins. We will start here in the east bend and work our way around. If memory serves, there should be a nesting area near the cove. We'll start there and, depending on our luck, we'll work our way back to the west segment."

CHAPTER 14

Greg patted around the walls, aiming the flashlight on his phone until he finally located the overhead switch. A single bulb lit up in the center of the room, unveiling the rows of stored wine, vintage vodka, and whiskey which were stored on several shelves.

"Oh, Andy Cornett," he muttered. The man liked his booze. Some was shipped in from various wineries and breweries, while some near the back were homemade. Glass bottles rang like bells as they shook. The entire house was vibrating. They could hear the creaking and battering of dozens of creatures climbing over the roof and walls.

Hannah found a stool and sat on it. Her legs and arms were shaking uncontrollably. It took several attempts to holster her weapon. The images of her Deputies being abducted taunted her mind. She clenched her hands together, trying to overpower the shakes.

"You good?" Greg said from behind a whiskey shelf.

"Yeah," Hannah said.

"How's your arm?"

The question seemed to reawaken the pain in her shoulder. Hannah had almost forgotten she had been grazed. She rolled her sleeve up to inspect the wound. It wasn't much more than a laceration, with some mild burns along the edge. She reached along her duty belt for some gauze she carried around with her and a roll of medical tape.

"Here, let me," Greg said. He knelt down and took the limited medical supplies, cocking a grin as he tore the packaging off. "I see you've copied my methods."

"What?"

"People used to make fun of me for carrying medical supplies in my duty belt," he said. "I found it handy on a few occasions when responding to medical emergencies, when I'd get there before the paramedics."

Hannah looked away. "I mandated all the Deputies to do that." She sighed. "As you said; it's come in handy."

He packed the gauze against the wound, then wrapped it with tape. "That'll hold until we get out of here."

"Speaking of which…" Hannah grabbed her speaker mic. "Unit One to Dispatch?" She waited. "Dispatch?" She looked at her speaker mic, then followed the cord to her radio. The lower half was missing entirely. Not only had she taken a bullet to the shoulder, but to the radio as well. "Great!" She felt for her phone, which wasn't in its usual place on her left hip. The clip was missing, having broken off at some point during the chase. "That's just perfect! I couldn't ask for a more perfect situation. I don't suppose you have your phone on you…"

Greg cleared his throat. "I have it…on the dashboard of my pontoon boat."

"Well done."

"Hey, I wasn't anticipating being overrun by a bunch of spider-squids."

"Probably should've thought of it before trapping us in here," Hannah replied.

"Hey, you wanna go back out there? Be my guest. Let me know how it goes."

The door shook again, causing both of them to jump. With weapons pointed, they waited. Pieces of wood chipped along the frame as the edge of a claw slid under the door. Like the dorsal fin of a shark, it traveled the width of the door, then slipped out of sight.

Greg and Hannah each drew a breath.

"Where the hell did these things come from?" Hannah whispered.

"They weren't here yesterday," Greg said. "That kid deputy of yours was the only smart one among us. He's the only one who considered a crevasse in this lake. Just like the one in Rodney."

"They can come on land, too," Hannah said. "How can they do that?"

"Do I look like a biologist?" Greg said. They watched the door for another minute. "They've stopped for now. But they know we're in here."

"That plank won't hold them for long. We need to figure out a plan," Hannah said. They listened to the battering sounds along the walls. On the other side of the east wall came all kinds of movement. They could hear splashing, as well as the rattling of a chain. It seemed as though the creatures were congregating.

Greg thought about their location, then realized that the boat garage was on the other side of this wall. Something was going on. Were they trying to break in? Whatever it was, he needed to find out, but without attracting unwanted attention. He studied the walls, seeing more unused lumber along the back corner, along with flakes of plaster and insulation. The wall on the back corner had been repaired recently, and not yet painted.

He pulled the items off of a shelve, then dragged it to the back corner.

"What are you doing?" Hannah asked.

"Getting a look," Greg said. He opened the toolbox, found a hammer and screwdriver, then used the shelf as a ladder. Balancing at the top, he slowly used the screwdriver to carve a hole in the plaster, right near the corner. Each movement was taken with caution. Even though the creatures were already aware of their presence, making too much noise might encourage them to press an attack.

Twisting the screwdriver, he widened a two-inch hole in the plaster. With the pliers, he tore at the insulation, dropping each chunk to the floor until he could see the other side. Reaching through the hole, he slowly chipped at the plaster on the other side like an icepick. That hole would only be a centimeter wide, but it was all he needed.

Immediately, a horrid smell filled the cellar. Greg winced, then peered into the garage. There was all kinds of movement. He could see the blue paint on Andy's boat, then a shade of dark green pass over it. There were multiple creatures climbing along the hull. Greg tilted his head left and right to get the widest view he could.

The boat was rocking in its berth. He leaned up an inch to see the waterline. There was something pressed up against the boat. Several somethings...whatever they were, they were white in color. Greg took the screwdriver and widened the hole by a few millimeters.

"What's going on?" Hannah asked. She was standing by the shelf now. Greg peered again, straining as he tried to make out what was happening. "Greg?" He kept looking. His expression turned to utter disgust. After a few moments, he looked away.

Hannah's shoulder throbbed. The shakes, which had subsided moments ago, were back with a vengeance. Whatever he saw, it wasn't good. Despite this, she NEEDED to know what was happening.

"Let me look."

"No, I don't think you want to."

"Greg. Step down."

It was obvious she wasn't going to let up. Arguing would simply increase tensions. Then again, so would letting her look, which was already inevitable. He didn't want to explain what he saw anyway. Greg stepped down, picked up Andy's shotgun, then moved aside.

Hannah ascended the shelves, hesitating as it trembled under her weight. A wave of fear struck. That nauseating odor invaded her nostrils. The sound of movement intensified. The Sheriff made her way to the top of the shelf, then leaned against the wall. Pressing her eye to the gap Greg made, she peered into the garage.

At the waterline were several white objects. They weren't paper-white, rather, they were somewhat clear. Below the water level, however, they weren't white, though she could tell they continued a couple of feet down. Slime. Below the water, it was relatively clear, while exposed to the air, it turned white.

Behind the layer of dried slime was a dark shape, like a shadow. Hannah strained, focusing her vision as though operating a camera. Not a shadow…silhouettes. There were people inside those casings. It dawned on her…she was looking at cocoons. There were several of them lining the berth and the fishing boat.

Focusing her attention to the right, she noticed a significant amount of movement. There were three or four creatures at the edge of the dock. They were in the water, their tentacles wavering in circular motions. Strands of slime stretched from pores in their undersides, coating fresh cocoons which were secured at the edge of the dock.

She could see the people through the clear slime: Gordon, Jake, Zach, Ross… BILL. They were bringing him in right now. His body was limp, his shirt partially ripped at the center. She could see his short brown hair, and when he was propped against the boat, his eyes—frozen open, staring blankly.

Immediately, the creatures pulled thick strands of slime from their abdomens and coated him with it. Hannah pulled away from the hole and started climbing down. Immediately, her quaking hands lost their grip and she fell to the floor.

She scampered to her feet and backed away from the wall. She sucked in several breaths, then pressed a hand to her chest. She coughed, barely resisting the urge to vomit.

"Sit down," Greg said. His voice was shallow. He knew what he saw, as it was the cocooning of Ross he had the misfortune of witnessing.

Hannah nearly fell on the stool.

"I can't believe it."

"Keep it together," Greg said. "You're the Sheriff now. The town needs you."

Hannah scoffed. "That's just it. This is what I get for what I did."

Greg glared at her. "Don't get superstitious on me."

"Stop joking. I just got four of my Deputies killed," she replied.

"Listen, dumbass," Greg said, "stop with the self-pitying. Nobody could've predicted this. I certainly didn't. Hell, the only one smart enough to suggest it was Bill. Hell, he was thinking of oversized fish. Not these things that could come on land and invade the lake in large numbers." The realization hit both of them at once.

"They can come on land. The whole town could be in danger," Hannah said.

Greg nodded. "God knows how far inland they can spread."

"You think they can go far from water?"

"Your guess is as good as mine." Greg shrugged. "We know they have no problems coming up on shore. They've invaded the entire north side on this segment of the lake."

The door shook again. Claws raked the walls. There was the sound of roots being ripped from the ground.

Hannah and Greg stood up again.

"Can't we get a damn break?" Hannah said. She watched as one of the creatures stuck its claw under the door. Fear and anger combined into an explosive outburst. She fired two shots through the door. There was a squealing sound on the other side, and suddenly, the claw was yanked back. "Eat that!" she said. She noticed Greg staring at her. "What? You said yourself, they already know we're here."

The scraping intensified.

"Yeah. And now they're pissed off," Greg said.

Sunlight streamed under the doorframe as a small chunk was ripped away. The claws returned again, acting like sawblades against the door.

There were more sounds of shuttering boards. Greg looked up and saw the ceiling starting to shake. Some of the damn things were inside the house, and were now cutting their way through the floor.

"Not fair," Greg muttered, aiming his shotgun high.

The siege had begun. They were coming in from all sides. It was only a matter of time before they got inside.

CHAPTER 15

At *Good Lake Resort*, the shore was alive with people in dismay. Several tenants started the process of packing up. It was unclear what was happening, or why the rescue team had not returned.

It had been several minutes since they heard the discharging of weapons in the distance. Joe Hall paced along the shoreline, passing several of his employees as he strained to see what was happening across the lake. Even with binoculars, it was hard to tell what was happening. It appeared that the pontoon boat had been run aground. All they knew for sure was that those distant *pops* were indisputably gunshots.

"Anybody see anything?" somebody called out.

"Nothing."

"I thought I saw movement on the roof of that house," a woman cried out.

"How can you even see that far?" somebody else said.

Joe Hall raised his hands. "Everybody, calm down."

"Easy for you to say," one of the account managers said.

"Those were gunshots," Ernie said. "Something serious happened."

"Maybe we should leave," someone else added.

"Best thing we can do is remain here," Joe said. "Please. Just keep calm. The police will handle the situation. They probably have backup coming in as we speak."

Further down the shoreline, the Kendricks and the Browns were watching from their docks. Everyone was terrified...except for Mr. Kendrick, who was half asleep with a margarita in his hand.

His wife approached, her eyes flaring with rage. "Harold! It's noon."

"Ever hear of day drinking, babe?"

"You know how that stuff messes with your intestinal lining," she complained. "And why are you so relaxed?! Shouldn't we be calling 9-1-1, or something?"

"That's already been done. The cops are already here. If they need help, they'll call for backup," Mr. Kendrick replied. He downed his margarita then stood up with a groan.

"Where are you going?"

"Fixing myself a couple of drinks. Ugh!" He held his breath as he entered the cabin.

"A *couple*?! Now?"

"It's called vacation, dear," he called out.

Mrs. Kendrick heard the pouring of margarita mix and the sound of the ingredients mixing. Then there was the sound of a beeping microwave, followed by the opening of a can. Two minutes later, Harold came out with a pitcher of margarita, and two microwaved hotdogs smothered in canned chili, one of which was half in his mouth already. As he stuffed his face, he proceeded to watch the events across the lake.

"Looks like they're backing the pontoon boat away," he said.

"I can't tell. It almost looks like it's drifting."

Mr. Kendrick shrugged, then ate the other chili dog. Moments later, there was the sound of gurgling, followed by a stench. Mrs. Kendrick sniffed, then glared at her husband.

He shrugged, picked up a magazine, then walked away.

"Where are you going?"

"Nature calls, babe."

"I told you to watch your diet!"

"It's vacation, babe. No such thing as diet."

"Tell that to our pipes." She pointed her thumb at the cabin.

"Don't worry. I'm using Cabin Two's. Nobody's using it."

"Jesus, Harold. Something serious is going on right now."

"The cops are handling it. The shooting stopped. It's probably over by now." He sucked in his gut and disappeared into Cabin Two.

****

It became a struggle for Ryan Hodges to hide his frustration. For the tenth time in a row, his cast had brought in nothing but a weird slime substance, which brought with it a few weed strands.

"Well, darn it, looks like I've struck out again," he said.

"Me too," Mandy said. She bit her lip, then whined as she tried to get the stuff off of her lure.

"What the hell is this stuff?" Katy said.

"It's probably just some residue from dying weeds," Ryan guessed. What else could it be?

"We'll catch something, I'm sure," Natalie said. She threw a cast out toward the lake's center. Like the others, all she brought in was more residue. Despite this, she smiled at the camera, much to David's delight. His gaze was fixed on her tan shoulders, her perfect figure carved from eight years of running track, enhanced by the color gifted to her by the sun.

David was lost in thought. Yeah, the slime stuff was weird, but unlike the livestreaming audience, he wasn't bored. He had Natalie to gaze at, after all. The realization brought a sense of self-pity and foolishness. Though she was well-balanced in terms of personality and attitude toward other people, she still wanted what she wanted. And that was a confident, enthusiastic, flamboyant man. Not a near cripple who lost his edge.

He found himself longing for the old jock days. Just a hint of it, if only to not be in pain anymore. Then again, watching the ladies all but ignore him completely in favor of the kid he used to pick on, was pain in its own right.

"Dave? Daaaave? DAVE?!"

He snapped back into reality at the sound of Ryan's voice. Keeping the camera on Natalie, he glanced at the *YouTube* star, who was counting down with his fingers. It was his way of asking 'how many viewers do we have?'

David wrote his answer on the pad. Two-hundred-and-thirty.

Ryan looked away, unsure whether the feed was fixed on him. If so, he didn't want the audience to see his panic and frustration.

Damn it, I should've done the livestream at Archer. Too late for that. He had to salvage what he had. Some of the people they lost might check in again later, but they needed progress. Progress meant reeling in some damn fish.

"You know how it is, ladies," he said. "Fishing is all about patience. Can't have them leaping into the boat all at once. I had a trip once, where I spent three hours on a boat, without a single bite. Right as I was about to call it quits, I decided to try one more spot. You know what happened next?"

"Got a bite?"

"Two bites...on one harness. Yeah, that's right. I caught two largemouths on the same crawler. Thought I was bringing in a freaking gator, they were so heavy," he said, laughing. "The point is, we've fished this whole side of the lake and caught nothing."

"Except this...whatever it is," Mandy said, disgusted.

"It smells horrible," Katy replied.

"Shh. Just crap from the lake," Ryan replied. "You can handle it, can't you, babe?" He rubbed his hand over the small of her back. Katy smiled, the touch making her tingle. Mandy glared openly.

Slut.

David leaned against the transom rail, his eyes locked on Natalie's similar expression. It wasn't as obvious as Mandy's, but it was there. All three of these hob babes longing for the same guy...right in front of him. It was the same song and dance every day, and each time, he felt more and more emasculated.

Ryan turned to the camera. "Stay with us, everyone. We're gonna head over to the next segment of the lake. With a little luck, we'll find a little more action for you to witness."

He pulled up the anchor and started the motor. Before engaging the throttle, he opened the cooler.

"In the meantime..." he passed beer along to the ladies.

"About time," Natalie said.

"Got a beer tab opener?" Katy said. Ryan pulled one out from his pocket and went to each of the ladies, popping open their beers in such a spectacular fashion that it caused several drops to spray their chests, sparking laughter. He turned to David.

"Need my help?" he said.

"I think I can get it," David replied. He took the tool and half-downed his beer, which did little to dull the mental anguish. He watched the comments rolling in.

"God, Ryan's so hot. I'd kill to be one of those chickas."

"I could watch Ryan all day, with or without the pike."

"Do more livestreams, Ryan."

The comments rolled on and on. Clearly, it was the female viewers that stuck around. The male viewers, though partially drawn by the hot babes on set, had tuned out due to the lack of progress. It would take more than their nearly naked figures and Ryan's personality to draw them back. It was the one thing the *YouTube* star hadn't quite wrapped his mind around. Yeah, the girls helped bring in the male crowd, but guys weren't interested in watching hot babes gush over another dude.

Nor was David, but he didn't have the luxury of clicking *exit*. He downed his beer and sourly watched the girls' chitchat with Ryan as he steered the boat west.

CHAPTER 16

The bottom edge of the door had become a serrated edge of wood. The ceiling and walls rattled, with claws protruding through the viewing hole Greg had carved.

"Oh, fucking shit," Hannah said. Once again, she was getting pissed off and hysterical at once. "Great idea, genius, locking us in here."

"Are you seriously on that again?" Greg said.

"We could've made it to the road," she said.

"We would never have cleared the yard," Greg replied. Something crashed above them, shaking the ceiling. Both of them pointed their guns high, then back at the door as three tentacles reached under the gap. The squid they belonged to was now trying to squeeze its head under the door, scraping its leathery flesh against the shards.

Hannah fired her pistol. The burst of sound in the condensed space rattled their eardrums. The squid retracted, trailing a stream of blood. There was the sound of struggle on the other side of the door, along with horrifying hisses and screeches.

"Sounds like they're taking on the weak," Greg said. "If you don't serve the colony, you become food."

"Like us," Hannah said. She repeatedly glanced at their surroundings. "We're totally screwed if we stay here."

"Then we need a plan," Greg said.

"There's a truck out there," Hannah said. "I can hotwire it."

"These things would be on you before you even got the panels off," Greg said.

"Can't run, can't drive…so, you'd prefer we just wait in here for them to break in?" Hannah's jaw was clenched.

"We can't outshoot them," Greg said. "What do you plan to do? Make false accusations against them? Tell the newspapers they're a bunch of homophobes, make them disappear to avoid the public backlash?"

"You CAN NOT be serious," Hannah said. "You're getting on that now?!"

"Makes as much sense as you blaming me for locking us in here," Greg said.

"Jesus! I can't believe I'm gonna die in here with *you*."

"*You* can't believe it?! Imagine my delight."

"Ugh!" Almost more out of anger than necessity, Hannah fired another three rounds at the gap in the door, hitting the squid that attempted to pry its way through it. It lay on the ground, twitching its jaws. The tentacles writhed along the stairs, shivering as the brain delivered its final signals.

Hannah checked her mag. Six rounds, and one other in the chamber. Already, the things were pulling the dead member away from the space. Shadows encompassed the sunlight. Claws raked the door.

"They're not gonna give up," she said. She wandered to the back of the room. Greg glanced between her and the door.

"Excuse me? What are you doing?"

Hannah looked at the bottles of wine, then at the whiskey. She pulled a bottle of Bruichladdich from the shelf.

"Thank God, he's got the strong stuff." She pulled the cork and drank from the bottle, wincing as it burned.

Greg's jaw dropped. She was seriously going to get herself drunk. On the one hand, it actually made sense. If it made her fate less horrible, then it served a purpose. Plus, it provided him a mild sense of amusement in this midst of terror. She was clearly not a whiskey drinker, judging by how hard she winced.

"Burns, does it?"

"I won't confirm or deny that," she replied, coughing.

Pieces of ceiling boards started to flake down. The creatures had broken through the floor beams and insulation, and were now breaking through the electrical pipes. Next was the thin layer of ceiling directly above them. It was a race between the creatures at the door and those above.

Hannah took another drink. "Listen, since it appears our fate is sealed, I might as well get this off my chest. Might not be worth much, but here it goes: I'm sorry for what I did. I was thinking about myself and not about how it would affect you. I was just trying to win the election, not destroy your reputation."

"You didn't consider that those accusations would stick around?" Greg said. *I can't believe that we're fixating on this in our last moments.*

"I wasn't thinking on that note. I was just thinking about winning. My mom and dad…winning was all they lived for. They hated it when I lost. All my life, it was about kicking ass. Get to the top. To hell with everyone else. But, after doing what I did, I realized it didn't just affect you and me, but it affected the whole department. Nobody trusts me, and I realized I can't run the department without the staff. In winning at all costs, I sabotaged myself."

Definitely half drunk, Greg thought. But the words were real. She just needed the extra push. Not that it mattered in the long run.

A chunk of door was torn away. Now, it took little effort for one of the squids to slip through. Greg hit it with a shotgun blast, nearly exploding its forward segment.

His ears rang again.

Tentacles breached the ceiling and reached down, forcing him to kneel out of reach. Hannah threw herself down as well, still clutching the whiskey bottle.

"So much for winning," she said. She raised the bottle, then took another slug. She coughed. "Okay, I'll confirm it. This stuff burns."

Her eyes widened. So did Greg's.

Burn…

She looked at the bottle, then back at him. "Does this stuff…"

"Let me see that." He rushed toward her, took the bottle, and smelled it. "Whoa, yes! This'll do it. What else do we have here?" They began sorting through the whiskey and vodka. "We got Jack Daniels, American Malt…Elijah Craig twenty-three years old?!"

"Is that flammable?!"

"Fuck that! I'm taking this for myself!" He tucked the bottle under his arm. "But the rest of this stuff will work."

"Oh, this is crazy," Hannah said. "We're just as likely to burn ourselves alive."

Greg scoffed. "What was that shit about doing whatever it takes to win about, then?"

Hannah nodded. "It's either that or be cocooned."

They began spraying the alcohol all around the cellar. In less than a minute, the whole place was soaked. Greg took a few more bottles and chucked them at the door, splashing the breach with whiskey.

Greg, a cigar smoker, always had a lighter on hand. He sparked a flame and applied it to the nearest spot. The alcohol lit up like gasoline. The vapor in the air ignited, causing large fireballs to shoot across the room, singeing the people inside. Greg and Hannah tucked their heads down and held their breath as the fire continued to spread around them.

A wall of flame consumed the cellar door. Behind that flame were whipping tentacles.

It was the hive's first exposure to the phenomenon of fire. It was visible heat, which brought intense pain to the slightest touch. Those nearest to it felt their skin dehydrate. Soon, this orange glow intensified. It began to consume the outer walls, and eventually make its way to the roof.

Smoke, much like those emitted by the vents in the world below, filled the air. Only, this smoke spread freely, unlike the toxins they had grown adept to. Behind that wall of fire were several loud crashes, each one seemingly causing the fire to spread faster.

Realizing this new 'enemy' was one they could not defeat, the swarm vacated the roof and yard. Whatever this was, it was a threat to the new hive. Like a single body, the creatures spread to the lake and adjoining properties, while some moved to retrieve the eggs and newly born larvae from the now-burning garage.

Greg threw another whiskey bottle into the ceiling, then another through the gap in the door. Both ignited upon impact.

It was like they were standing in hell itself. Their whole world had turned into fire and smoke. Most of the floor had gone up, leaving them little space for protection.

They hugged each other like a loving couple, savoring the small bit of space they shared. Fire rolled like demon claws, singeing their clothes and arms. The ceiling began to crackle.

"Alright, let's hope the plan worked," Greg said. They rushed to the door, and realized the board was encased in flame. Not willing to suffer third-degree burns to unlatch it, Greg simply put a shotgun blast through it. The board, and much of the door, exploded into fragments. Greg kicked what remained off its hinges, then sprinted out onto the grass, with Hannah right behind him. They scanned the yard and tree line with their weapons, saw that the creatures had vacated, then dashed for Andy's pickup.

Hannah dove into the driver's seat, checked the visor and glove compartment in hopes that Andy was the type to leave his keys in the vehicle. Unfortunately, that was not the case, which forced her to hotwire.

Adrenaline and booze messed with her vision, and she couldn't stop coughing from the smoke she inhaled.

"Might wanna hurry up there," Greg said.

"I'm working on it," she replied.

"Work faster," Greg said. Hannah heard the scurrying from the adjacent property. The creatures were circling back, having sensed the movement of prey.

"Oh shit."

****

"Holy shit, look at that?!" Ryan Hodges pointed at the large bloom of smoke rolling up from one of the lakeshore properties.

"Oh my God!" Mandy said.

"Does anyone have a phone? We ought to call the Fire Department," Natalie said.

"Already on it," David said. He dialed 9-1-1 and waited for the operator to answer. "Yes, I need the Fire Department. We have a large structure fire. Don't know the address, but it's on Peanut Lake, west segment, northside. Believe me, they won't miss it when they get here."

"Thank you. Please stay on the line."

David turned to Ryan, then whispered, "Hey, I think we should kill the feed."

Ryan shook his head, then stood in front of the center camera.

"Don't be alarmed, everybody. I'm sure nobody's hurt. As you probably heard, my cameraman has already notified the Fire Department. Let's just keep out of the way and not get involved."

David gave him a sneer. *You seriously want to record this? What if somebody's in there?*

Seeing his friend's expression, Ryan stepped behind the camera to speak with him. He glanced at the monitor to assure himself he was out of view—and to see the view count. He removed his mic, then tapped David on the shoulder. "We can't cancel the livestream."

"There's a burning house, Ryan."

"Shh! Not so loud. We can release clips from this. They'll get a bunch of views."

"This is a fishing channel, Ryan. You of all people should know that! We shouldn't be filming this."

"Ryan?"

The star turned around and saw Natalie facing him. Out of respect for the show, she stepped out of view and removed her mic from her bikini strap.

"I think David's right."

Ryan sighed. "Let's just sit back and wait…"

"We're not catching anything anyway," Natalie interrupted. "Except this slime shit."

The 9-1-1 operator returned. *"I've alerted the Fire Department."*

Ryan held a mic to David's lips, hoping to record the conversation. Unable to focus on fending him off and relaying information, David relented.

"Do you know if anyone's inside?"

"I can't tell from here. I'm out on the lake. I think the driveway is behind it, but I can't see from where I'm at." He studied the shoreline, squinting at the various shapes moving along the property on the west. "I think I see movement, but I'm not sure…what the hell am I looking at?"

"What's that?!" Katy said.

"It's a fire," Ryan said.

"No. In the water." She pointed at the garage door, and the large swells rolling away from it. Then there was another set, followed by another. Something broke the surface, disappearing before they saw what it was.

Ryan reattached his microphone, then approached the bow.

"Fish?" Mandy asked.

"I don't know," Ryan said. The girls shrieked as something touched the boat from underneath.

Katy heard a splash behind her. She turned around and screamed. The tentacles unveiled like a flower and latched onto her waist. In the blink of an eye, she was pulled over the railing and under the waves.

"Katy!" David rushed to the rail, while the others backed away.

Having spent much of their energy collecting hosts for the larvae and their mother, it was time for the creatures to hunt for their own sustenance. The squid-creature easily overpowered its victim, impaling its flesh with its claws. There was no need for the proboscis. The jaws would do all the work this time.

The human writhed as teeth sliced through her midsection, spilling intestines and gallons of blood which billowed into a dark red fog. Ribbons of flesh were suctioned into its throat and into the digestive tract in its mantle-like abdomen.

Mandy pressed her hands to her face as she watched the lake turn red. "Oh my God!"

Panic struck the pontoon boat. Mandy continued to scream, while Natalie attempted to comfort her, while suppressing her own terror.

Ryan peered over the port rail. The blood cloud thickened under the thrashing waves. Between those waves arose a series of tentacles, each one several inches thick, flexible as a rubber band.

"Jesus, God!" Ryan went for the helm. His hand fumbled over the throttle. The water exploded in front of him, preceding the arrival of several more tentacles. More appeared around the stern. Then the starboard side.

The boat shook as though caught in a whirlpool. It shifted back and forth as new weight tugged on the railings. Metal groaned behind them, simultaneous to the tremors of violent action beneath the waterline.

"Oh my God!" Mandy screamed.

"Ryan! Get us out of here!" Natalie said. Ryan engaged the throttle. The engine roared to life. There was a slicing sound. The boat vibrated as the propellers cut through bloated flesh. The water around them turned to black.

The pontoon boat moved forward. It was very slow, the engine groaning with strain. He clenched his teeth, looking for a place to go. The whole north shore was alive with movement.

He looked to his left, seeing the crowd of people by the resort. As far as he was concerned, that was the safest place to run aground. He cut the wheel to port and gunned the throttle. Again, the boat shook violently. They were moving slowly, but they were moving.

The creatures, whatever they were, were everywhere. They were keeping up with the boat, like orcas ganging up on a large grey whale.

Mandy screamed again. Ryan looked back, then gasped as two of the creatures heaved their drooling, bloated bodies over the transom. With his attention on them, he almost didn't notice the beast hoisting itself over the bow.

He felt the wetness of a tentacle brush over his shoulder. Ryan reacted with speed he didn't know he was capable of. He ducked under its grasp, then made a bounding leap onto the center of the deck. He looked over his shoulders, seeing the tentacles still coming at him, making squiggly lines in the air as if caught in a current.

His mind was gone. It was everybody for themselves.

There was no thought behind his next action beyond basic instinct. Ryan grabbed Mandy and Natalie and threw them in the way. Both girls screamed as the tentacles brushed over their bare waists and shoulders.

Drawing a folding knife from his back pocket, David lunged at the tentacles. He slashed like a barbarian hunter from Stone Age times, hacking the demon tentacle repeatedly. Like engine oil, blood spilled from the various slits, until the arms retracted, freeing Mandy and Natalie.

"Get back," David said. Mandy was in hysterics, unable to form sentences or thoughts. Natalie, though terrified, was able to hold it together. She nodded, staying close to David, who held his knife out, 'warning' the squids to stay back.

The creatures on the stern rail raised their front arms, revealing their jaws. Together, they pounced, knocking the center camera, the computer console, and Ryan Hodges to the deck.

The *YouTube* star screamed and punched at the beasts. Wet flesh coiled over his arms and legs, then squeezed. There was intense pressure, resulting in pain, which intensified at the snapping of bones. Like executioners from the Middle Ages, the creatures tugged at his limbs, while a third hovered over him. It raked its scythe-like talons over his stomach. Innards spilled over onto the deck.

Gurgling blood bubbles, Ryan convulsed one final time. Femurs cracked like toothpicks, then with a squelching sound, the flesh pulled apart. He was drawn and quartered, leaving a wobbling trunk on the deck, whose abdomen was now being ravaged by ravenous jaws.

Ryan turned his head, his mind going numb from blood loss and shock. In his final moments, he found himself gazing at the computer screen, watching the footage of his own demise, and the comments section scrolling along the bottom.

"Holy SHIT!"
"Is this real?!"
"Oh my God! Get the police!"
"What are those things?!"
"Giant squids?!"
"Fake!"
"Staged!"

CHAPTER 17

Rodney, Michigan

"Okay, take it down," Mike Wilkow instructed. Joel Pobursky bit his lip. Never in a million years did he think he'd be taking instructions from a nutjob like the guy standing behind him. But it was a job, and the guy was generous enough to recommend him to N.E.C.T.O.R. Piloting drones certainly beat filleting fish in a closed lodge resort.

Three years ago, in early afternoon, Ridgeway Lake would've been teeming with activity. Jet skis and motorboats would be zipping past them. The shoreline would be alive with people wading hundreds of feet out. Aluminum boats would be all over the coves and weeded areas, and when the sound of boat motors settled, the splashes of struggling fish would take their place.

Since the arrival of the Carnobass, and the carnage it brought with it, that all changed. Many of the lakeshore homes were vacant now. The lodge closed that following winter. Once in a while, people would venture out onto the lake, only to be chastised for taking such an unnecessary risk.

Whenever he came near the artificial ledge, he could still smell the diesel from the helicopter crash. There had been talks of new buyers for the lodge. Since tourism came to an abrupt stop, so did the revenue that came with it. The newly elected town Mayor was already making noise about getting businesses running again.

Joel didn't know how he felt about that. On the one hand, there hadn't been an incident in three years. On the other, what if people started going on the lake, only for the same thing to eventually happen again?

Do understand this, they needed to know more about the crevasse and the world beneath it.

Joel lowered the drone into the water, then took the control pad. "Drone lowered."

"I gathered that by the water on my screen," Wilkow remarked.

"Just following procedure."

"We're not in the military, Mr. Commando," Wilkow joked.

"I was a pararescue."

"Point is, it's just us here. Dr. Nevers is in the lab, and the other agents are waiting on shore. No need for the 'I'm doing this.' 'Oh look! Now I'm doing that!' 'Holy smokes, I just made a left turn!' 'Oh my God, I'm going bald now!'" He grinned nervously, realizing Joel didn't take the hair thing very well. He cleared his throat and looked to the west shore. "Better get going, though. They look rather impatient."

"From the comfort of their beach chairs. Bunch of wusses," Joel remarked. He had to give Wilkow credit there: at least *he* had the nerve to stand on the deck of this boat and monitor the situation. Then again, knowing Wilkow, it probably wasn't bravery, but pure insanity.

He thumbed the joystick, steering the two-foot drone deep into the lake. It was the deepest section, the floor being over three-hundred feet down. The light gradually faded as he neared two-hundred feet.

"Engaging the lights," Joel said.

"Like an angel," Wilkow said. "The fish down there might think you're their savior!"

"I'm leaning on the side of hoping we DON'T find anything down there," Joel said.

"Well that's boring," Wilkow said. "This mission is all about discovery!"

"It's about determining level of threat."

"We're not para trooping into Korea. We're just taking a peek into a speck of dirt."

"Korea?" Joel shot Wilkow a glare. "How old do you think I am?!"

Wilkow pretended to cough, then focused on the monitor. "Watch where you're going. I can see the bottom. I think you need to go a little bit north."

Joel exhaled. He gently steered the drone, maintaining a ten-foot height over the bottom.

"There it is," he said. "Let's hope this prototype works. This is the tenth time."

"First two were on you," Wilkow said.

"I wasn't a professional drone operator," Joel said.

"I thought you were a jack of all trades?"

"I blame Chief Sydney for that title. Besides, you gotta learn the trade first." Joel groaned, thinking about his first dive attempts with these drones. It seemed simple enough at first glance. Joystick, accelerators, left, right, up, down, lights, etc. But the device always went faster than what he intended. It seemed the slightest touch on the joystick would send the thing shooting like a rocket. The first trip, he accidentally crashed the drone into the lake bottom. The second time went slightly better; he at least got the drone two feet into the mouth of the crevasse before striking a ledge.

"We're in," he said. "Already beats the first two days." He watched the monitor intently, seeing the soft soot turn to hardened rock as the drone descended a hundred feet. "Alright, this is where the next three lost their signals. So far, we're holding up pretty well."

"Don't forget about the shards dangling from the ceiling," Wilkow said.

"I remember."

"Once we're in the lake, I'll activate the sonar ping. Maybe today, we'll *finally* get an idea of how big this son-of-a-gun is."

"God-willing. Just give me a few minutes. I'm taking it slow," Joel replied.

"I'm aware."

Moments passed. Joel watched the tunnel passing by the screen, as though he was piloting through a wormhole in deep space. Or the throat of some gargantuan beast. How a twenty-five-foot fish made its way through here was…impressive!

A tiny splash over to the side nearly hindered his concentration. He shrugged. It's a lake. Fish jump. What *did* break his concentration was the cranking of a fishing reel. He looked over and saw Wilkow standing at the transom, tugging at a fishing line.

"Are you SERIOUSLY fishing?!?!"

Wilkow shrugged. "Why not?" He pointed his elbow at the monitor. "I've seen this part already. We've got a few minutes to kill. More than a few, since you're driving like an old grandpa."

"Oh, you're funny. Bet you'll be laughing as hard as I am when you're eating corn on the cob with no teeth."

"What's to be offended about?! You *are* a grandpa! Remember?"

Joel stared. Was he being sarcastic with the 'remember' part? *How old DOES he think I am?!*

He focused on the monitor. "Could've left out the 'old' part."

"How's the youngster?"

"Got me wrapped around his little finger."

"They still living at home?"

"For now."

Wilkow performed a small dance. Joel tried not to look, despite being cursed to see it in his peripheral vision.

"I would ask what it is you're doing, but I'm not sure I want to know."

"Celebrating. I'm allowed to feel good that this job was willing to put the grandbaby on the insurance policy," Wilkow said.

Joel couldn't deny that. As annoying as Mike Wilkow was, Joel was in his debt. Now, if the kids could get on their feet so he wouldn't have to endure this knucklehead's antics any longer. Plus, he was ready to retire and kick his feet back.

"I see Viper Seven. What's left of it," he said. The silver remains of the drone were spread across the tunnel floor. He was careful to keep low, remembering the formations that hung from above. He steered the drone around the bend.

This was where the last two lost their signal.

"Alright, it's our moment of truth. Fifty feet to go..."

A series of splashes broke the water.

"Fish on!" Wilkow said. He tugged on his rod, which bent into a semi-circle.

"You're kidding, right?"

"I've been working so much, I gotta get recreation when I can," Wilkow replied.

"Working? All you do is stare at a screen!"

"Hey, don't forget about all the lab work on Carnobass. The dissection. The mapping of the tunnels. The designing of the drones."

"Yeah, you did a real bang-up job there," Joel said. As Wilkow conducted his 'task', Joel gradually took the drone into the abyss. So far, the screen wasn't getting fuzzy. The controls were responding as though the receiver was right next to him. This might be the successful expedition they were waiting for.

Joel held his breath. The tunnel went straight down. This was where Viper Ten lost its signal. Another meter, and this would be the furthest they'd ever gotten.

Like a helicopter descending onto a landing pad, the drone sank, guided by its vertical propellers. He counted the depth marker. The drone was three-hundred-and-seventy-meters below them, and counting.

Finally, the tunnel widened. All of a sudden, there were no walls around the drone. He was no longer looking at hardened stalagmites and columns. He was in open water now, with almost no sign of earth except for ceiling above. He expected to see darkness. Instead, he saw vibrant lights all around him. Tiny shrimp danced around the camera, inspecting the alien lifeform visiting their world.

"Doc! DOC! You seeing this?!"

Wilkow glanced back, realized that Joel had reached the destination sooner than he anticipated, then whooped. Still, he didn't want to lose his prize. He reeled the largemouth in a few feet, then with a fling of the rod, he launched it into the boat like a catapult.

The fish arched in midair, then flopped against Joel's right cheek.

"Lord above! Are you serious, dude?!"

"Nineteen inches! These guys have been growing since nobody's been catching 'em!" Wilkow said. He stood by his monitor and took his first glimpse into the world below.

"Would you look at that!"

Joel wiped the water from his face, then resumed control. "Should I take it further in?"

"Turn three degrees port, then take it at one-fourth speed. I don't want to attract the attention of any predators yet."

"Yet?!'

"Sooner or later, we're gonna have to see what lurks beneath," Wilkow said. He gazed at the bright green algae on the rock surface. To the right were colors ranging from blue to purple, and even red several feet down. The bottom almost resembled molten lava, though Wilkow knew that this was something else. Rocks? Coral? Algae? Probably something new entirely. They had just discovered an entire ecosystem.

"Finally! We did it," Joel said. "You ready to send that sonar ping?"

"Charging it up. Three…two…"

Suddenly, both monitors turned to fuzzy grey. Joel tapped on the joysticks, while Wilkow tried typing on the keypad. No response. He tried enhancing the signal. The signal struggled briefly, only to die again.

Wilkow squeezed his eyes shut and groaned. "Dead in the water."

Joel leaned back. "Son of a gun!"

"Back to ground zero," Wilkow said. Joel rubbed his hands over his eyes, then looked down at the largemouth flopping at his feet. He picked it up, dislodged the hook, then tossed it back into the water. Wilkow spun to grab it, but was too late. "HEY! That was my dinner!"

"You seem more pissed about losing your precious fish than what just happened," Joel said.

"I've recorded the footage. Today was a major milestone. I bet you no longer consider that submersible training a waste of time."

"Only as long as the paycheck rolls in," Joel replied. "And no stinking way am I going down there until we have a map of the area."

"Well, with the recorded footage we have, we can prep a new, better detailed simulation," Wilkow said. "We might send some drones to try and widen the passage and—" He paused, then looked at his phone. *Dr. Nevers.* "Oh, great." He answered it. "Thank you for calling Dominos! May I take your order?"

"Mike, get on the internet right now!" Nevers was frantic. *"Get on YouTube. NOW! You've gotta see this for yourself!"*

Wilkow didn't waste time with quips or other various methods of annoying the professor. He got on his laptop, logged onto *YouTube*, and immediately saw the trending video right there on his home page.

"Oh, the *Ryan Hodges* channel is having a livestream," he said. "The guy's good, but you can tell with some of the coastal stuff he doesn't really know what he's talking about."

"Will you shut up and click on it!"

"OOOKAY!" Wilkow activated the video.

Joel watched his expression harden. His eyes narrowed at the screen; the grin immediately vanished. He stood alongside the biologist, then felt his jaw drop at the sight of the horror on the screen.

"Nevers? Where is this?" Wilkow asked.

"Some lake in the UP. Schoolcraft County, I believe. We're investigating right now."

Wilkow looked at Joel. "Mind taking us in? I have a chopper ride to catch."

Joel gave one last glance at the screen. These creatures were nothing like the Carnobass, or even like anything he saw in the footage. They looked like something from another world entirely. And though smaller in size, their ferocity made the Carnobass look like a damn flounder.

"You *sure* you wanna go there?"

"Damn straight. You coming?"

Joel almost choked on his spit. "Heck no!"

"Oh, come on. N.E.C.T.O.R. is paying you top dollar. You might get a bonus out of the deal."

"Yeah, I think I'm good. I've got chili in the crockpot at home, and frankly, I'd rather spend my evening enjoying that than fighting monsters."

"Oh, I'm sure you won't have to fight monsters," Wilkow said.

"Look at that!" Joel pointed at the monitor. "You see that?! They can come out of the water. How many of them are there?"

"That's what I'm gonna find out," Wilkow replied.

"Wait...you think they came from the crevasse?"

"Obviously not this one."

"You know what I mean."

Wilkow shrugged. "I think it's safe to assume they didn't wander in from the woods." He got on his phone and brought up the arrowhead prototype. "It might be a good opportunity to try this out."

"Should've recruited my youngest son. With all the video game practice, he'd probably be a natural at piloting these things."

"But *you're* the jack of all trades, remember. And didn't your wife have a honey-do-list that was gonna cost a pretty penny?"

Joel tensed. His wife had been bugging him about building a new addition to the house, which he needed a few extra grand for.

"We might get a special grant from the State for investigating this. Nevers is negotiating it," Wilkow continued. The unspoken phrase was 'tag along and you might get some of it.'

"I hate you," Joel said.

Wilkow smiled. "Great! Let's get to it."

Joel looked at the laptop screen again. "This place is across Lake Michigan. It's three hundred-plus miles away, easy. You think there's another underwater lake up there?"

"That... or this world below is much bigger than we've ever thought possible."

CHAPTER 18

Greg Goodman pumped his shotgun. He had three shells left—not nearly enough to deter the dozen creatures gathering on the neighboring property.

"Feel free to take your time," he said to Hannah.

"Get off my case!" she said, fumbling over the wires. She shook at the sound of a shotgun blast. One of the creatures flew backwards, spraying blood onto its brethren.

The others started coming toward them, stalled momentarily by the intense heat radiating from the house.

The Sheriff linked the wires together. The engine turned a few times, though it didn't quite spark.

"Need me to take over?"

"Shut your face, Goodman! I've got this!" She tried again. This time, the engine came alive with a mighty roar.

Roused by the vibration, the squids scurried in their arachnid poses. Hannah seated herself and slammed the door shut. Greg fired his last two shells, taking out the two leaders, then dove into the truck.

"Floor it!"

She did. Tires screeched as they carried the truck along the driveway. One of the creatures raised its tentacles and bared its teeth. The truck jolted as Hannah plowed into it. Wiggly arms waved in every direction for a split second before the thing was pancaked onto the pavement, the tires leaving long black trails.

With its grill packed with flesh, the truck raced through the two-hundred feet of driveway onto Circle Drive. As they came out of the patch of woods, the two occupants noticed a series of *thumps* coming from behind them.

Greg looked back, then ducked. Another drone, having hoisted itself aboard during the escape, was peering right at them through the glass.

"Oh SHIT!" He aimed his shotgun, only to remember he was out. "Give me your pistol." Hannah handed it to him, and he aimed back. Before he could squeeze the trigger, the creature lifted itself over the cab. Water and slime dripped down the windshield. Tentacles assaulted the hood, their claws grooving the metal.

Hannah hit the brakes in an attempt to throw it off, but the creature maintained its firm grip. It lowered itself onto the hood, then assaulted the windshield.

Greg fired all remaining rounds in, punching holes through its face. It reeled backward, twisting and turning in impossible motions. Hannah floored the accelerator, splattering the thing against the pavement.

"Are they following us?" she asked.

Greg looked back. "No. Looks like we're good." He squinted. "Turn us around."

"What? You insane?"

"Look in your mirror."

Hannah slowed the truck, then looked at the mirror, immediately seeing the flashing lights of a Fire Department truck on the verge of serving themselves up as the next course.

She performed a U-turn and floored the accelerator. She honked the horn, waved a hand through the window, and flashed the brights. It was enough to slow them down at least. Hannah brought the truck to a screeching stop across the road, blocking the Fire Department from entering the driveway. She immediately stepped out and held up her badge.

"Sheriff?" the Fire Captain said. "What's going on?"

"Captain, DO NOT go in there, you will be killed. There's a deadly situation. I need to borrow your radio right now."

The Captain didn't argue. Judging by the minor burns and smoke marks on Hannah's uniform and face, she had seen the fire up close, and knew something he didn't. He handed his radio over.

Hannah changed the frequency to her station. "Dispatch?"

"Sheriff? Where have you been?"

"Dispatch, we have an outbreak situation at Peanut Lake. Multiple officers are down. Alert the State Police immediately. Any Deputies not on duty are on duty. We have multiple biological organisms. If they ask questions, tell them we suspect a situation like Rodney."

The Fire Captain stepped past the truck and saw the squelched body in the pavement. The tentacles were still twitching, the blood forming little rivers in all directions.

"Jesus! What the hell is that?"

Greg shook his head. "*That* is why you don't want to go to the lake."

CHAPTER 19

Rivers of blood flowed along the feet of the three remaining occupants of Ryan Hodges' pontoon boat. Mandy was grabbing fistfuls of her hair, watching the creatures climbing up around her. Natalie clung to David, not crying, but still frozen from sheer terror.

Tentacles were all over the guardrail. The creatures on deck were feasting on Ryan's mutilated corpse. Already, there was barely anything left to identify him as a human, other than his basic skeletal form.

David tried to think fast. They had moments before they would be like Katy and Ryan. They were completely surrounded. Swimming would be useless, as the lake was full of these things. There was nowhere to go but up.

He glanced up at the canopy, then squatted. He cupped his hands together and looked to Natalie. "Step up!" Understanding what he meant, she let him boost her onto the thick tarpaulin. Already, it folded inward slightly, forcing her to stay close to the supports.

"Mandy!" David called. She was facing away from him, almost catatonic. The creatures were over the bow, now poised like tarantulas. The ones on the port and starboard rails were completely out of the water, with more taking hold behind them. "MANDY!"

He grabbed her by the shoulders in an attempt to get her attention. Instead, all it did was drive her into a mad panic, as she thought it was one of the creatures seizing her. That reality came a split-second later, when one of the beasts pounced on her from the bow, knocking her and David over.

Natalie screamed, watching the world of squirming tentacles beneath her. David, his hip flaring, his shirt red with Ryan's blood, pushed himself up on his hands and knees. Immediately, he felt warm blood splash his face. Mandy hollered while two creatures mutilated her. Jaws cut through her limbs, with muscles rolling the teeth back and forth. Her screams were silenced, not by death, but by the squeezing of a tentacle around her neck. The pulling motion, and the subsequent removal of her head, made the silence permanent.

"David!"

He looked up and saw Natalie reaching down at him. Before he could reach back, he felt the wetness of several arms flooding the air around him. He slashed with his pocketknife, hitting a couple of them. However, he only delayed the inevitable by a few seconds.

Natalie screamed, watching the cameraman being torn limb from limb. She cursed herself for being part of this channel, for not going back to college and pursuing education—for not being anywhere but here at this very moment.

She heard the tearing of tarp, then saw the claws passing through the middle like dorsal fins. The tarp slit, sending her freefalling into the swarm below. There was a series of ripping and pulling, as the pontoon deck became host to a violent feeding frenzy.

****

"What in the name of—" Joe Hall muttered. Like everyone else, he was watching the burning house in the distance. Over the course of the next few minutes, the flames grew larger and larger.

Then came a series of screams from the pontoon boat. With everyone's attention on the fire, most of the crowd didn't notice the activity on board, until it came within a couple hundred yards of the shore.

"What the hell is that?!" Ernie said.

"A fire. What else?" one of the account managers said.

"NO! *THAT!*"

All eyes went to the pontoon boat. Several employees screamed when they saw the swarming movement and the blood dripping over the hull. The creatures were swarming over the boat as though parts of one body, the tentacles discarding bones and clothing over the side.

"Oh my God!"

"What are those things?!"

"They're coming right for us!"

Joe Hall raised his hands and stepped between the group and the shore to get their attention. "Listen carefully! We're leaving. Let's head out in an organized fashion." He spoke calmly, trying not to contribute to a panic. But it happened anyway. People screamed and started running around the yard. "Hey! I said don't panic…"

Then he heard the rolling waves behind him. He looked over his shoulder, saw the army of arachnoid shapes scurrying up the beach toward him. All sense of reason was lost. Joe Hall screamed, then started to run. He only gained two meters before one of the creatures drove him to the ground.

Following the pontoon boat to the shore, the drones still in the water detected new movement from the world they had not yet explored. Chemical signals spilled from pores in their bodies, alerting more drones from the crevasse, and directing them to the landscape. New members that arose from the depths were further spurred by the scent of blood. This world was rife with sustenance, and it was time to harvest.

Mrs. Kendrick gasped as she realized the swells rolling up on shore were, in fact, not swells. Huge creatures emerged from the lake, coiling their tentacles and pumping fluid into their muscles like hydraulic presses.

"Harold!" she screamed. She ran to Cabin Two and pulled on the door. It wouldn't open. The pudgy bastard latched it shut!

"Be out in a few minutes, babe!"

"Harold! Let me in!" She turned around, then threw her arms over her eyes as the creature tackled her against the door.

Harold grunted, shifting on the toilet. The heavy impacts on the door were not helping with making space for the chili dogs. He groaned, irritated. Why was she so eager to get in? And by the sounds of it, she was practically trying to break the door down.

"No wonder that Greg guy charges a security deposit," he said. He heard the door shutter again. "Jesus! I'll be out in a few minutes! If you need to go that bad, just ask the Browns." The commotion didn't stop. Cursing under his breath, he downed his margarita, hoping the buzz would help the process.

The room spun. He closed his eyes and smiled, barely noticing the sound of the front door splintering. There was a sticky sound, along with that of heavy movement.

Harold squinted as a big spider emerged at the door. Except, it wasn't simply a spider. It was dripping wet, and the legs, when raising over the floor, looked more like octopus arms than an arachnoid.

He looked at his empty glass. "Did I overdo it?"

The sensation of flesh being stripped away answered his question.

Seconds passed before the beach was swarming with squid creatures. A few became a dozen. Then a dozen became dozens. In less than a minute, there were a hundred squids scurrying across the beach property, each with the same goal in mind.

Every which way he looked, Ernie saw movement. Creatures with outstretched tentacles wrestled his coworkers to the ground. Some had the flesh ripped from their bodies, others were stung, paralyzed, then dragged toward the water.

It was everyone for themselves. He raced up the hill for his car. Someone screamed in the distance. The cabins further to the west were now being invaded. The Browns were racing up the hill, with the eighteen-year-old twenty feet ahead of his parents.

Right behind them were the creatures, easily closing the distance. One sprang like a cricket. Even the screams of his nearby coworkers couldn't drown out the hollers by Mrs. Brown.

"Get it off of me." There was a high-pitched squeal, then suddenly, her cries ended…only to be replaced by those of her husband. Their son didn't look back. Yet, Ernie couldn't take his eyes off the event, even as he ran for his own safety. The squids overpowered the husband, snapping his limbs, and eventually engaging in a tug-of-war. There was a shriek of pain, followed by the crack of a spine. Mr. Brown was torn in half, his entrails as wriggly as the tentacles that disemboweled him.

When Ernie turned his eyes to the ground ahead of him, he saw a river of red. The creatures were all over the hillside, darting back and forth, tackling his staff, and stinging them. Humans stiffened and frothed at the mouth. Meanwhile, body parts were strewn among the trees as other victims were eaten alive. It was as if the devil had risen from the lake and unleashed hell upon the Earth.

Everywhere he looked, he saw leathery flesh and flailing tentacles. He stopped as one of the creatures emerged from behind a tree to his right, ready to spring. He turned on his heel and ran left, only to see a couple more scurrying a few meters ahead. Within seconds, they circled around him. He was cut off. The only way to go was down. Or so he thought.

He spun toward the lake, ready to make a hail Mary sprint to the cabin, where he'd lock himself in. He never took the first step. The drone was right there to intercept him. Its stinger struck his abdomen, the shock and pain knocking him to the grass. Ernie tensed, spasmed, his heart pulsing rapidly. His vision blurred. All he could feel was wetness and the grinding of dirt on his back.

CHAPTER 20

"Dispatch, this is Car One-oh-Two. I'm at Circle Drive near Good Lake Resort. There's something going on over here. We have people running about. Cars flying out of the driveway. I'm pulling over to investigate."

Sergeant Arnold Thorp of the Michigan State Police brought his car to a screeching stop. The screaming civilians barely took notice of his towering frame and blue uniform. His blood surged, the first thought racing through his mind being that a mass shooting was taking place. In his twelve-years in the state police, he had encountered two violent shootouts, both of which left their mark on his psyche.

He stepped toward the crowd. "What's going on?!" Only a few stopped long enough to answer, before disappearing in a sprint.

"They're everywhere! My God! They're just EVERYWHERE!!!"

"Who's everywhere? What's going on?"

More screams erupted, and the civilian simply raced away for his own safety. Arnold's partner, Trooper Vince Bickford, already had his hand on his holster.

"Sarge, this isn't the address of that fire," he stated.

"Something's going on," Arnold said. He sprinted through the driveway, winding between fleeing bodies. He came to the hill, where he saw the bloodbath taking place below. "Jesus, GOD!"

Vince stood beside him. Both men were silent, briefly glancing at the other to assure themselves they saw the same thing.

"All available units! Converge on Good Lake Resort. There are…animals coming out of the lake and they're killing everybody.

Multiple casualties. Dispatch, alert SWAT, and get ahold of the Governor's Office. We're gonna need the National Guard."

"Car Ninety-seven on site."

The Troopers heard tires on gravel, then the slamming of doors. Two Troopers ran up alongside them, then immediately froze upon seeing the swarm ascending toward them.

"Is this real?!"

"Get your rifles out of your trunk, Trooper," Arnold bellowed. He drew his Glock and started down the hill. He opened fire, punching holes in the nearest drone. After several shots, he heard Vince join in. Together, they fired round after round into the horde. The other two Troopers started joining in with high-powered rifles. Dozens of *cracks* filled the air. There was a smell of gunpowder and sewage. Squids coiled up and rolled over, their bodies gushing blood. Yet, their brethren continued up the hill.

More State vehicles packed the driveway. Soon, the Troopers formed a firing line. What was once a quiet, sleepy resort, had become a battleground in the span of a few minutes.

More drones fell over dead, yet the swarm was still coming. Not only were they scurrying like roaches, but they were springing forward, gaining several yards each time.

"Don't break ranks!" Arnold said.

"Sarge! They're not holding back!" one of the Troopers replied.

"DON'T break ranks! Keep at 'em!"

Empty magazines littered the ground. The creatures crawled over their dead brethren and sprang. As they closed within five yards, Arnold realized his tactic of winning by attrition was not possible. More were still coming in from the shore.

"Withdraw. Top of the hill. Form a barrier with the vehicles…"

Already, the men broke ranks. The more disciplined Troopers provided cover fire, only to be swarmed by the squid creatures. Men screamed and gagged as they were violently torn apart. Fountains of blood coated the hillside like something from a satanic ritual.

Arnold suddenly longed for the prospect of a mass shooter. As terrible as those were, at least it was usually ONE person whom the police could corner. But this? He was dealing with an impossible force. A swarm of pure terror.

He reached the top of the hill, where a few of the Troopers had formed a new firing line.

"Dispatch, we have multiple officers down. These things are all over the resort! We need the National Guard on the double."

"Sarge! They're not stopping!" Vince said. Blood splattered from each gunshot. But like ants, the swarm never stopped. The creatures reached the top of the hill, then leapt into the firing line. Bullets whizzed into the air as Troopers were wrestled to the ground and stung. It became a close-quarters battle, with rifles and batons battering the creatures after the mags ran dry.

Troopers cried out for God's mercy, even the nonbelievers, as limbs were severed and torsos carved like turkeys.

****

Greg gripped the seat as Hannah performed a sharp turn around the southeast bend of Circle Drive. Their radio was on the State frequency, where they heard the countless transmissions of panicking Troopers. It was obvious his resort had turned into a bloodbath

"You sure you wanna get close?" he asked through gritted teeth.

"Don't you hear what's going on? We have to help," Hannah replied.

"Yeah? How?" Greg said. "Last I checked, we don't have any ammo. And by the sound of it, we're as likely to be killed by the Troopers as by the horde."

"Think, then!" Hannah said. "And think fast! How can we drive them back into the lake?"

"Clearly gunfire isn't doing the trick. They don't give a shit. They'll happily die for the good of the group. Mindless drones."

"They've got to be afraid of something," Hannah said.

"The only thing we've seen them retreat from is fire," Greg said.

"That's it," Hannah said.

"What's 'it'?" Greg asked.

"Fire."

"Fire? Great...except we don't have any flamethrowers. Maybe if the National Guard gets here, but until then, we're on our own."

"There's got to be a way," Hannah said. She squeezed her eyes shut. Beads of sweat rolled down her face. There HAD to be a way to drive them back.

"Pay fucking attention!"

Hannah opened her eyes and realized she was running off the bend right toward the tree line. She swerved to the left and hit the brakes, nearly planting Greg's face into the dashboard.

He rubbed his forehead then grimaced. "Not going to help much if we kill *ourselves*." They sat silently, listening to the nearby gunfire, and the sound of fuel splashing within the tank. The truck had been recently fueled.

The Sheriff's eyes lit up.

"There are several vehicles in the driveway. We can light the gas tanks and roll them down the hill. Block these things off at the shoreline."

Greg groaned. "We? I seem to forget the part where I'm a cop."

"Quit your bitching. I'm deputizing you, whether you like it or not. If you want the paycheck, I suggest you like it." Before Greg could grasp what she had said, she floored the accelerator, knocking him against the back of his seat. As she drove, she relayed instructions to her Deputies through the fire department's radio. "All units, use fire to repel these things. Use whatever you can: propane tanks; car tanks; wood; hell, charcoal. Get a fire burning around the entire lake. Or else they'll keep coming."

Hannah swung the truck into the resort parking lot.

Despite the warnings from radio chatter and rapid gunfire, neither of them were ready for what they saw. The squid creatures were everywhere, slashing their tentacles at the police, whose numbers were quickly dwindling. Weapons were lying all over the hilltop and driveway, the remaining cops retreating to Circle Drive.

Hannah honked the horn and floored the accelerator, while waving an arm through the window, yelling "Out of the way!" A small group of Troopers dispersed, allowing her to ram the two squid creatures right behind them. Their bodies compressed against the earth then burst. Blood, like tar, spat from underneath the tires. Hannah cut the wheel to the left, ramming another squid, then stopped by Greg's garage.

He hopped out of his seat and ran through the open door. Immediately, he grabbed a rag and coat hanger, made a small hook at the end, then strung the rag to it. He returned to the truck and stuffed the rag deep into the gas tank, soaking it with fuel, then withdrew it.

"Fucking domino day," he said to himself.

"What?" Hannah said.

"Nothing," Greg replied. He held his lighter to the rag, then watched the horde advance to the hilltop, only nine yards from where he stood. "Hope you're all set."

"Do it!"

He sparked the flame. "Go!"

Hannah sped the truck to the hill, winding around a couple of Troopers, and smashing another squid. She lined up the truck along the center of the hill, facing the driver's side to the lot so she could make her escape. The rag vanished behind a large orange glow, trailing flame into the gas tank, which ruptured into a deafening blast.

The earth shook. Glass shattered, and smoking pieces of frame zipped across the lot like meteors. The swarm broke apart, snarling at the bizarre fiend that halted their advance.

Hannah saw Greg scoop up a discarded rifle, checked the mag, then aimed high at a couple of creatures climbing over his roof. After shooting them down, he disappeared back into the garage for more rags. As he did, Hannah searched the ground until she found another rifle, then rushed toward the new firing line. Sergeant Arnold Thorp was easy to spot due to his frame. They had crossed paths on a number of occasions in the past few years and were on a first name basis.

"Arnold!"

"Hannah? Good to see you're still kicking. What the hell is going on here?"

"Long story." The Sheriff and Troopers proceeded to blast the few remaining creatures up on the lot. They had seconds before the rest of the swarm would make their run. "Listen, help me roll these vehicles to the edge. We can repel them by igniting the fuel tanks."

Arnold glanced at the vehicles. Even in this situation, he knew he would catch hell for willingly destroying private property. But to hell with what the judges and internal affairs personnel thought.

Let them make judgements from the comfort of their offices.

"Come on, boys! Let's set up a little cookout!" He pointed at a few Troopers at the end of the line. "You, you, and you, keep at 'em, while we get the barricades into position."

Already, the creatures were swarming around the fire, ready to make their second go at the fresh meat. Gunfire shook the officers' eardrums as they rolled the vehicles toward the lot.

Meanwhile, Greg emerged from his garage, carrying a gas can in each arm. He smashed the lids with a hammer, then tucked a rag into each one. After lighting them, he tossed the cans with all of his might. They hit the hill and rolled a few feet before bursting like grenades.

Creatures scurried in all directions, some encased in flaming gasoline. Greg shouldered his rifle and picked off one that tried to make its way around the burning truck, rupturing its head like a melon.

Hannah and the Troopers pushed the other vehicles along, using Interceptors as bulldozers. Tires kicked up gravel as the police vehicles strained against the stationary weight.

The first vehicle to make it to the hilltop was a Buick. Immediately, Greg sprinted to the vehicle, rags in hand, along with a bottle of fuel for the grill. He soaked the rag, stuffed it into the fuel tank, then lit it.

"Floor it!" he shouted to the Trooper driving the Interceptor. The officer shot him a confused look, then gunned the accelerator. The Buick slewed onto the slope, where it proceeded to roll a few yards before bursting into flames. Already, Hannah and Arnold had another vehicle on standby. Greg loaded the gas-soaked rag, and lit it while they pushed it over. Another fiery explosion followed.

As though pushed by an invisible wall, the horde gradually retreated to the safety of the lake. Some tried to brave the assault, but could not take the intense heat, which increased as the land-dwellers pushed more obstacles down the hill. More fire erupted, hindering their path.

Then, a distinct chemical signal raced through the water. Acting like a bullhorn, it called the soldiers back to the lake. Not a full retreat, but a temporary withdrawal. After all, there was no such thing as defeat. Only setbacks. Once the swarm discovered new territory, it was theirs for the taking.

"They're retreating!" Hannah said.

"Good! Let's reward that idea," Arnold replied. "Let's get some fire burning around the shoreline."

Hannah got on her radio. "All units, report status."

"Unit Ten here. We're over by the Cornett fire. The things are withdrawing to the lake."

"Unit Twelve, at the east cove. Same here."

"We can't keep burning stuff forever," Greg said. "We're gonna need an electric fence. Something we can string up along the shore to keep them at bay."

"I can handle that," Arnold said, pulling his speaker mic from his collar. "Captain, give me a call on my personal." Hardly five seconds passed before his phone vibrated. "Yeah. Hey...I'll explain when you get here, because you won't believe this until you see it for yourself... I don't know where they came from...Listen, I'll explain later, BELIEVE ME, it'll make sense. Right now, you need to get with any fencing company you can locate. We need to string electrical fence all around the lake... NOW, CAPTAIN!... Thank you!" He clipped the phone to his hip. "Jesus."

"Like pulling teeth?" Greg said.

"Wouldn't stop asking about the casualties," Arnold replied. He looked at the blood and body parts all over the place. He turned his gaze back to Hannah and Greg. "So, about that long story?"

CHAPTER 21

By three in the afternoon, the sky was full of helicopters. State Police and Sheriff Deputies patrolled Circle Drive, with barricades set up along all intersecting roads. The few residents lucky enough to survive the mass attack were forced to evacuate. Troopers from other precincts arrived at a rapid pace, with still no word given on the status of the National Guard.

It was four minutes past the hour. The Troopers and Fire Department were about a third of the way complete with stretching the electrical barricade along the shoreline. High voltage generators were set up at various places along the lake to deliver power, both to the fence, as well as the various outposts.

****

"Alright, Captain. Do what you need to do," Arnold Thorp said through the radio.

Captain Beau Meyer of the Fire Department rode in the first firetruck onto the Cornett property. The fire was still blazing high, the roof partially collapsed. Several State Troopers were on standby with shotguns and automatic rifles aimed at the lake. So far, none of the creatures had made an appearance since their withdrawal.

High-powered hoses sprayed the building, gradually extinguishing the fire over the course of the next ten minutes.

"Sheriff reported seeing victims in the garage," the Captain said. "Let's tear into it and check it out."

Some firemen continued spraying the building, while the Captain, Lieutenant, and a few others proceeded through the main entrance. The front door broke off the hinges with a mild impact from his axe. He proceeded into the building, waving his hand back and forth to brush the smoke away. He found a hallway on the left side and followed it past a few bedrooms. The door on the end was completely torn away, revealing the inside of the garage.

He stepped inside, then stood, flabbergasted at what he was looking at. Bodies were propped against the fishing boat, the terrified expressions frozen on their faces. Through the dried slime-substance that cocooned them, it was difficult to tell whether they were still alive.

"Come on." With the help of his crew, he pulled the cocoons from their place.

"There's only three here," the Lieutenant said.

"They must've taken the others," the Captain replied. "Let's get these people out of here and see if they're still alive." The other firefighters checked on the other side of the boat. The Captain noticed them staggering backward, staring blankly into the water.

"What is it? What do you see?" the Lieutenant asked.

"Sir, there's a—" the fireman simply pointed into the water. The Captain and Lieutenant approached to look. Like their subordinates, they couldn't help but stare in stunned silence.

"What the—"

At first, he thought he was looking at a canoe or a kayak. Then he noticed the fins, the scales, the gill lining, and ultimately the eyes. It was a large fish, roughly ten feet in length, completely encased in the slime substance.

"Situation just got weirder."

CHAPTER 22

Greg Goodman tucked his black button shirt into a set of jeans. It took twenty-minutes to wash the stench of squid monster and smoke off of himself. However, he didn't mind the time so much, as it allowed his body to work through the jitters of everything he had experienced up till now.

When he stepped into his kitchen, he saw officers, state and county, all over his yard. EMTs had been called in from nearby counties to help with the mess. The cleanup process was not a pleasant one. The vomiting brought many setbacks all by itself.

He dug through his cabinet and found his regular coffee maker and grounds, while prepping his Keurig to make a cup for himself. As he filled the other with water, he was drawn to the sound of helicopter rotors.

He clipped the badge, given to him by Hannah, to his shirt, then ran outside. Immediately, he saw Arnold Thorp and Hannah looking up. The droning sound intensified. There were two choppers, completely black, landing on Circle Drive behind the trees.

"Is that the National Guard?" he asked.

"Doesn't look like it. They don't have the markings," Arnold replied. The three of them hustled past the driveway entrance and turned to the right. Past a string of police vehicles were the choppers, the rotors slowing to a stop. The fuselage door opened. Greg expected to see an older government official, probably someone from the federal government. Instead, he saw someone in his mid-thirties, dressed in jeans and a bass-fishing t-shirt, and a ball cap. Had he not arrived in a damn chopper, Greg would've assumed this guy was here to cast a line.

"Hey!" The man waved. Other people disembarked behind him, carrying computer equipment, drones, and briefcases. They looked more official looking, wearing black outfits and sunglasses.

Hannah and Greg shared the same confused glance.

"Can we help you?" Hannah said.

"Actually, it's I who am here to help you." The man spoke with an enthusiastic tone of voice. He held out a hand. "Dr. Mike Wilkow. Pleasure to meet you all."

Hannah reluctantly shook it, as did Greg and Arnold.

"Who are you with, Dr. Wilkow?" Greg asked.

"I'm with an organization called N.E.C.T.O.R. We specialize in studying the world beneath the crevasse. I'm the one who helped discover the Carnobass in Clare County, three years back."

"N.E.C.T.O.R., I've heard of it," Arnold said. "What the hell does that stand for?"

Wilkow thought for a second, then shrugged his shoulders. "You know what? I really don't know! But hey!" He tapped the Sergeant on the shoulder, "It sounds cool, though. Very science-y."

"National Explorers of Caverns, Tectonics, Organisms, and Resources," said a man in his sixties. He stepped off the chopper, carrying two drones, a control pad, and two briefcases. "Wilkow, I'm not your mule!"

"Oh, Joel, you're always complaining about not getting enough exercise," Wilkow replied.

"No! I'm always complaining about *you*!"

Hannah held her hands up. "Hold on a sec. What exactly are you doing here? Is this organization privately run, or government run?"

"Privately, at the moment, although we're working on contracts with the State and Federal governments," Wilkow said.

"Well, until we get State or Federal authorization, you all are civilians, and right now, we are not allowing civilians near the lake," Hannah said.

"It's an extremely dangerous situation," Greg said.

"I know. That's why it's imperative I get an idea of what these things are," Wilkow said. He glanced back at the drones. "Not to mention, we need to get a view of the crevasse."

Greg's expression softened a bit. The Doctor had a point there. No way were any divers gonna go anywhere near the water.

"So, do you think there's another subterranean lake?"

"It's possible," Wilkow said. "Better yet—I have a hunch these systems are all connected."

"One big underground lake?" Hannah asked.

"Michigan is the Great Lakes State," Wilkow replied. "We've always assumed there were five. I'm suspecting we have a sixth, right under our very feet." The flabbergasted expressions on the three officers was enough for Wilkow to assume they were willing to let him and his crew onto the perimeter.

The three shared another glance, shrugged, then followed the Doctor onto the property.

Joel Pobursky groaned as he continued to drag all of Wilkow's equipment.

Wilkow looked at the aftermath of the attack. Strobing lights streaked across the gravel as paramedics loaded bodies off of the hill. He stopped, gave a moment of silence to the dead. After all, he wasn't a heartless bastard. Eccentric, but not cold.

After his gesture, he studied the ground, noticing the streaks of black blood. Definitely not human, even after hours of exposure. He turned to face the Sheriff.

"How many have you guys killed?"

"Not enough," she replied.

"Dozens," Arnold said.

"More than that, even," Greg added.

"And more kept coming?" Joel asked.

"Yeah," Greg said. "I'm telling you; it was like an organized effort. They invaded the shorelines and *knew* what they were doing."

"Where are the bodies?" Wilkow asked.

"The ones up here have been cleared out. However…" Hannah led the Doctor over the hillside, where he saw several other corpses lying about.

"Wow. At least I won't have to worry about screwing up the dissections," he said. He glanced about. "You have any suggestions where I can set up a workshop?"

"Wait…you're gonna cut into one of them?" Hannah asked.

"To give us an idea about what we're dealing with, I'm gonna have to understand a bit about their anatomy. We need to understand how they communicate. How they reproduce. If each one has a separate function. The sooner I can get started, the sooner we can take more definitive action."

Greg sighed. "I can clear off some tables in my garage."

"Perfect!" Wilkow said. Greg entered the garage and started clearing off his worktables.

Wilkow and his crew started following Hannah to the shore. The area had been marked off with steel fencing, with electric cables on standby.

"We have to wait before the rest of the perimeter is complete," Hannah said. "Don't want to be zapping our personnel as they set it up."

Wilkow snickered. "I remember touching my grandmother's hotwire fence one time. Knocked me right on my ass. Before I could move, one of her horses cornered me, and accidentally pressed me up against it. Zapped the shit out of me for ten minutes straight."

Next, it was Joel that snickered. "That explains a lot."

"This should provide more than a little jolt," Arnold said. "If that horse were to knock you into this fence, the voltage would be enough to stop your heart."

"Good deal," Wilkow said. They made their way past the cabins near the shore. The Doctor stared across the lake at the still smoking remains of Andy Cornett's property. "What happened there?"

"That's where the bastards were making a nest," Hannah said.

"A nest?"

"Yeah. Almost like a spider's nest. They were cocooning bodies and storing them in the boat garage."

Wilkow nodded. "Probably came up during the night and needed a spot to protect them from the sunlight until they adapted."

"Oh, they adapted alright," Arnold said. "The way they invaded this shore, there were no reservations about sunburn. They came up as if they've done it a hundred times before."

"Yeah, that brings to mind a question, Doc," Hannah said. "If these things really do live in an underground lake, how could they adapt so quickly to land environments?"

"To get an answer for that, I need to get a look into the crevasse," Wilkow replied. "BUT...I do have a theory...and that is, depending on the geological structure of the location, there might be pockets of space above the water. The lake might have a consistent water level. If you have areas of high elevation, there might be dry regions above the water where things can 'come ashore', so to speak."

"I wanna get back to the subject of making a nest," Joel said. "You said they were loading *bodies* in there?"

"Correct," Hannah said.

"So, they produce web?" Wilkow asked.

Hannah shrugged. "It seems to perform the same function."

Joel turned to the Doctor. "Why would they cocoon their victims?"

"They might be bloodsuckers," Wilkow said. "Like some spiders, they like to store their victims, they suck the fluids out when they're good and ready."

"No, I can assure you that's not the case," Arnold said. "I saw them rip people to chunks. They are as ravenous as a lion." He pointed at the pontoon boat and the deck smothered in blood and skeletal remains. "Case and point."

They heard muffled coughing. One of the N.E.C.T.O.R. crewmen had turned pale. He covered his mouth, realized he couldn't stop what was coming, then turned around. Cabin Three was the nearest sanctuary. He rushed inside, found the bathroom, then found the toilet.

What he saw was actually *worse* than the pontoon boat massacre.

After clearing off the workstations, Greg went into the kitchen to collect his coffee. He had sweetened it up just right when he heard intense gagging down by the cabin. He stepped outside and hurried down the hill. By the time he got there, he saw the N.E.C.T.O.R. agent staggering out of Cabin Three, sweating profusely.

"Oh, shit. Sorry, I should've warned you guys about that…"

Joel shrugged. "I worked at a resort in Rodney. Cabin tenants can be a pain."

Wilkow watched the water. "Where's the deepest region?" Greg pointed to the center of the west segment.

"Goes down about thirty feet."

"Is it like that anywhere else?"

"Not that deep. A few twelve and fifteen foot areas, but that's by far the deepest zone."

"Then that's where the crevasse is. That'll be next on the agenda. But first, I need to get a look at the specimens."

"I got the garage set up," Greg said, holding his mug out, gesturing to the Doctor that he could get started.

"Perfect," Wilkow said. As he turned, he saw the outstretched hand and the coffee in its clutches. "Oh! Thanks a bunch! I usually have a cup of joe around this time." He took the mug and started downing it as he started up the hill, leaving a bewildered Greg Goodman staring at his now empty hand. His gaze went to Joel Pobursky, who shrugged.

"Hey, get used to it. I have to endure it every day."

Greg sighed, then followed the others up the hill. *This guy better be worthwhile.*

CHAPTER 23

At four-thirty, Arnold Thorp finally got the call he was waiting for. The National Guard had been activated and were en route to Tonette. Thirty minutes later, the first Chinooks arrived, each one carrying dozens of trained guardsmen. They set down on the west end of Circle Drive where the canopy was more spaced out. Hannah, Greg, and Arnold were right there to greet them.

Guardsmen spilled out of the ramp and immediately converged on the lake. Their commanding officer, a short, but grizzled-faced man in his late thirties, barked orders to the troops.

"I want a perimeter set around the lake. I want M240s set up on all sides. I want snipers on the rooftops, and comm posts on the corners of the lake. Move it."

With their M4 Carbines at their shoulders, the troops converged on the lake. Sergeants barked at their squads, leading them to their designated locations. Meanwhile, the leading officer stepped toward the three cops.

"I'm Major Sierra. I'll be taking over from here on," he stated. He looked at Arnold, read his name tag and insignia. "You're Sergeant Thorp, I imagine."

"Correct."

"I've been in constant contact with your Captain. He's been relaying to me all of your radio transmissions and reports, keeping me up to date." He glanced at Hannah. "Sheriff Tyler?"

"Correct."

"I understand you've all lost many people today. My condolences. That said, we need to stay focused on the mission at hand. So, let's get to work. We have a hundred more guardsmen coming in from Battle Creek, and another thousand on standby. The way the governor sees it, the situation is under control at the moment."

"Explains why she dragged ass getting you here," Greg said. "These things will make another attack, Major. It's just a matter of when. We need to order an evacuation of the entire town. Maybe the county."

Sierra narrowed his gaze at the Deputy. There was no insignia, no clear indication of rank. As far as he looked, this guy was just a reserve who was called into service. "Pardon me. Who are you, exactly?"

"He's with me," Hannah jumped in. "He helped me develop a tactic to drive these creatures back into the lake. If not for him, this town would be overrun by the horde, and you would've arrived guns blazing. I suggest you listen to any advice he has to offer."

"Fine," Sierra said. "In that case, I need a full briefing. As stated, your Captain has kept me informed, but I want to hear it from somebody on the front lines. Tell me what you know, and let me get a look at this perimeter you've got set up so I can update my squads."

"Let's go," Hannah replied.

They rode together, followed by two armored Humvees to Greg's resort. Upon arrival, they immediately walked to the shoreline.

"The wire fence was completed twenty-five minutes ago," Arnold said. "We've got high-voltage electricity coursing through it at the moment."

"It surrounds the entire lake?" Sierra asked.

"Affirmative," Arnold replied. "We came up with the idea to maintain bonfires at the beach areas, hoping to keep the creatures at bay."

"A bit primitive. I like it," Sierra said.

"Good, because fire seems to be the only thing that'll hold them back," Greg said.

"Have they made a run at the wire perimeter yet?"

"No, but they haven't yet experienced electric shock," Greg said. "As far as those things are concerned, this is just a piece of mesh in their way."

"Still, we'd rather warn them off with fire, if possible," Hannah added.

"Understandable," Sierra said. He looked around at the corpses scattered around. Most were still on the hill, where the clash with the cops took place. He radioed his men, informing them to set up the comm units near the property. "I saw that black helicopter around the bend. Is that one of yours?"

"No. There's people here from N.E.C.T.O.R. They specialize in exploring these underground lakes."

"I've heard of them. Have they confirmed the existence of a crevasse in this lake?"

"Not yet. Their main scientist has a workstation in my garage," Greg said. "He's performing a dissection as we speak on one of them."

"Good. I want to speak with him asap."

Hannah turned around and walked toward the hill. "Follow me."

In all of his travels, Joel Pobursky had been exposed to a hundred odors from a hundred different species, in a hundred different terrains. One was always worse than the last. Then there was his private business as a maintenance contractor, where he cleaned out the filthiest homes and apartments imaginable. Never once did he feel the need to plug his nose, until now.

"You playing that recorder?" Wilkow asked.

"Yes," Joel said. "You really need to film this?"

"Better than spending two hours on the phone with every government bureaucrat who'll have me explain every detail ten times."

The dead creature was sprawled out over two wooden tables. Mike Wilkow had just run his scalpel over the mantle, exposing its inner organs. Joel winced, not from the smell, but the sight. There was actually mist coming out of the thing's body, as though it had been cooked.

The tentacles and head section had already been opened up, completely exposing the oddly shaped jaws and the enormous stinger, as well as the veins it was connected to.

"Alrighty, what do we have here," Wilkow said, his voice muffled by his facemask. He proceeded to dig around. "Ah-ha! I think I found your stomach! And your heart! So many other goodies to choose from. First, let's find where *this* trail leads to." He found the tube-like veins connecting to the fleshy sack at the end of the barb, then followed them through the body. Using suction equipment, he drained the excess blood. "There we are." He set the scalpel down and with his gloved fingers, began to examine a membranous sack of flesh. It was as soft as a waterbed, with thick fluid swirling around within.

The door opened. Hannah and Greg stepped in, only to wince at the atrocious smell.

"Oh, Jesus!" the Sheriff said. "Maybe we should've waited."

"No time for that." Major Sierra somewhat regretted those words when he stepped in. For a split-second, his hardened expression became one of disgust. His jaw clenched, his face wrinkled. He cleared his throat and regained control. "You the scientist from N.E.C.T.O.R.?"

"Yes sir, I am! Good to meet you, Colonel! Doctor Mike Wilkow, at your service." He stepped around the table and extended his hand. Sierra looked at his glove dripping fluid, then back at him. "Oh! My bad." Wilkow yanked the glove off, tossed it aside…where it landed on Joel's boot.

The former pararescue grimaced, then inhaled slowly, preventing himself from hulking out as he stared at the guts on his pant cuff.

I could be home eating chili right now…

Sierra reluctantly shook Wilkow's hand. "It's Major, actually. Tell me everything you know about these things."

"Come take a look," Wilkow said. The group surrounded the table. Everyone, including the Major, helped themselves to the facemasks available. The tentacles were sprawled out and flayed open, with clamps keeping the flesh peeled back. "First thing's first; these things are drones, like your typical ant or bee. They scout, they hunt, they seek out new territory. Their brain is roughly the size of a dime. Considering that they're almost as large as a person, that's pretty small. They have a base instinct—essentially, they're drones, with just enough intelligence to do the jobs to preserve the swarm. Or hive, whatever you want to call it."

He pointed to the head, which was split down the center. With forceps, he pointed at the jaws.

"Major, I'm assuming you want to know the weapons your enemy uses. While they don't have projectiles that we know of, they are fast, and they will flay the tissue from your body with these teeth. For creatures with no skeletal structure, they have teeth made of bone harder than anything I've ever seen. Same thing with the claws. These can cut through the hull of a boat, no problem. Major, don't let your troops get in close quarters with these things, because THEY WILL LOSE. If you think Kevlar will protect them, well, ask the Sergeant how well that worked for his fellow Troopers."

Sierra glanced at Arnold, who nodded.

"They ripped through my friends like they were paper."

"How could they be *that* sharp?" Sierra asked. "Evolution?"

"I've studied the scales of the Carnobass down in Rodney," Wilkow said. "Let me tell you, those things are tough. Joel will even tell you; he was there."

"I've seen bullets bounce off those things," Joel said.

"The point is, you're right. They *did* evolve, because they prey on creatures with similar defense systems. They need to bust through those scales. We have evidence of this, actually."

"How so?"

"With the help of the Fire Department, our people have sorted through the remains of the nest they made in the Andy Cornett property," Hannah said. "We located a few cocooned people, as well as a large creature. A species of fish, roughly ten feet in length. We needed a crane to lift it out. The N.E.C.T.O.R. agents cut through the webbing, and found wounds reminiscent of the claw marks, as well as a stinger piercing."

"It's being stored in a container across the lake," Greg added.

"Probably explains why they like humans so much. No exoskeleton, easy pickings," Wilkow said.

"How are they able to stand up?" Hannah asked. "You said they don't have any skeleton or exoskeleton. You'd think they'd be crawling, like an octopus."

"By the looks of it, they have two layers of muscle tissue. The first layer controls the actions, like reaching, stepping, and so forth. The second layer more like a hydraulic press. They pump fluid into the tissue, swelling it up at certain points, allowing the arms to take on a rigidity, which in turn allows them to stand up like bugs."

"I wanna get back to their feeding habits," Sierra said. "You said they've been collecting *bodies*?"

"You heard right," Hannah said.

"And they do it with that," Wilkow said, pointing to the stinger. "I was just examining this when you arrived. If you see here, these veins connect to this sack in the abdomen, where the venom is produced. They fill up this into this other sack, located at the end of the rod. These muscles here are connected to tiny nerves located at the tip. Once they're triggered, the muscles contract, immediately shooting venom into the host."

"Are the victims alive?" Sierra asked. Wilkow shook his head, then shrugged.

"I mean, in a sense, but as far as we know so far, once this stuff is in your system, you're brain dead. Blood samples show a chemical, which we have not identified yet, but it's something in the venom. I suspect it keeps the blood circulating just enough to keep it viable, kinda like a bypass machine. But the host has no brain activity. They're gone, simply reduced to—with all due respect to the victims - meat sacks."

"But why?" Sierra asked.

Wilkow took a breath, then grabbed his forceps. He peeled back some tissue located at the upper joint of one of the front tentacles. He rolled the appendage over slightly, then gestured for Sierra to step around and look.

"See these pores?"

"Yeah."

Wilkow rolled it back over, then sliced through some of the muscular tissue to get to a rounded blob of membrane. It was thick, but almost see-through. In its center was a white object, shaped almost like a shrimp.

"Hand me that jar over there, please," he asked Hannah. She passed the glass jar over. "Lid too." Hannah paused, then slid it across the table. Wilkow gestured for the Major to step back, which he did. Wilkow ran his scalpel over the strange flesh, immediately triggering movement from the kidney-bean sized thing inside. Fluid spilled out, carrying its little body. Wilkow scooped it up with the jar, then sealed it…right as the thing attempted to flee.

It was alive.

"Good God!" Greg said. Even Joel was on his feet.

"Is that what I think it is?"

"Yep. My study shows that these bastards carry little embryos. Once they sting a victim, they put a couple of these bastards inside. There, they initially feed on the blood. Then, once that's gone, they probably eat the tissue, until they're grown up into—" He froze, then looked over at Hannah. "Sheriff? Where are the bodies located?"

"They were taken to the Flower Hospital," she replied.

"Call them right now and make sure they are quarantined. Tell the Doctors that they need x-rays of the victims immediately. And don't forget QUARANTINE!"

The goofball Doctor was suddenly as serious as a drill sergeant. She stepped out of the garage and proceeded to make the phone call.

"You suspect those bodies are carrying these things, Doctor?" Arnold said.

"I guarantee it. And I'd like to see the x-rays as soon as they're made available."

"To prove your point?"

"That, and to see how rapidly these things grow," Wilkow said. "Yeah, the police recovered a few bodies, but not all of them. Where do you think they went? More importantly, why do you think they haven't attacked yet?"

"I'd like to think they realize they can't win this fight," Arnold said.

"Ha! I wish," Wilkow replied. "Depending on the growth rate of these embryos, it's possible they're just gathering more troops for another assault."

"Jesus," Sierra muttered. He stared at the claws, teeth, and stinger, before settling on the little walnut-colored brain. "You said they were drones. Even things with a hive mind take command from something. I doubt they just decided all at once to withdraw into the water. You think something called them back?"

Wilkow nodded. "Same thing laying these eggs."

"Wait…what?" Greg exclaimed. "It looks like this thing is carrying the eggs."

"It's carrying the embryo," Wilkow said. He took a look at the mantle, draining some more fluid with his suction. "There doesn't appear to be any egg sack. These pores are just storage units. I think these guys take the eggs from the mother, then inject them into the hosts after stinging them."

"The mother?" Greg swallowed, thinking of the ant swarm in Cabin One. "You've got to be kidding me."

"Not even I would kid about this," Wilkow said. "We're facing something we were never prepared to deal with. Unless we get a look into that crevasse, we won't know the magnitude of what we're facing until it's too late."

"So, we seal the crevasse," Sierra stated.

"That would be preferable," Wilkow replied. "However, we won't know how until we get a peek at the thing. Can't just drop bombs on it, or else we might widen it further."

"You're absolutely certain they'll keep attacking?" Sierra asked. Wilkow nodded. "Why? For food? There's got to be easier prey for them down there."

"Because I don't think they're simply hunting. I mean, they are, but there's more to it than that. They're expanding—they're an invasive species. We've seen this in the rapid pace they've overtaken the lake, and how quickly they've set up a nest. These types of organisms are quick to wipe out any life currently occupying the territory they're invading. This isn't scouting behavior. They're here to stay, and they'll keep coming."

"Okay. Worst case scenario, they'll remain in the lake and perhaps the surrounding area. Circle Drive, perhaps," the Major said.

"No, that's best case scenario," Wilkow explained.

"Excuse me?"

"There's plenty of lakes in the county, not to mention this county connects to Lake Michigan," Wilkow explained. "If you think these things won't overtake lake after lake, town after town, until they're in the Great Lakes, you're out of your mind."

"How could they do that?" Arnold said. "You seriously think they can travel that far from water?"

"Of course, I'm speaking in theory, but these things do share certain similarities in physiology as cephalopods," Wilkow said. "You ever see videos of octopuses coming up on land?"

"I thought it was octopi," Joel said.

"Eh, the science community can never seem to make up their minds about that," Wilkow said, shrugging.

"Yes! I've seen them," Sierra said, getting them back on point.

"Well, some species of cephalopods can stay out of the water for over thirty minutes. These things have already proven they can stay out of water for that long, *while* engaging in a fight. It's possible they can remain out of water for hours at a time, though they might do it at night."

"Lake Archer is not far from here," Greg said.

"That would be their next target," Wilkow said. "Then, they'd move on to the lake south of there. Then the next. Hopping along, until they're in Lake Michigan. Meanwhile, everyone who remains in the general vicinity will be devoured, or taken to be hosts for more embryos."

Sierra crossed his arms. "I know you're a scientist, Doctor, but you seem to be making a lot of assumptions."

"Well, every scientist does when dealing with a new discovery. You start off with physiology, observations of actions, feeding habits, general behavior, then compare it to other species. You've obviously heard of the murder hornets. They're an invasive species. They kill species of bees and dominate their territories. And don't get me started on the snakeheads. Those didn't originate here; they came all the way from Asia. So, Major, my suggestion is to not underestimate these things' ability to cross long distances."

"Snakeheads have air lungs," Sierra said. "These creatures do not."

"No, but I did find these tubs here." Wilkow pointed at some thick veins located at the joint between the head and mantle. He took a knife and severed it, spilling water across the table. "They store water. I don't get the impression it's because they're thirsty. They suck in water, circulate it as they need, kind of like an air cannister for divers." He shrugged. "Of course, you can just write this off as another assumption."

Sierra watched the water drip off the edge of the table. Finally, he grabbed his radio. "Oscar Charlie to Central Command, come in."

"We read you."

"We're going to need additional personnel on standby. We need to form a strong barricade between the county and Lake Michigan, stat."

"We'll have to get authorization from the Governor."

"We'll send her the data." He tucked his radio to his uniform, then eyed Wilkow. "You better be right about this."

Right then, Hannah stepped back into the garage. "Greg, do you have a fax machine?"

"Yeah."

She handed him the phone so he could relay the information to the Doctor on the line at Flower. Immediately after, he went through the backdoor into the house. Wilkow pulled off his gloves and followed them, along with Sierra, Arnold, and Joel.

The faxes came through.

Greg held them up where they could get a good clean view. On the upper left edge was Bill Hoskin's name, the date and time. The image had been taken an hour ago.

"There. You see that?" Wilkow said, pointing under the ribcage.

Greg nodded. "I see it."

Wilkow looked at the Major, making sure he could see the seven-inch lifeform burrowed in Bill's abdomen.

"Should we *assume* they have a fast growth rate?"

Sierra's eyes burned into the image. Finally, he nodded. "Let's figure out how to close that crevasse."

CHAPTER 24

Rotor drafts whipped Mike Wilkow's brow as two UH-60 Blackhawks descended onto Circle Drive. Each one was armed with two M134 miniguns, as well as a swivel-mounted M60, manned by a guardsman. A crew member stepped out of the nearest one and approached Wilkow.

In the Doctor's hands was the Model 11 Arrowhead drone. It was silver in color, its shape matching the name.

Major Sierra stood beside him, eyeing the device, particularly the cameras mounted on the wings and underbelly.

"You sure we'll get a clear image from that thing?"

"As sure as the sunrise," Wilkow replied. "If it doesn't, Joel here will have to owe us all dinner." He tapped the operator on the arm, failing to spark any amusement. Major Sierra glanced at Joel.

"Perhaps I should ask *you*."

"Just today, we've conducted a descent that went over four-hundred feet down, through a winding pathway. Signal held until we got to the bottom, and that was with three-hundred feet of earth in the way…and three hundred feet of lake water on top of that. If this passage is straightforward, then there should be no issue maintaining the signal."

"Alright. We have a workstation set up down by the cabins. Our chopper unit will lower the device into the lake. From there, it's all on you guys," Sierra said.

"Fine with me. Let's get started before we lose daylight," Wilkow said. He handed the drone to the guardsman. "Whatever you do, don't drop that." The guardsman rolled his eyes, then hustled back to the chopper.

Joel, Wilkow, and Sierra returned to the resort property and started down the hill, joining Greg and Hannah at the shoreline.

Greg couldn't take his eyes off the fence. The high-voltage generator hummed consistently, reminding the world of the intense voltage coursing through the metal barrier.

Hannah crossed her arms. While Greg's attention was on the fence, hers was on the water and the activity on the opposite shore. She could see guardsmen moving about, with snipers resting, like little green dots, on the roofs of houses. There were two mounted machine guns placed around the Cornett property. Even with the security of the fence, nobody was taking any chances. By now, many of them had seen the released bodycam footage. The Governor had recently made her first press statement about the issue, stating that everything was under control, and that there was no need for mass panic.

The broadcast was repeating, the audio echoing from the smartphone of a N.E.C.T.O.R. employee standing nearby. Two of her Deputies and a state Trooper were standing by him, watching the broadcast.

"Nobody's buying her bullshit," one of them said. "Look at that. The whole state's in an uproar. Like clockwork, she's stating there's nothing to be concerned about, and in the same breath, stating how she's considering a mandate for all lakeside properties."

"Hotels are already closing down all along Lake Superior," another said.

"No shit. Everyone's seen that *YouTube* footage by now. People are losing their minds."

"This'll have a lasting effect for years. People are gonna stay out of the water like it's 1975."

"I have a friend who works at the Concord Luxury Rentals in Manistee. He texted me and said they've already had twelve cancellations for the upcoming week. People are crapping their pants because of this."

"I got a call from a pal I worked with in Emmet County," the Trooper said. "He said he drove past a few state and private lakes that are normally teeming with boating activity. He said he's never seen them so calm, even at midnight."

"It's been several hours. No sign of them so far," Hannah stated.

"You think Wilkow's wrong?" Greg asked. "You think they've moved on?"

"Maybe I just *want* to believe that," the Sheriff replied. Greg noticed her scraping her boot along the dirt. The nervous energy couldn't be more obvious.

"What's on your mind? Those things?"

"Huh? No…well, yes, obviously," she replied.

"What is it?"

"I still need to visit the families of our fallen deputies. I've…never had to do that before."

"Well, that's important…but you're a little busy at the moment with, you know, trying to contain an outbreak," Greg replied.

"The National Guard's here for that," she said.

"Ah-ah, no," Greg retorted. "This is your job as well. *You're* the Sheriff. You have a duty to the town and the county. *That's* your priority right now. You can visit Ross' family tomorrow. And Jake, Zach, and Bill's."

"I'm surprised you see me as a legitimate Sheriff."

"Well, technically you are," Greg said. "You used a shitty tactic, but the votes were legitimate."

"Well, I guess you'll get the last laugh after all of this," she said. "This whole event will probably cost me the re-election."

"Give me a break," Greg replied. "Nobody was prepared for this. I would've run into the exact same trap. This outbreak would've occurred no matter who was in office. Yeah, your opponent might try and use it against you, but that's not what's important right now."

Hannah smirked. "I sense foreshadowing."

"Not sure what you mean."

"You gonna try and run again?" She then shrugged her shoulders. "Probably won't have much trouble beating me out."

Greg shook his head. "No."

Hannah stared. Yeah, she deputized him, but he had no obligation to stay on with the department. He had every reason not to support her holding the position.

"No, you won't have much trouble?" she asked, seeking clarification.

"No—I don't want to run," he said. "I'm fine where I'm at."

"As…a business owner?"

"A Deputy."

Hannah was tired of the word games. She needed it spelled out in plain English. Why would this guy want to work for her after what she did to him?

"I don't understand why—"

"A good Sheriff needs good sense as well as humility," Greg said. "I think you've learned a thing or two since the campaign. Particularly in the last eight hours."

Hannah was quiet. Unbeknownst to Greg, she had actually learned of another factor she was lacking—something he proved he had in abundance. Character. It took character to forgive such an atrocity, let alone offer to lend support.

Greg Goodman was the clear choice for the office, but Hannah knew to face the facts. She was the Sheriff, and she had to handle the looming threat.

Speaking of which…

She looked back in time to see Wilkow and Joel approach the workstation, which had been set up to the left of Cabin One. There was a military tent, with several computers and monitors set up on desks arranged in a U-shape. Joel sat in the middle, taking a moment to appreciate the luxurious seat cushion.

"Didn't have these things in my day. DEFINITELY better than the brick stools provided by somebody I know," he quipped, glancing briefly at Wilkow. He placed the control pad in front of him.

The lake rippled as the choppers took position. Sierra stood two meters behind the fence, guiding the birds with radio instruction. The group watched as one of the choppers gradually descended into the water, while the other provided cover.

Heartbeats raced. Beads of sweat wetted the brows of everyone on shore. It felt as though the water would erupt at any moment.

"Right there," Sierra said. "Deploy arrowhead."

The guardsman placed the device into the water. Its silver hull reflected the sunlight as it sank.

Joel immediately engaged the thrusters. "We're a-go."

"Chopper units, elevate to seventy-meters. Keep a bird's-eye view. Let us know if you see any activity not human." He stepped back around the workstation to view the monitors. "Mr. Pobursky, let's take this slow. Take the drone around the lake, particularly near the garage. Let's see if any of these things are in the surrounding area."

"Be careful though," Greg said. "They've coated the weed beds with their webbing. Get too close, and you'll get snagged, easily."

"Good to know," Joel said. He increased speed and steered the drone to the northside of the lake, while keeping close to the surface. The image was dark, making it difficult to see. It was after six-o'clock, and while they still had plenty of daylight, the trees to the west were casting huge shadows onto the water.

"Go ahead and engage the lights," Wilkow said. Joel flipped a switch. Immediately, the image brightened, showing a world of slime-coated weeds. Sierra leaned forward.

"They did all of this?"

Greg nodded.

The drone proceeded to pass over the weed forests. The light bounced off the scaly bodies of hundreds of dead fish caught in the swarm's deadly trap. Wilkow whistled.

"Oh boy. Yeah, these guys were building a nest, alright. And it's worse than we thought."

"*Worse?*" Arnold Thorp said. He was coming down the hill after making a phone call to his wife. He joined the others and found himself glued to the footage.

"Yeah, way worse," Wilkow said. "We thought they were using that garage as a nest. Look at this—they were turning this *entire* lake into their nest."

"Expanding territory," Greg said. He found himself looking at Cabin One, and the little black dots scurrying along the open window.

"No sign of the creatures, other than this substance," Joel said. He took the drone around the property, finding nothing but residue. He steered to the west, but found nothing but the same. This lake was completely void of life. "I can take it over to the east segment."

"Don't bother," Sierra said. "Let's find that crevasse."

Joel took the drone to the surface to gauge its location, turned it to face the resort, then accelerated to the center of the lake.

Wilkow pointed at the monitor. "Hey! I see me."

"At least we're not the only ones who suffer that misfortune," Joel replied. The biologist winced, mouthing "ouch!"

"Right there," Greg said. "Go straight down. You're right above the deep zone."

Joel descended the drone, his light shining down on a world of slime. The bottom angled down into a narrow cavity, lined with thick weed beds. Chunks of earth lay all around, as though launched from a volcanic blast. Between it all was the crevasse.

"Good God, there it is," Hannah said.

"It's got to be at least fifteen feet wide," Sierra said. "How did this go unnoticed?"

"I can answer that," Wilkow said. "See the sediment? The chunks? The coloration? I bet this crevasse was waaayyyy smaller, until our new friends decided to kick in the door. Judging by that fish we found, my guess is that they chased him up here, and inadvertently found a new haven."

"No movement so far," Joel said.

"Proceed," Sierra said. "Take it slow. I want to see the rock walls. With a little luck, we can plant bombs near the top and seal this entrance."

Joel began the descent.

First, there was nothing but rock walls. Water, filled with sediment particles, swirled about. His light found nothing but granite and darkness.

"We're a hundred-and-thirty feet down, if you take the lake depth into account," he said. "The rock wall looks like it goes down for another couple hundred feet at least."

It was exactly what Sierra was hoping to hear.

"Proceed a little further and confirm." He turned around to speak into his radio. "Echo Five, start prepping your charges."

"How do you plan on setting them, Major?"

"We'll lower them to the crevasse by cable. Tracking monitors will confirm the depths. Once the charges are at seventy-five feet, we'll detonate. The opening will cave-in on itself. Once that's done, we'll get in touch with the Governor's Office to construct a barrier to place over it as an extra precaution." He turned to watch the monitors. "Before we do that, I just want to make sure this passageway is narrow enough to support a cave-in."

"Looks like it," Joel said. "It starts to widen at two-hundred-and-fifty feet past the opening."

"Joel?" Wilkow said.

"What?"

"Set off a ping," Wilkow said. Joel realized what he was thinking. He flipped open a plastic cover, then pressed a button, sending an echo blast through the underground cavern.

Like a sonar monitor on a submarine, the computer tracking the range lit up with a hundred green dots. The blast continued on. Joel set off another.

"The sonar echo is going straight *down*," he said. "This place is deep."

Wilkow opened his personal laptop and hooked it up to the control pad. "Turn toward the south and set off another one," Wilkow said. Using the vertical thrusters, Joel leveled the drone and turned it around. The echo ping traveled endlessly.

Wilkow watched as several geological images formed like drawings on the computer screen. "Look at that. You guys see this?"

"What the hell are we looking at?" Hannah said.

"The world beneath the crevasse," Wilkow said. "Our range is limited, so it's hard to say for sure, but this lake runs for miles at least."

"So, it's fair to assume these lakes are all part of the same system," Greg said.

"Correct. God only knows how far it goes to the north. There's no way to tell without an expedition."

"Yeah, that's not happening," Sierra said.

"No, I don't mean here, or today," Wilkow replied.

"I understand, Doctor, but there's already talk about having investigations to every body of water to find any more passageways. The public does not want to risk another outbreak like what we nearly endured here today."

"Looks like N.E.C.T.O.R. will be doing some press conferences in the near-future," Wilkow said.

"I've seen enough," Sierra said. "Bring up the drone. Time to seal this crevasse. We still have the whole rest of the lake to inspect."

Wilkow considered making an argument for exploring further, but he knew it would be a debate he would lose. He still had the crevasse in Rodney to explore, assuming the government didn't order that one to be sealed as well. He could already picture the public forums in his mind. Fear had already been sparked in the hearts of the populous, as well as those in the adjacent states. Knowing human beings, fear was a better motivator than reason. Who knows what resources could be discovered down in that world? The vaccines that could be obtained? Even potential power sources. Renewable clean energy? The secrets came from the earth. Instead of possibly having to travel seven miles down to the Mariana Trench for answers, they might just have to go a few hundred feet.

That was an argument for another time, with other people.

"What was that?" Hannah said, pointing at the upper right corner of the screen. Wilkow turned to look but was too late.

"I missed it."

"I saw it. Something whipped by," Joel said. They waited in silence. After ten seconds, Joel started to ascend. Then it appeared again, whipping in front of the camera like a bird. Everyone watching recognized the dark green colors caught momentarily in the white light.

"Oh shit. Joel, they think your drone is food," Greg said.

"Bring it up," Sierra said.

"No! Wait!" Wilkow said, holding his hands out. "You'll lure them back up here." Sierra considered this possibility, then nodded. Technology could be replaced after all. Hell, it wasn't even the National Guard's property.

Joel released the controls. There was nothing else to do but let the creatures swarm over the drone. He activated the aft cameras, splitting the screen into four monitors, showing viewpoints from all sides. The creatures, using jet-propulsion like cuttlefish, flocked around the drone. After a few quick moments, one of them closed in, stinger protruding from its jaw. The images flickered as the drone shook. The hull was breached, but the electronics continued to function.

"Shut down the motors, Joel," Wilkow said. "Let them think it's paralyzed."

Joel couldn't help but snicker at what they were attempting. He shut down everything but the camera systems. To the squids, the drone's 'heartbeat' essentially stopped. Tentacles seized it and began dragging it deep into the abyss. Joel's grin faded as the world started coming into view. He saw green vents and rocks glowing with blue and green algae. Rocks stretched for miles like mountain ranges. Some, he wasn't even sure were rocks, as many had particular shapes that couldn't have been circumstantial. There were rows of landscape that were like giant mushrooms, glowing with various colors. Others were like teepees, some like tubes, laying across the bottom.

"My lord," Greg muttered. It dawned on him that he was among the first people to lay eyes on this new world. Only a percent of a percent of the population ever received such a privilege, even if this one was home to the worst thing he ever imagined. This place, at first sight, was beautiful. He even started to smile, as did Hannah, and Arnold. The astonishment was overwhelming. For a moment, they almost forgot about the dreaded events that preceded this moment.

Greg glanced at Wilkow, expecting the eccentric scientist to be over the moon with joy at this discovery. Instead, he watched the screen with a dead stare that almost appeared to display fear rather than astonishment. Greg raised his eyebrows, and even considered asking what was wrong. Then it dawned on him...

Despite this vast world they were observing, one thing stood out. There was no life—aside from the horde. Greg had seen videos of deep trenches in the past, and every single one of them always showed the deep worlds teeming with all kinds of life. But this place was dead. Only empty water, and tentacled creatures, filled the screen.

Wilkow and Joel, having seen the abundance of life in the cavern beneath Ridgeway Lake, knew this wasn't right.

Twenty-seconds passed when they saw a vast stream of silk, identical to those coating the lake floor. Instead of weeds and lily pads, it was the rock structure below that was taken over. But it wasn't those that the group was fixated on.

Countless species, of all shapes and sizes, were encased in silk cocoons. It was a forest of bodies, some 'balancing' on their tailfins as bodyfat attempted to float them. There were species of fish, similar to those fished from typical freshwater lakes, only much larger in size. Others were completely different. There were fish with horns, fish with suction cups for mouths, while many were too securely wrapped for a decent view.

But the bones protruding from a few deflated cocoons couldn't be missed. Wilkow usually enjoyed being right: this was not one of those times. The larvae had eaten the hosts from the inside out. He had noticed that some of the other fish appeared to be shrunken, though he couldn't determine for a fact since he had no real knowledge of the species. But he knew sickly looking fish when he saw them—and many of these hosts were clearly being drained from within.

"They've completely taken over this region," he said.

"Killed everything in it," Joel added.

Those fears were confirmed as the drone was carried to the right. Several meters of underwater landscape passed over the monitor. The next colors they saw were red.

Everyone leaned in for a better look.

It was like a series of tiny lightbulbs, strung together in enormous bushes. Several squids hovered over the bushes, expanding their tentacles, and pressing their bodies to them.

"Eggs," Wilkow said.

"My God, there's thousands. MILLIONS!" Hannah said. She covered her mouth.

Greg pointed at one of the squids, which appeared to be pulsing its tentacles against the egg. "Doctor, you mentioned before that they collect the eggs."

Wilkow nodded. "That's how they do it."

The drone was carried over the field, where countless squids lurked. The group went silent as they witnessed the entire screen fill with tentacled beasts. Greg Goodman felt the need to scratch all over his body. He felt as though he was trapped in a wasp nest. His understanding of the basic structure of these hives came back to him. As though to confirm his fears, he saw the mountainous shape.

It was like Cthulhu from the ancient depths. Its tentacles were coiled to her sides. Her color was darker than the others, the abdomen massive and glowing red along the underbelly. They couldn't see her face, as two tentacles, like elephant trunks, coiled in front of it.

"There she is—her majesty, herself," Wilkow said.

"That can't be right," Arnold said. "She's got to be a hundred-and-fifty feet long!"

"More than that. Two hundred. Those tentacles have a reach equal to that," Wilkow replied.

Sierra's facial muscles stiffened. He stepped away from the monitors and snatched his radio.

"Echo Five, are the charges prepped?"

"Ready to go, sir."

"Lift off now."

CHAPTER 25

Echo Five lifted off the southeast bend on Circle Drive. Its rotors bombarded the trees below with powerful drafts, causing the branches to sway wildly. Dangling below the chopper by a cable was a hundred pounds of C4 explosives, activated with a depth meter and camera unit. The lake surface trembled as the Blackhawk passed over it.

Major Sierra held his radio to his lips while he watched the chopper move into place. "Echo Three and Four, fan out one hundred meters. Have gunners in place. Five, you all set?"

The chopper descended to fifty meters, then held position. *"We're ready to commence."*

"Begin descent. Once it's lined up, I'll give you the go-ahead to disconnect cable."

"Copy that. Proceeding to lower package."

Greg Goodman stood by the Major. The explosives didn't look much bigger than a Labrador retriever. "Sir, you saw the tunnel. You think that'll be enough?"

"That's affirmative, Deputy," Sierra replied, slightly impatient. "We have more explosives on hand in case we need to hit it again. But, judging by the entrance layout, if we get the explosives fifty feet below the entrance, we should be able to trigger a cave-in. By this time tomorrow, we'll have construction crews here to seal a dome or a steel plate over the crevasse. One way or another, these things are NOT getting out again."

The explosives touched the water.

"Descend to eighty feet," Sierra instructed.

"Copy."

They could hear the whine from the winch. A moment later, the explosives disappeared. Sierra turned to the workstation to his left, where a monitor had been linked to the feed. Immediately, it was getting too dark to see.

"Damn it. Hold it there, Echo Five. Echo Three and Four, put your spotlights on the crevasse. Visibility is too low," Sierra said. White beams of light burst from the choppers and waved across the water's surface. The lake floor lit up, revealing the silky bottom below. Sierra panned the camera to the right, then down a bit until he found the crevasse. "Echo Five, turn six degrees starboard, then reverse fifteen feet. You're almost there." He waited a moment until the chopper got into place. Echo Three and Four adjusted position as well, focusing their spotlights down on the cable.

Wilkow stepped toward the monitor. His eyes lit up as he watched the spotlights pierce the crevasse opening, lighting up the cave walls.

"Major, you might want to be careful about that," he said. "It's very likely those things are attracted to lights. Might be how they located the drone so quickly."

"Doctor, in less than two minutes, that crevasse will be sealed. Until then, I need visibility so my men can do their job." The Major directed his voice to his radio. "Echo Five, continue."

The winch turned again, lowering the explosives into the crack in the earth. Wilkow watched the edges pass by the frames of the monitor. They were looking straight down into the throat of the earth. The background was black, save for some hints of the bioluminescent ecosystem, and some tiny stars.

Hannah noticed them too. She looked at Wilkow, his expression triggering the same concern she currently felt. Those 'stars' were getting larger rapidly. Suddenly, there wasn't simply a dozen—there were tens of them. Hundreds. In seconds, the cavern was alive with swarming beasts.

"Major?!" Wilkow said. Sierra looked toward him, his throat primed to let out an angry bellow at the Doctor. Then his eyes went to the screen.

"Twenty feet to go. Almost there."

"Echo Five, pull up!"

The camera feed vanished as the creatures swarmed around the package.

Like a fishing line, the cable started tugging back and forth. A hundred squid creatures tugged at it in a hundred different spots. Next, the lake started to sizzle. Water lapped in opposing directions, as though caught between two category five storms. Like worms bursting from the earth during a rainstorm, an army of tentacles stretched above the lake.

The cable lashed back, then descended, taking Echo Five down with it.

"Five, pull up!" Sierra ordered. He could hear the groaning of struggling rotors. The chopper was now rocking heavily, while slowly sinking to the lake.

Echo Three and Four opened fire with the M60s. The gunmen concentrated their fire near the cable, hoping to dislodge the creatures pulling it downward. The crew detached the package, but the creatures maintained their deathly grip.

There was no explosion. The depth reader must have been dislodged.

Echo Five's gunman began firing frantically into the water below him. The line whipped to the side, causing the chopper to spin, inadvertently causing his weapon to send dozens of rounds whipping to the air.

Tiny glass fragments exploded into Echo Three's cockpit. Smoke billowed from the rotors. The chopper spun out of control.

"Fuel cut off. Engine failure." The pilot's transmissions ended simultaneous to the violent crash. Walls of water climbed over a hundred feet high, while rotor fragments zipped in all directions.

Joel Pobursky was the first to dive to the ground, followed immediately by everyone else. Metal shrapnel crashed into the fence, ripping entire sections free. One fragment struck a guardsman right in the chest, the tip punching through his spine.

The horde swarmed the crashed chopper, invading the fuselage and seizing the personnel inside. Rifle and pistol shots pummeled the air for a couple of brief seconds, replaced by the screams of their operators.

Meanwhile, Echo Four attempted to shoot the creatures around it, to no avail. They were showing up by the tens each second. The lake, which had been quiet barely sixty seconds ago, was now teeming with squids from shore to shore. The rooftop snipers went to work attempting to pick them off. There was almost no point in aiming. A bullet would now whiz into the lake without hitting some sort of flesh.

Sierra was the first to be back on his feet. His eyes went to the crash, then to Echo Five, which was still struggling to fight against the pull. It was losing ever so gradually, the landing skates less than six feet above the thrashing surface.

Finally, Echo Four activated its miniguns. The twin death machines unleashed their fury into the swarm, causing chunks of flesh and waves of blood to splatter with the water.

Despite the mounting casualties, the horde did not relent. Echo Five's crew fought back with all of their might and resources, only to find themselves right at the water's surface, and at the mercy of countless wiggling tentacles. Several creatures secured a hold on the aircraft and hauled themselves in. The gunman was the first to be seized and tossed into the water. A feeding frenzy ensued, with limbs being torn from their roots, and his chest and midsection slashed open by teeth and claws.

Pistol shots rang out as the second crewmember made his last stand. Screams filled the fuselage before it was splattered with his blood. Claws and teeth went to work, slicing through flesh and bone as though it were made of cardboard. Next were the pilots.

Either by frantic movement or deliberation, the pilot swung the chopper around once, then plummeted into the water. Again, the air above was dominated by a hundred pieces of shrapnel, many of which assaulted the shorelines. Water flooded the Blackhawk, allowing the squids to overtake the pilots with ease.

Sierra stood up on his knees after diving for cover a second time. When he looked to the shore, he saw an army of squids with swollen tentacles, marching at the shallows. The bonfires did nothing to deter them this time. Across the lake, they converged on the fence. Those that made contact were flung backward, their flesh scorched by the electric surge carried within that barrier.

Machine gunners opened fire, tearing the front line of creatures apart. Blood spurted all across the sand, the dead bodies appearing deflated as their brethren marched over them. Infantrymen closed in on the fence and opened fire on the moving bodies behind it.

Hannah and Arnold Thorp immediately flooded their radio frequencies with orders to their officers across the lake.

"All units, maintain perimeter at Circle Drive. Do NOT come near the shore. Let the National Guard drive them back," Hannah said.

After giving similar instructions to his Troopers, Arnold turned to the Major. "Sir, you're gonna need more men."

"I just made the call," Sierra replied. "They'll be here within the hour."

"Not soon enough," Greg said.

Sierra tensed. He watched wave upon wave of tentacled beasts race toward the defenses. The electric current knocked them back, but it was clear that they could continue until they broke it down. His eyes went back to the water. There was no way of knowing where the explosives landed, but at this point, he needed to try something to weaken the horde's advance.

He pointed at a guardsman stationed near the desk. "Corporal, detonate the C4."

The Corporal didn't hesitate. He activated the switches on the device, then activated the triggering mechanism. Everyone braced for a booming explosion, believing the device ended up somewhere along the lake floor. Instead, what they heard was a distant rumble far below their feet. Had the guardsman not activated the device a moment prior, they would've assumed it was some small-scale earthquake.

Wilkow found himself stepping back toward the hill, unable to take his eyes off the insanity in the water. The squids were withdrawing at a rapid rate.

"They're retreating," Sierra said.

"No...I don't think so," Wilkow replied.

"What does that look like to you?" the Major retorted.

"Those explosives fell into the crevasse," Wilkow said. "You just detonated that thing near their nest. Near their *Queen.*"

"Good. Maybe we fried her ass," Sierra replied. He raised his radio. "Echo Four, keep hitting them. Pick off as many as you can. Echo Six, prep your explosives. We're gonna give it another go."

"With pleasure, sir."

Greg couldn't take his eyes off of Wilkow. The Doctor's body language said it all. Joel Pobursky must've been thinking the same thing, because he was backing away from the workstation as well. Greg's stomach tightened. Those squids withdrew almost immediately after the blast. His memory flashed to the Brown's kid. His mind's eye focused on the welts he suffered as a result of assaulting their Queen.

"Mess with an ant Queen, or a beehive Queen, and you're in for a rude awakening. She'll send signals that she's in distress, and all the workers will rush to her defense."

He tapped Hannah and Arnold on the shoulders.

"We might head to the hilltop."

The military radio sounded off. *"Major? You hear that?"*

Everyone stopped to listen. There was a faint echo from down below, like footsteps deep below the earth. Gradually, that sound became more intense. Soon, it was clear it was coming from the center of the west segment. The vibrations had definitive repetition, with grinding sounds following each tremor.

"Standby," Sierra warned his men. His confidence was threatening to fade. He looked back at Wilkow in search of an explanation, only to realize the man gave it in the form of his actions.

"Major, we have new activity."

The water, having calmed after the horde's withdrawal, was now teeming with life. Like ants emerging from their hill, the squid-creatures burst through the surface and expanded. Immediately, a swarm of them formed a line to the east, heading into the next segment.

"What the hell are they doing?" Arnold said.

"Don't know, but that's a deliberate formation," Hannah said.

"They're probably attempting to breach another point in the perimeter," Greg replied.

"They're in for a rude awakening," Sierra said. "Echo Four, hit 'em with everything you've got."

"Wait...wait...Major!" Wilkow, who was halfway up the hill, was suddenly sprinting to get Sierra's attention. Echo Four turned around and opened fire on the horde. Fountains of water and guts sprayed several feet high in a soupy mixture. Echo Four continued its assault, concentrating its miniguns at the head of the pack.

Behind it, the lake was rising.

Sierra raised his binoculars, unsure whether his eyes were playing tricks on him. It was as though a mountain was forming in the lake's center. "The hell?"

"Major!"

Finally, Sierra turned toward Wilkow.

"Turn them back around and fire whatever explosives they have at the—"

By then, it was too late. The water parted ways, revealing the gargantuan mass that lifted it. Tentacles, ten feet thick, with claws extending fifteen-feet from the tips, stretched to all sides, revealing the hideous face of the queen.

Unlike the soft, leathery flesh of the servants, her body was protected by a bony carapace. A horned crest, like that of a triceratops, covered her head, with thick spines curving over her eyes. Unlike its main body, her tentacles had no armor, allowing for maximum flexibility.

Her servants swarmed around her. Despite her advantage of a shell, they used their bodies as shields against the land-dwellers.

"Goddamn!" Hannah shouted.

"Echo Four, bank to port..."

Tentacles, like sea serpents, sprang fifty-meters into the air. Hooked claws snagged Echo Four by the landing skates and tail. Emergency lights flashed in the cockpit. The pilot yelled at his crewmates to brace for crash landing. The chopper turned sideways and plummeted near the shore along the bend. The armaments erupted, consuming the chopper into a bright yellow flame.

Soldiers fled from their positions near Cabins Eight and Seven as shrapnel ravaged that area. Glass shattered as the shockwave passed under the buildings. The generator sputtered, its ventilators spewing smoke.

"Someone check that unit," Sierra instructed. Guardsmen, dazed, confused, and overwhelmed, rushed the generator unit. One immediately waved back at the Major.

"Shrapnel damage, sir!"

Before the Major could respond, he heard the rotor rotations of Echo Six speeding into the combat zone.

M134 miniguns spat bullets, each of which struck uselessly against her shell. The Queen tucked her head down, deliberately pointing her shell at the assault. Thin fragments of shell broke away, though not enough to endanger the soft flesh and internal organs beneath it.

"Six, hit it with rockets," Sierra ordered.

"Copy that, sir. Stand by."

The Queen sank further into the water, completely submerging her face. After a few short moments, she raised her bulk and turned to face the chopper. Her tentacles coiled back, revealing the tremendous jaws and black slimy eyes. The jaw hyperextended, the fleshy throat twisting behind it.

Echo Six got into position, making sure to stay out of reach of those arms. The pilot locked on target then put his finger on the trigger.

"Good, I see you're opening wide, you fat ugly—"

The Queen's mantle compressed, expelling thousands of gallons of water through her mouth. The thick stream sliced through the air like a laser, striking Echo Six with enough force to shatter the windshield. The pilot screamed, inadvertently squeezing the trigger as he fought to keep the chopper from spiraling out of control.

Rockets pummeled the south shore, blasting holes in the perimeter fence, and causing the soldiers to scatter. Cabin Seven was struck dead center, instantly becoming a crater from which hundreds of debris fragments were launched.

Hannah's ears were ringing. She could hear a thousand screams from everyone surrounding her. Ranking soldiers barked orders to their subordinates, attempting to get the men into defensive positions.

The world was then rocked by another explosion. Echo Six whipped overhead, circling repeatedly until it struck a tree, which ended any hopes of the pilot regaining control. It struck down on Circle Drive and exploded. Fuel and rockets combusted, spreading fire to the trees and property all around it.

The world around her turned to chaos. All available Blackhawks were down, leaving only ground units to fend off the advancing horde.

Major Sierra barked orders to his men, while demanding a radio tech to request assistance from across the state.

Photos snapped as news reporters recorded the horrible event. However, those people, who were the most eager to be on site, were the first to flee when they saw the swarm converge on the perimeter line.

Soldiers fired at will, killing creature after creature. But for each one that fell, two more took its place. Like a tsunami, they rolled ashore as one unit, packing overwhelming numbers against the defenses. Meanwhile, more were still emerging from the crevasse. The fence buckled under the combined weight of a hundred squids, who proceeded to sweep inland.

All-out warfare began.

Soldiers screamed as they were seized by tentacles and shredded like tissue paper. Within seconds, the creatures advanced past the cabins and workstations, and were engaging National Guardsmen at the foot of the hill.

It all seemed to be happening in slow motion. The rapid gunshots and bloodcurdling screams caused the Sheriff to freeze. There were creatures all around her. And at the shoreline, the mountain of a Queen was making landfall.

With the sight of her, Hannah's senses returned.

She aimed her Glock at an advancing squid and ruptured its head with six hollow points. A few meters behind her right shoulder, Greg was emptying a mag into another squid. Hannah gasped, seeing another sneaking up behind him.

"Greg, look out!" She aimed and fired several shots into its abdomen. Greg spun on his heel, shrieked at the flailing tentacles, then fired a single round into its head.

"Too close," he muttered. He loaded a fresh magazine, then froze briefly after seeing the wall of dark green that was the Queen. "Oh...SHIT!"

Arnold Thorp was the next person dashing for the hill. Behind him was Major Sierra and a few other soldiers. Gunshots echoed from all across the lake. All major shores had been breached. The infestation had begun.

People screamed as they were either torn apart or carried off into the water to be made hosts for new spawn. Squids, like worker ants, started coating the shoreline with their slime webbing, as though placing a flag atop an enemy fortress.

"Up the hill!" Greg shouted.

The swarm overtook the few remaining guardsmen at the foot of the hill and began ascending. Greg, Hannah, and Arnold passed a firing line of soldiers at the top, who proceeded to fire. It was a similar chain of events as the last, except the National Guard had fifty-caliber and M60 machine guns on swivel mounts. Immediately, the first lines of creatures were cut into shreds.

It was only a momentary delay, as no one, including Wilkow, predicted the rapid advance of the Queen. Six of her eight tentacles filled with fluid, inflating her muscles to support her immense bulk, while the forward arms served as weapons of war. She darted up the hill with incredible speed, lashing at the firing line with those tentacles.

Dismembered soldiers flew apart in bloody chunks as the claws passed through the line. Machine guns were smashed into fragments.

Major Sierra finally had his weapon drawn. He emptied his magazine into a couple of drones, while barking orders for his men to fall back. The radio tech ran toward him.

"Major! I got Battle Creek on the line."

Sierra snatched the radio. "Get the Governor on the line. The attempt to seal the crevasse failed. These things are coming out in swarms. We need more troops! We need air support and heavy artillery. There's no choice; we need to coat this entire end of town with napalm, or else all of Michigan will be one big nest!"

Several creatures were converging on him, eliminating all ability to focus on communication. The Major snatched up a dropped M4 and began blasting away.

"Get out of here!" he ordered the tech. "All units, fall back. Take position at—"

The two halves of his body took to the sky like softballs.

The Queen retracted the claw that sliced the biped creature across the middle, only to lash again at the others running about. Killing them was an easy task for her. Her brain, adjusted for size, was far larger than the thousands of servants. This species, whom her colony had never encountered before, were dwindling in numbers. Beyond their defenses was a world of green. Never had the Queen experienced such openness that wasn't completely occupied with water. Her respiratory cycle had been recently filled with water, giving her several hours to invade, and possibly find a new body of water. Her ever-increasing colony needed space and sustenance. Here, they found both in abundance.

"All units, fan out. Clear Circle Drive. There's too many of them!" Hannah screamed into her radio. She ran beside Greg and Arnold through the driveway and into the road, where Joel and Wilkow were waiting.

"Need a lift?" Wilkow said, pointing to his chopper. The N.E.C.T.O.R. pilots were inside already, getting the engines started.

The cops looked back and saw the driveway area teeming with creatures.

"Yeah, I won't complain!" Greg said. They sprinted for the chopper and dove inside.

Wilkow tapped the pilot on the shoulder. "Don't wait for us to buckle in!"

The chopper ascended, while the remaining N.E.C.T.O.R. staff filled the other. It lifted off just as the creatures were about to pile themselves on it.

Wilkow found a headset and put it on. "Bravo Unit, don't worry about us. Get the hell out of dodge. There's nothing you can do here."

"Roger that. Returning to home base."

"That's where we ought to be going," Joel said.

"Not us," Greg replied. "We're not letting these things infest our town."

Joel leaned his head back. "I could be home eating chili. But noooo..."

"Guys, look!" Hannah said. The group pressed their heads to the window. Down below, the swarm had overtaken Circle Drive and were rapidly overtaking the main roads.

Arnold was immediately on his radio. "All Troopers, evacuate every resident for five miles."

"Where do we direct them to?" a Trooper responded. Arnold opened his mouth to answer, but couldn't come up with one. Watching the swarm below, it was clear these things were going *everywhere*. There were plenty of ponds spread across the vicinity to act as 'outposts' for the swarm to take refuge in. Then, of course, there was Lake Archer.

"Away from Tonette," he said.

"Sierra asked for a napalm strike," Hannah said. "I don't see how that'll work at this point. Just look at how they're spreading! They're all over the place! It would take so much napalm, they might as well drop a nuke."

"We need to do *something*, because there's nothing stopping them," Arnold said. "Doc! You're the expert. What do you suggest?"

Wilkow shrugged. "At this point, there's no one answer. The simplest solution is to kill the Queen. That'll at least prevent the production of eggs, assuming these creatures only rely on one Queen per colony. That said, we'd still have to deal with the aftermath of her drones. They might not stop pillaging because she's dead. They'll see *us* as a threat and pull all of their members into a final assault."

"*Us* a threat?" Arnold said. "I don't recall us busting through their front door."

"They don't have that self-awareness," Wilkow said. "All they care about is what they can gain and how they can expand. Remember, they're an invasive species. Everything else is either food or resources to them."

"Do we know if more guardsmen are coming?" Hannah said.

"I'm picking up some transmissions," the pilot said. "The Governor's Office is issuing executive actions. The Air National Guard has been deployed. Evacuations are being ordered for the entire county, with surrounding areas on standby."

"They don't understand what they're walking into," Greg said. "They're just gonna bomb every horde they see and hope they can contain this thing."

"You have a better idea?" Hannah said.

Greg scoffed. "You do realize that they won't bomb until the evacuations are complete, right?"

Joel raised his hand. "He's right on that."

Hannah rested her forehead against her palm. "Those things will be all over the town before we even get close to evacuating it." She took a breath, glanced out the window, then sat straight. "We need to stop these things ourselves."

Joel squeezed his eyes shut. "I'm starting to miss the Carnobass."

"What's the matter, Joel? I thought you were the hunting type," Wilkow said. "I remember seeing photos of crocs you've wrestled to death, and you were pretty eager to go headfirst against the Carnobass."

Joel glared at him. "Did you even *see* all the craziness that happened back there? That's not hunting, that's Word War Two level chaos, except this is an enemy that doesn't fear the bullets we fire at them."

"Come on, Joel. Greatest generation, remember!" Wilkow said. "You'll help us beat these things just like you did the Nazis."

Joel stared at him with unblinking eyes for several seconds.

"How old do you think I am?!?!"

"Let me be honest, we don't have the manpower or the resources to fight these things," Arnold said. "We just watched the National Guard get overrun. And call me crazy, but I think that Queen bitch knew what the hell she was doing back there."

"She's a lot smarter than the drones, that's for sure," Greg said.

"And you'll be lucky to get near her," Joel said. "Unless you have an armory full of flamethrowers, you're not gonna get past the creatures guarding her. And even if you do, she'll cut you in half. You'd need a bulldozer! Or a semi."

Greg's eyes widened. He leaned into the cockpit.

"Take us into town! Hurry!"

"What's in town?" Hannah asked.

"A way to stop these things. Doc, these things communicate through chemicals. Do you think they can do the same thing out of water?"

"Seems to be working so far," Wilkow replied. "They couldn't coordinate an attack like this over such a large area without some sort of constant communication."

"And if the Queen was *severely* injured, would they converge on her location?"

"She, and the drones accompanying her, would probably let off signals to the others. The Queen is the priority, so it's highly possible all colony members would converge on her location."

"What are you thinking, Greg?" Hannah asked.

"I'm thinking of hosting a little barbeque," Greg replied.

CHAPTER 26

Within ten minutes of the perimeter breach, the Governor's Office got on a secure phoneline directly to the President. The Cabinet was called in for an emergency briefing. Military experts were brought in to evaluate the situation. Senators and Congressmen from both major parties took to *Twitter*. Some stated that they believed the situation to be a hoax, others simply expressed their support for Michigan, while a few took advantage of the scenario to push their own agendas.

The meeting commenced with audio recordings taken from Doctor Mike Wilkow during his examination of a squid's corpse. These recordings were taken by Major Sierra of the National Guard. When asked about the Major's whereabouts, it was revealed that he had not made contact since the colony came ashore.

Satellites aligned over the upper peninsula and zoomed in on the town of Tonette. The images centered on Peanut Lake. What they revealed was a dying sunset overlooking a world of moving bodies. The lake itself was almost invisible, as it was completely dominated by the swarm. The surrounding area showed police forces retreating from an expanding wave. Meanwhile, news footage of the invasion dominated the television stations. An emergency broadcast was issued to the public. A press statement was prepared for the President, which would be broadcast after his next call to the Governor's Office to authorize additional military force.

With the information at hand, and the rapid spread of the colony, the government saw no other choice but to launch a full-scale military strike on the County of Schoolcraft.

****

The horde branched out from Peanut Lake like an expanding spiderweb. Those on the northside led an assault on the neighborhoods in Bellner and Rockwell, taking the residence by surprise. Some further down had gotten word to evacuate. Others, closer to the lake, were not so lucky.

The creatures killed without mercy. The few cops guarding the barricades made their last stand, only to be overwhelmed by the superior numbers. Those who were lucky were torn apart and killed on the spot. Others were stung and dragged back to the new hive, where they would be impregnated with embryos.

Some steadfast homeowners tried to make their last stand, locking themselves in and defending their property with privately owned weapons. Some lasted longer than others, depending on their security measures and firepower. However, the common denominator was defeat. It was only a matter of time.

SWAT units arrived on McGrain Street, which intersected with Circle Drive on the west side of the lake. The officers in the armored vehicle immediately engaged the horde, only to suffer instant casualties. The creatures advanced without regard for their individual preservation. They were a hive-mind, dictated to by the chemical signals received from their Queen.

McGrain Street became a bloodbath.

National Guard personnel carriers soon arrived on scene, deploying troops to McGrain, Zolciak, and Rockwell. Drones passed overhead, relaying footage to military and government officials.

By seven-ten, the creatures had expanded roughly a mile in all directions, sweeping the roads and wooded areas. Homes were taken over with force, their occupants seized and skewered. The only thing that spread faster than the colony was the confusion, which worked in favor of the creatures. Even with the unusual military presence, the populous was unclear about what was happening. Creatures emerging from under the ground? It seemed unreal. Many didn't bother taking it serious until the creatures were bashing in their front door. Others tried fleeing once they saw the National Guard and local law enforcement battling the horde in the streets, only to be snatched and stung.

A quarter-mile southeast of Peanut Lake, the horde discovered a small neighborhood on a street called Quincannon. During their fight with ground units and the forced entry of the six houses in that stretch of road, they discovered two thirty-foot ponds, which instantly served as havens for the creatures to rehydrate and store hosts.

Similar 'outposts' were formed a mile up in McGrain Street. In the backyard of the Anthony Caris property, the creatures seized took refuge in his pool, where they stored his paralyzed body, and that of his wife. Two-hundred meters north, they located a large pond and invaded it, killing the local fish with their webbing.

A mile south, hundreds of creatures traveled down Guy Street, escorting their Queen to the intersection at Zolciak. The ground was wet with the blood of human bodies the first wave had encountered, and the air was rife with chemical signals alerting them to a larger population further east.

The Queen made the turn and continued on, stopping briefly to hydrate herself in a small pond the warriors secured. This had been the longest she had ever been out of water, and it was proving to be an exhausting task. However, her sensory receptors detected large bodies of water in the vicinity. She would be able to find a new haven to rest and lay more eggs, before ultimately moving on to new territory.

Two miles south of the business area of town, Archer Lake was in turmoil. National Guard units deployed from Chinooks and went door-to-door, ordering the residents to evacuate. Several people were still out on the lake, completely oblivious to the current events surrounding their town. Those who came from out-of-town failed to get cell-service, which prevented them from receiving any news broadcasts.

Some residents complied, while others made arguments about government overreach, which led to forced removal from the premises. This led to further outcries, which in turn, led to a small-scale insurrection from the residents.

The town area itself was in utter chaos. The initial wave of squids arrived, scurrying about with incredible speed, seizing prisoners and leaving their paralyzed bodies on the pavement to be collected later. Sheriff Deputies and State Troopers engaged the beasts with handguns, shotguns, and rifles. Claws slashed through Kevlar vests and the flesh they protected. Casualties mounted, and not solely from the swarm's doing. People fled the streets, trampling each other, while vehicles raced through red lights, resulting in collisions and injuries.

Police vehicles raced down Zolciak, filling the radio channels with reports of the Queen's advance, along with her escort. She would arrive within minutes. Once the area was overtaken, she would move on to Lake Archer, where she would spawn thousands of new warriors. Meanwhile, the colony would continue its advance, seizing every inch of land for miles, and every body of water within it.

****

"Oh God! Look at that!" the pilot said.

"I see it," Greg said, watching the Queen down below and her hundreds of servants.

"My God, they're fast!" Hannah said.

"They're not wasting time," Wilkow said.

"Can I ascend now?" the pilot asked.

"No!" Greg said. "Keep going a little further. Just to the next intersection."

"What's there that's so important?" Hannah said.

Greg pointed ahead through the windshield. "That." Hannah saw the fuel truck parked along the side of Crabb Road.

"Holy shit! That might work. You can drive that thing?"

"Just gotta make the turn and drive in a straight line," Greg said.

Joel looked at the truck, then back at the invasion, then at Greg. "Let me make sure I understand your plan: you're gonna drive that truck into the horde and, I assume, detonate the fuel load?"

"Yep."

"Will that be enough to kill her?"

"Maybe. I'm hoping not," Greg replied. He turned his gaze to the sky above them, as Air National Guard fighter jets passed above. "We need to get ahold of the military."

"And tell them what, exactly?" Arnold asked.

"They're going to start bombing the hell out of this area. If we can draw the swarm to this plain to protect their queen, we can condense their population, thus making an easier target for the bombs. Any stragglers can be picked off by ground troops afterwards."

"I don't have the National Guard's frequency."

"Yeah? So?" Greg glared at her.

Hannah nodded. "Do whatever it takes to win. Looks like I'm gonna be flooding the Governor's Office with phone calls."

"Want me to set you down in the intersection?" the pilot asked.

"No," Greg replied.

"NO?"

"No?!" Hannah said.

"Kinda hard to drive that truck from up here," Joel remarked.

"Yeah, problem is, it has a power-steering issue. I need to get fluid in it first, or else, that truck's not going anywhere."

"Why not just pull it into the middle of the intersection and wait for the Queen to get close?" Arnold said.

"Because she might move around it. I need to make sure she's front and center when that thing goes boom. Pilot, take us into town. Land in the grocery store parking lot."

"Don't forget the produce," Joel said.

"Very funny." Greg watched the landscape pass beneath them as they sped further east. "I gotta say; I did NOT expect this day to take this turn. I thought my biggest problem would be a clogged toilet."

"Don't jinx it. You'll make it worse," Hannah replied.

"It's worse," Arnold said. He was looking out the window at the town. Creatures were scurrying all about, attacking people and vehicles. Windows and doors were smashed, with slime and blood coating the pavement.

"Good God. I can't believe they've made it this far already," Hannah said.

"Scouts," Wilkow said. "They advanced ahead of the Queen. Essentially, they're the pawns, sent to thin the enemy forces before the big boss shows up."

"We don't have much time. Get me down onto that lot," Greg said.

"No way!" the pilot exclaimed. "We'll be swarmed."

"If we don't stop these things, a hell of a lot more people will die," Hannah said. She stepped into the cockpit, making it clear her hand was resting against her sidearm. The pilot looked at the threat wide-eyed, then glanced back at Wilkow.

The Doctor shrugged. "Don't look at me."

The pilot looked back at the Sheriff. "I'm calling your bluff, lady. You shoot me, and there'll be nobody left to fly the chopper."

An annoyed Joel groaned, then stood up. "Yeah—that's not true." He made his way into the co-pilot seat, then clicked his tongue at the pilot while directing him into the back. "Out."

"You're not serious!"

Hannah yanked him from the cockpit and forced him into the passenger seats. Joel put the headset on and resumed control. He steered the chopper over the town, then hovered over the store parking lot.

Arnold opened the fuselage door, then aimed his Glock at the dozen creatures below. He, along with Greg and Hannah, opened fire on the drones, killing them as they gathered under the chopper. Fountains of blood splashed the hull, the stench filling the air.

Joel set the chopper down. "Alright Greg, I hope you're fast on your feet."

Greg handed him his M4. "Cover me...and keep these fucks out of the chopper."

The former Air Force pararescue took the freshly loaded weapon, then stepped onto the pavement. Right away, he took aim at a couple of drones moving onto the lot from across the road, their front tentacles waving high above their heads. With short, controlled bursts, he erupted their heads, which opened up in a display of black fluid, jaw fragments, and brains.

Hannah and Arnold stepped outside and assisted him in holding other swarm members back, while Greg sprinted toward the building, Glock in hand. Squids writhed, their tentacles lashing uncontrollably as their deflating bodies gushed blood.

Hannah got on her cell phone and put it on speakerphone as she continued shooting at additional creatures.

A secretary answered the line.

"Yes, this is the Schoolcraft County Sheriff, Hannah Tyler. I need to speak with the Governor."

"Sheriff, the Governor is on another line with the National Guard. We're working to contain the outbreak."

"I'm right here in the middle of it, jackass! We know how to stop the spread, but we need to get in contact with the Governor, or at least whoever's leading the National Guard operation."

"Sheriff, the government has evacuation plans in place. Your instructions are to evacuate the town and the surrounding areas. The Air National Guard has been ordered to deploy bombs on the area…"

"You don't understand! I have the N.E.C.T.O.R. researcher here with me. He concurs with our plan. We can converge the horde into one general location, but you need to grant us time."

"That's not up to me, Sheriff."

"Then get the Governor on the line."

"She's not available. I have another call to take, Sheriff."

"Not as important as this one. For godsake! At least connect me to the base of operations so I can speak to the Military Commander."

The secretary paused.

"One moment please."

His voice disappeared, instantly replaced by a generic piano tune.

Joel put another three-round burst into a squid, then noticed Hannah's irritated expression.

"He put you on hold?"

She nodded.

Joel shrugged. "Figures."

CHAPTER 27

When Greg Goodman walked into the store nine hours prior, it was a clean building with a half-dozen or so staff, and an equal number of customers. What he walked into at seven-thirty was a mess of fallen aisle stacks, screaming victims, and tentacled bodies. Many of the overhead lights were broken, and several aisle units had toppled over on the left side, causing a domino effect.

He stepped into the checkout lobby, where a civilian lay face-down with a stinger in his back. The creature injecting the venom identified its next target, and retracted the barb.

The first eight inches of that stinger snapped free as a bullet passed through it. Greg followed up the shot with five others, shredding the squid's insides. It wiggled then rolled backward on its mantle, its tentacles coiling into a deathly pose.

Greg looked at the signs above each aisle, his heart skipping a beat when he saw the four rows on the far left completely collapsed. If the auto section was there, he would never find what he needed through that mess. Then he remembered that the automotive supplies were to the right.

"Focus, you dumb idiot," he said to himself. He ran through the lobby and moved around the corner, only to stop in his tracks. Two squids stood in his way, munching a dismembered corpse. The first one turned around to face him, its jaws clasped over a forearm. Tentacles lashed forward, ready to hook the human with its talons.

Greg hit the creature with several rounds, blowing chunks from its face. As the dying creature rolled to the side, he aimed at the next one. Its slashing tentacle matched the speed of his aim. Only luck of distance saved him from its grip. Still, the tips of those claws grazed his arm, knocking the pistol to the side.

Greg staggered back, his right forearm bleeding, his hands empty. "Oh SHIT!"

He pivoted to the left and sprinted for the nearest aisle. The crashing of merchandise behind him alerted Greg that his pursuer was a few short steps behind him. He arrived at the intersection and followed the center aisle to the right. He only ran a few steps before seeing another set of tentacles emerging directly ahead of him. The drone crawled out from an aisle on the left side, immediately turning right to intercept him.

Not fair!

Greg turned right at the nearest aisle, then dove, narrowly avoiding a lash by the creature behind him. He landed in a summersault, which brought him right back to his feet. Ignoring the pain in his lower spine from a bulging disc, he sprinted to the end of the aisle...only to stop again as a third creature appeared. Inadvertently snagged in one of its back legs was a shopping basket, loaded with brownies, bread, and milk.

"And I thought I'd seen everything," Greg muttered, backing away from the creature. He looked over his shoulder at the two others blocking his exit from the other side. He had no weapon, no exit, and no time.

Greg's eyes went to the aisle shelves. He didn't see displays holding Oreo cookies and pop tarts—he saw steps. With a bounding leap, he threw himself onto the shelves and climbed. The creatures raced into the aisle, lashing their tentacles toward him.

Greg yelled as one of their claws sunk its way into his calf. A barrage of curse words escaped his lungs. He clung to the top of the shelving unit, screaming more as he felt his flesh ripping down to his heel. With one hand grasping the top, he reached out for anything he could find. He felt something plastic, grabbed it, and swung back at the claw.

He struck it several times, failing to dislodge it. He looked down just in time to see one of the other creatures about to scale the shelf. It reached at him with its claw. Shrieking, Greg swung the store item at the claw, catching it right at the tip.

The item burst, splattering liquid all over the two creatures below.

The claw retracted from his leg. The creatures scurried backward, flailing their arms and clawing at their own bodies.

Greg glanced at the plastic bottle that served as his club. *Ortho Home Defense.*

"Look at that, they have it in stock now."

The squids thrashed below, shaking the chemical liquid from their bodies, while the third began scaling the shelf. Greg hauled himself to the top, then looked back again to see the other two starting to circle around. He looked for anything else he could use to fight. Sprays, fog bottles, mosquito traps… nothing that would hold these things off. The creatures were now on the other side, ready to climb to the top. Once again, Greg had nowhere to go…except to the next shelf. Grimacing from the intense pain in his leg, he squatted, then leapt to the other side of the aisle. His body slammed against the next shelf, rocking it back and forth, spilling pots and pans.

The creatures turned around and continued pursuit. Already, they were closing in around him.

"Son of a bitch," Greg muttered. Once again, he hauled himself to the top, then reached for anything he could use to fight with. The first thing was a spatula. He scoffed, then threw it at one of the creatures. Next was a skillet, which he used to whack an outstretched tentacle away. He batted the arms for several seconds before one of the claws snatched it from his hands. He grabbed numerous miscellaneous items and chucked them down. Desperation took hold. He threw spoons, can openers, even kitchen scissors. He crawled along the shelf unit, which shook as one of the creatures climbed aboard.

Finally, Greg collapsed. He was losing blood rapidly, and no amount of adrenaline could dull the pain in his leg. He lay face-down on the shelf, watching the creature in his peripheral vision. Its jaw opened, revealing that bony stinger.

No…no way am I gonna get one of you things stuffed inside me.

He reached down the shelf, grabbing the first thing his fingers felt. He sprang to his knees and raised the item over his shoulder like a softball. He stopped, noticing the near weightlessness of the package.

Matches.

Greg looked down, seeing the rows of stick matches…and the lighter fluid stacked beside them. He grabbed a bottle, popped the cap, then aimed at the creature. Gasoline sprayed the beast, the chemical sensation and vile taste driving back in the split-second before its tentacles reached its prey. Greg emptied the bottle over the creature, yanked several matches out of the box, then sparked a flame.

"Nibble on *this.*"

With a flick of the wrist, the burning matches were chucked onto the gas-soaked flesh, igniting the creature into a writhing ball of fire. Flailing its tentacles, the creature fell off the shelf, landing between its brethren, who quickly distanced themselves from the heat.

Greg snatched up several more bottles, ripped the caps away completely, and splashed the contents into the aisle, coating both creatures. Match heads ignited and fell onto the dripping masses. The aisle was alive with moving flames, which raced across the store as the creatures scurried about in agony.

Greg caught his breath, tossed the empty bottles aside, then climbed down the shelf. Limping heavily on his left leg, he hobbled into the automotive section, where he finally located the transmission fluid. He wasn't wasting time. He scooped several bottles and tucked them under his arm, then hurried to the front lobby. After stopping briefly to pick up his pistol, he rushed out the door.

"Warning. Please return to the checkout counter. Apparently, you have an unpaid item in your—"

"Oh, shut up," Greg moaned. By now, the pain in his leg was unbearable. He could feel the torn, blood-soaked pantleg brushing against his flesh. He would have noticed the blood trailing behind him were his eyes not fixated on the chaos taking place in the streets.

Several squad cars, a SWAT vehicle, and two National Guard personnel carriers had raced into town while he was in the store. Gunfire completely filled the air. In the middle of it all was Hannah Tyler, who was fed up with waiting for the idiot on the other line to connect her with the National Guard Chief.

She emptied her magazine into a squid creature, then spotted him limping from the store. "Greg!" The relief in her face faded when she saw his condition. "Oh God!" Joel saw it too, and rushed with her to help the guy along.

"Hang on there, partner," Joel said. He looked at the huge gash in Greg's calf, then winced. "They did a number on you. Hang on, this'll hurt a bit." Greg yelled out as Joel ripped a section of the pantleg free, making a strap which he tied around the laceration.

"You even know what you're doing?!"

"Done this a hundred times before, though not quite in scenarios like this," Joel said. "You need stitches…and maybe a surgeon."

"To hell with that. We need to get back to that truck," Greg replied.

"Hang on," Hannah said.

"Hang on for what?! We gotta get going," Greg said. The sound of choppers whizzing overhead drew their attention.

"We have to do this *right*, or this'll get a whole lot worse. Joel, get him on the chopper and GO." Hannah sprinted to the chopper, then grabbed Wilkow. "Come on. I'm gonna need your help."

The two of them raced toward the guardsmen, who took position at the intersection. Hannah waved to get their attention, after failing to shout over the intense gunfire.

Finally, one looked over.

"Master Sergeant?" he said. The soldier in charge, after unloading into a drone, stepped forward to greet the Sheriff.

"Ma'am, you'll wanna get the hell out of here. Fighters are deployed. They'll be leveling this entire area with explosives."

"I know, I need your help, Master Sergeant," Hannah said. "You HAVE to get in touch with Senior Command."

"Plan's already in place, Sheriff. These creatures are spreading like wildfire. They've already occupied neighborhoods two miles north of the point of origin. It's just a matter of time before they reach the Great Lakes."

"Listen! We know how to get these things in one centralized area! If we don't, the air units will be dropping bombs over this entire county, killing God knows how many people who haven't escaped yet."

The Master Sergeant shook his head. "This isn't a discussion. I have my orders."

The Doctor raised his hand. "I'm Dr. Mike Wilkow of N.E.C.T.O.R. Hate to break it to you, Sarge, but if you don't get us in touch with Senior Command, we're in for a long night."

"Master Sergeant, if we don't do this, your forces will be here all night bombing the UP," Hannah said.

"We need to postpone the attack, just long enough to get the bastards around the Queen," Wilkow said.

The Master Sergeant groaned, then climbed into the back of the carrier.

"Get me Command Central," he said to the radio tech. He looked back at the Sheriff. "You better not be pulling my chain or I'm gonna catch hell for making this call."

A gust of wind struck them as the N.E.C.T.O.R. helicopter lifted off. Hannah looked back in time to catch a brief glimpse of Greg and Arnold in the fuselage, the former giving her a thumbs up.

Joel angled the chopper to the west and pushed it to full speed. In the far distance, he could see the river of creatures marching through the fields, making a B-line for Lake Archer.

CHAPTER 28

Major General Allen Grayson, Adjutant General of the Michigan Army National Guard, watched the aerial monitor as F-16s flew over the farmlands of Tonette. What he saw was a river of spider-like creatures, guarding a giant one.

"It's continuing southeast, sir."

"Has there been any other contact with Major Sierra?"

"Negative. The containment point has gone dark. We're picking up transmissions from other security forces. Evacuations are on the way, but sir, I don't know if we can get everyone out faster than these things can spread."

"No, we can't. They're already closing in on Lake Archer. There's more of these than our ground units can handle," Grayson said. "According to that scientist Wilkow, these things can keep spreading until they get into the Great Lakes. If they do that—Get me the Governor again."

"Sir?"

"There's no choice. We're gonna have to commence the operation now if we're going to contain this. Order all units out of the area. Strengthen the perimeter at Lake Michigan. Get armored units and artillery there. We WILL NOT let these things into that lake."

"General?"

Grayson saw the nervous communications officer raising his hand. "What is it?"

"I have an incoming transmission from Master Sergeant Ryan Bankowski. Says he has urgent information to share directly with you."

Interesting. The Master Sergeant should've known there were several channels to go through before going directly to the Major

General. If he was willing to bypass all of that, then it must be extremely important.

Grayson gestured to the officer to put it through. The receiver went to speakerphone, blasting the echo of running footsteps through the compound.

"This is General Grayson. Speak fast."

"General, this is Master Sergeant Ryan Bankowski. I've got someone here who needs to speak to you about these things."

"Tell them there's no point," Grayson replied. "We're about to launch our attack. Load them onto your trucks and fall back to perimeter six near the county line, then await further instructions."

****

"Y-yes sir." The Master Sergeant pulled away from his radio to look at the Sheriff. He shrugged. "He's ordering us to pull out. Sounds like the attack's about to begin. Sorry, Sheriff, there's nothing I can do." Hannah's blood boiled. Her face wrinkled as though she was suddenly possessed by some demonic spirit. She hauled herself into the truck and snatched the radio from the Sergeant. "HEY!"

"Shut up, dude. I'm making your job easier." She hit the transmitter. "This is Sheriff Hannah Tyler. Give me the guy in charge of this operation."

There was a moment of silence before the General answered.

"Sheriff, this is a military frequency. Get off this line, and evacuate. There's an airstrike about to commence, and you're about to be caught in the middle of it."

"Yeah-yeah, I get that, General, but you're about to make the situation a hundred times more difficult," Hannah said. "You need to hold off the attack. My team and I have a plan that's likely to work. It involves your bombers, but you have to *wait* for the right moment."

"Sheriff, this is not a negotiation. We don't have the luxury of time. We have to stop that horde before they reach Lake Michigan."

"Listen to me, General!" Hannah said. "You don't understand. You start the attack now, you'll be launching bombs all the way until next week."

"If that's what it takes to stop these things…"

"General, we have intelligence on these creatures. We have a way of injuring the Queen. My team are initiating our plan as we speak. We can stop her advance on the business sector and Lake Archer, and draw the rest of them in."

"You're wasting your time, Sheriff. My team can eliminate that Queen in a heartbeat. Her shell might deflect bullets, but there's no way it'll resist hellfire missiles."

"You kill her with explosives, then this whole town is as good as dead," Hannah replied. She looked to the back of the truck, where Wilkow stood, gesturing for her to hand the radio over. "I have Dr. Mike Wilkow with me. He's the one who's provided the analysis of the creatures so far. Maybe he can articulate this better." She tossed the radio to the Doctor.

"Wilkow here."

"Doctor, I don't know what scheme you're cooking up, but you're putting many lives on the line by attempting to delay my operation."

"Sorry, Colonel, but you're about to make the situation a helluva lot worse."

"It's Major General. Are you ACTUALLY a Doctor?!"

"Listen, Major General, you may launch the attack and kill the Queen, but then that'll leave nobody to control her colony. You see how fast these things have spread and how quickly they've adapted to our environment."

"There's not much we can do about that, Doctor. Except act before it gets worse."

"What if we could get the entire colony in one centralized location?"

There was a brief pause. "How can you do that?"

"If we severely injure the Queen, it's highly probable the whole colony will gather around her for protection. Can't propagate the species without mommy-egg-layer. The key difference between our plan and yours is the emphasis on *injury*. You blow her up with missiles, there won't be a chance for her to communicate with chemical signals. The hive will simply continue to invade until every last one of them is picked off. The trick is to cause the right amount of damage. A little love tap won't alarm her much, but if we immobilize her, then the colony will create a defensive position. Then your jets can come in with their bombs and missiles and do the rest. Or—you can just blow up the entire upper peninsula and hope for the best."

"Don't patronize me, Doctor. There's a lot of HOPING on your part, judging by what you just told me. If this plan doesn't work, then we're allowing the horde to spread even further, thus widening the range of our strike."

Wilkow scratched his head. "Fair point." There was a pause. "General? You still there?"

"I've got the Governor on the line. She wants me to initiate the airstrike now."

"And...?"

"How confident are you in your plan?"

"I'd say sixty-forty...you know—make that eighty-twenty!"

"Put the Sergeant Major on the line." Wilkow tossed the radio back to Bankowski.

"Awaiting instructions, sir."

"What's the status on the business sector?"

"We've cleared out the scouts, finally. Lot of civilian and law-enforcement casualties, but the area's secured...until the Queen gets here."

"Move your forces toward Crabb Road and provide support for these guys. I'm probably gonna kill my career for this, but if their plan works, it'll save hundreds of lives."

"Aye-aye, sir. We'll keep you updated." The Sergeant Major hopped out of the truck. "Listen up, boys. We're providing a welcoming party for the Queen bitch! Mount up! We're going west!" As the soldiers filed into the vehicles, he looked over at Hannah. "This plan better work or we're all dead."

Wilkow tapped him on the arm before climbing into the truck. "Tell you what: beer's on me if this works."

"I'm good with that," one of the guardsmen shouted.

"Stow it." The Sergeant Major then pointed at Wilkow. "I'm holding you to that."

CHAPTER 29

Joel lowered the chopper on the intersection at Crabb and Zolciak. He never took his eyes off the horde, which were now a quarter-mile ahead to the west and closing in fast.

"Greg, you think you can get that truck ready in time?" he asked. Greg was already out the door and limping to the vehicle.

"Just do whatever you can to hold them back," he said.

Joel gritted his teeth. The supply run at the store had taken longer than he anticipated. His faith in their plan was quickly fading.

"I can help," Arnold said.

"No!" Greg replied. "Joel needs a gunner. Attract the Queen's attention. Shoot it. Spit at it. Sing to it if you have to! Whatever works to keep it off of me!"

Arnold checked his rifle. He had collected two additional mags off the pavement near the store. It would hardly be enough to faze the Queen, but it would have to do. He clung to his seat as Joel ascended the chopper.

"Did he imply I have a bad singing voice?"

Joel shrugged. "Wouldn't know, Sergeant. I never met you till this afternoon."

Arnold took firing position at the fuselage door, then started humming a couple of tunes. He settled on Stevie Ray Vaughan's *Life by the Drop*.

"Hello there, my old friend. Not so long—"

"Yeah, you suck," Joel interrupted.

"Well, aren't you a peach," Arnold replied. He watched the ground through the sights of his rifle. The green farmland reeled to the left, only to become a river of tentacles surrounding a giant bulk. His stomach churned. The combined smell of these creature permeated the air. The sticky sounds of movement overwhelmed the drone of the rotors.

Joel circled around and lowered the chopper toward the Queen. Arnold centered her in his scope and fired several bursts, each of which crashed uselessly into her thick shell.

"Focus on her eyes," Joel said. "No shell around her eyes."

"Yeah, but she has a bunch of thick arms around them," Arnold replied.

"Without shell," Joel added. He steadied the chopper two-hundred feet above the Queen. Arnold took aim at her forward appendages and squeezed off several rounds.

A high-pitched hiss made him wince. The beast leaned up high and extended its tentacles at the chopper. Joel yanked up on the joystick, throwing Arnold and the N.E.C.T.O.R. pilot back into their seats. The tentacles stretched like rubber bands, their reach stopping a couple of yards shy of the landing skates.

"Jesus, this is insanity!" the pilot cried out. "Let's get out of here."

Arnold, his temper rising, and patience deflating, turned toward him and knocked him out with a solid blow to the chin. "Grow some balls, why don't ya?" He harnessed the unconscious pilot into a passenger seat, then reloaded his rifle. Meanwhile, Joel veered the chopper to the south, putting a world of drones underneath the skates. It was like shooting fish in a barrel. He fired into the horde, killing drone after drone, focusing on the creatures nearest to the Queen. With the magazine nearly dry, he planted the last few rounds into her side. Judging by the way one of her tentacles flailed, he suspected one of those bullets found its way into the soft flesh.

The Queen turned and followed the chopper to the south, the colony following her lead.

"We got her attention," Joel said.

"Greg better act fast, because we won't hold it for long," Arnold replied.

"All he has to do is get some fluid into that truck and get it started. Should go smoothly…"

"Son of a bitch!" Greg shouted. He tugged at the door handle. The damn driver had locked it before evacuating. He looked back at the field. Joel and Arnold were successfully leading the chopper away from him, but the time they bought would be gone quickly. He slammed his fist into the window, only to nearly fall back in pain. He knew movies were fake in their depictions of glass shattering, but now he REALLY knew how inaccurate they were.

He looked at his knuckles and immediately knew he broke something in his hand.

"Can't anything go right?!"

He took his pistol, gripped it in his left hand, and fired through the window. Rather than shattering the glass, it simply punched holes through it, the sheet still remaining fairly sturdy. He emptied his mag around the frame edges, weakening the window until he was able to club it with the pistol muzzle.

The glass flew apart into the truck. He brushed the glass off the leather seat and popped the hood. He scooped up the power steering fluid and climbed the engine and searched for the components. He found the oil cap, coolant, de-icer...where the hell was the power-steering intake cap?

On the other side, of course!

Unable to reach it from where he stood, Greg had no choice but to go around. His calf felt like it was on fire at this point. The bandage Joel had wrapped was caked with blood. The adrenaline was not helping to slow the bleed. But Greg had bigger problems to focus on.

He climbed the engine and unscrewed the cap. Immediately, he dumped the entire first bottle into it. Immediately, he could smell the leakage. As the bottle emptied, he started loading the next. He couldn't risk losing control of the vehicle when he made his run.

"Come on, drink it up," he growled at the truck.

Arnold watched the thrashing bodies roll over dead after being pumped with lead. He had switched to semi-auto, sending one round at a time into the horde. A few of those bullets crashed into the Queen, successfully pissing her off. Joel was sure to keep out of reach, but not so high that the bitch would lose interest.

Arnold looked over at the intersection. No headlights. No roaring engine. It should've been done by now. "Is Greg jerking off over there, or what?!"

"How should I know?" Joel replied. He swerved to starboard, going behind the Queen. The chopper pointed east at the intersection. He could see the Deputy working on the engine. "He's there. Should be almost done."

Joel's eyes caught movement on the ground between the chopper and truck. He moved forward for a closer look.

"Sergeant? How many bullets are in that mag?"

"I'm down to ten rounds," Arnold replied.

"You're gonna need 'em. A bunch of drones have broken off from the group and are heading for Greg."

"Goddamnit," Arnold said. He clung to the seat harness as Joel whizzed the chopper over the colony, then lowered it to allow proper aim for the gunner.

Arnold centered the leading drone in the crosshairs, then fired a single round into its head. The squid slumped and twitched. He fired at the next one. It jolted, but kept going, its brain untouched by the lead. A second shot cemented its fate.

Seven rounds to go.

Arnold put two in the next squid, then panned left to aim at the next. "Fuck!" Right as he squeezed the trigger, the damn thing made a grasshopper leap, causing him to miss. The next one did the same, though this time, Arnold was able to time his shot right. He fired as soon as it landed, rupturing its head.

The earth rumbled under intense weight. The Queen was advancing with haste, still determined to swipe the chopper from the air. Joel had no choice but to lead it to the north, or else end up drawing her and her brood right to Greg. He banked to starboard, barely avoiding the reach of those whips.

"Ha! Nice try," Joel said.

Like a crab, the Queen scurried after them, only to stop abruptly. She cocked her body back several meters. Joel watched the bizarre movements, only to notice the springing motion of some of the small drones heading for Greg.

Joel ascended. The creature made its leap.

"Hold on!" he yelled to Arnold, who strapped himself into his harness.

One of the tentacles struck the hull, ripping the landing skates from the chopper. Alarms flashed on the control monitor. Gauge needles whipped back and forth. Red lights flashed in the fuselage.

Baring teeth, Joel struggled to keep the machine in flight, while simultaneously getting out of reach of the beast. His efforts resulted in a catastrophic spiral which took the chopper to the east. A yank on the joystick successfully pulled the nose up, but failed to level the chopper completely.

"Cover your head!"

The chopper smashed down and rolled. Rotors hit the dirt and broke into dozens of projectile daggers. The chopper rolled repeatedly like a log, settling a few hundred feet east of Crabb Road.

For a moment, Greg couldn't move. The shock of seeing the chopper smash down overwhelmed him. He tensed, half-expecting to see the thing burst into flames. Luckily, it didn't. Joel managed to control the crash just enough to preserve the integrity of the fuselage. Whether it was enough for the occupants inside, he couldn't tell.

The Queen resumed her eastbound campaign, with less than three-hundred yards to cover before passing the intersection. The sound of claws on gravel drew Greg's attention to the other side of the engine. A dozen or so creatures were coming right at *him*.

Immediately, he slammed the hood shut, then fell backward as one of the creatures hauled itself over the truck. Landing on his back, he pulled his pistol and put several rounds into the beast. As its corpse drooped over the hood, another crawled around the front. Greg put several rounds into that beast, killing it. He could hear the others advancing. He got to his feet and stumbled for the vehicle.

He had to stop that horde. He HAD to.

Greg reached for the passenger door, only to stop and shoot another drone poised on top of the truck. The slide wasn't locked back yet—there were still bullets in his mag. How many, he had no idea.

Movement to his right drew his attention to the drone propped on the hood. Greg shrieked and fired the few remaining rounds right as the thing sprang. It absorbed the bullets mid-leap, dying right as it crashed into the Deputy. Its dead weight struck like a battering ram, knocking Greg several feet back. The world spun. His chest felt tight, as did his legs and abdomen. He groaned, then gasped after seeing the dead creature lying on top of him. The momentary relief of knowing it was dead disappeared. Several more creatures were advancing toward him. Greg aimed his pistol and fired. Nothing. The gun was empty.

The creatures closed in, the one in front revealing its stinger.

"No!"

Lost in a world of desperation, he kept squeezing the trigger.

Gunshots echoed overhead. The drone exploded into a fountain of blood. All at once, the creatures behind it were struck by a hail of gunfire.

Tires screeched on pavement. Automatic rifles sent wave after wave of bullets into the horde. Then there was the sound of running feet, followed by Hannah Tyler's voice.

"Greg!"

She ran from the two Army personnel carriers, while the guardsmen continued to blast the remaining drones near the truck. She pushed the dead thing off of him with her boot, then helped him to his feet.

"Lazing around on the job? Who do you think you are? A night-shift worker?"

"Very funny," he groaned. They ran to the truck together. "We only have minutes left before I'm unable to drive this thing in any direction but a straight line. Who's in charge of this unit?"

"Sergeant Major?!" Hannah called out. Bankowski, after directing some guardsmen to the crash, ran to her.

"You injured, Officer?"

Greg looked at his leg. "It can wait. Sergeant Major, you have any C4 explosives to strap to this tank?"

Bankowski's face wrinkled. "You going to attempt what I think you are?"

"That's right."

The Sergeant Major glimpsed at the advancing horde. There was no time to talk about how crazy this idea was. Besides, the Michigan National Guard Adjutant General had already committed to this plan.

"One explosive should do the trick." He rushed back to the truck, got a C4 explosive, and stuck it on the tank. "Detonator's armed. All I need to do is hit the button once this thing is close enough."

"Do it *right* as this truck gets within a few yards of the Queen. Remember, we're not trying to kill her at this moment."

Hannah shook nervously. "Greg? You sure you want to—"

"No time to argue," Greg said. "I'll bail out once I've got it lined up." He climbed into the semi, then dug around in the glove compartment. Like many of the trainees in his trucking days, the driver had a spare set handy. He started the truck and floored the pedal.

He drove it past the intersection, then past the crashed chopper. After another hundred yards, he found level ground where he could angle the truck without plummeting into a ditch.

Guardsmen set up fifty-caliber machine guns and began blasting away at the horde and the Queen. Two Guardsmen helped Joel, Arnold, and the unconscious N.E.C.T.O.R. pilot from the chopper.

"I'm alright," Joel said, brushing the medic's hand away from a scrape on his forehead.

"Hey, Joel! You survived!"

Joel saw Wilkow standing by the Army personnel trucks. He looked back at the medic. "On the other hand, you have any morphine?"

Greg made a wide turn, circling the truck back and lining up with the Queen. She was five-hundred feet off the intersection and closing fast. Already, the steering wheel was getting stiff. It was now or never.

He stomped on the accelerator, launching the truck like a rocket. He opened the door, only to be assaulted by the wind. He leaned out, keeping one hand on the steering wheel. The truck crossed the road and entered the bumpy farmland on the other side. Several creatures formed a barrier around the Queen, who coiled her front tentacles in preparation to do battle with this new enemy.

Greg looked at the ground rapidly moving beneath him. "Oh, what was I thinking?" He closed his eyes, tucked his head down, and dove. He struck down and bounced repeatedly. He felt ribs crack, his joints sprain, and his bandage rip away. Cursing repeatedly, he propped himself up on his knees, saw the truck continuing on toward the Queen, then sprinted as fast as he could in the opposite direction.

Bankowski watched the truck smash through the barrier of squids, bursting their bodies into jelly. The final stretch of distance closed within the span of a heartbeat. A hundred feet...fifty...twenty-five... Bankowski triggered the explosive. Ten thousand gallons of gas combusted at once, sending a fiery tidal wave splashing over the Queen and her loyal cohorts. What was once lush green farmland was now a hellish river of flame. Moving fireballs zipped about, only to fall over and die after a few meters.

The Queen fell backward. Her tentacles lashed at the fire, unable to brush this strange 'enemy' off of her body. Her face was lost in the flame, as were her four front tentacles. The rear appendages deflated their musculature, allowing flexibility for the arms.

Immediately, hundreds of drones swarmed around her. Many climbed over her, only to be encased in the very fire which was killing their Queen.

Several guardsmen rushed out into the field and helped Greg behind the defense line. Medics waited with proper equipment, ready to get stitches and bandages on his calf.

"Greg? You alright?" Hannah asked.

"Just in desperate need of a beer," Greg replied.

"That's on *him*." Bankowski pointed at Wilkow. Together, they watched the Queen roll over in agony. The troops assembled underneath her, guiding her back away from the fire. Her front tentacles were completely black and deflated. Her head was marred in black, oozing blood and other disgusting fluids. Her functional tentacles were also severely scorched, unable to lift her immense bulk.

"What's that smell?" Joel asked.

"She's letting out a distress signal," Wilkow said. "She's alerting the rest of the colony."

"Damn, Officer, it worked," the Sergeant Major said. "Well done."

"He needs to get to a medical center, pronto," the medic said.

"Aww, don't I get to watch the fireworks?" Greg said.

"We'll record it for you," Arnold said. "But the medic's right. If Joel hadn't tied that bandage around your leg, you'd have bled out by now."

The Queen continued to flail. Like a mountain of fire, she barrel-rolled, crushing several of her subordinates in the process. Slowly, the fire subsided. The Queen fluttered on the ground, slowly crawling away from the burning truck. Her abdomen pulsed, filling the air with chemicals.

"We got her. She's not going anywhere," Wilkow said. He looked to the sky at the numerous Blackhawk helicopters rushing to the scene. Miniguns fired at squids that branched out from the main group. Like shepherds, they herded the squids near their mother.

"Keep them at bay," Bankowski said. "Do NOT fire at the Queen. I need eyes on the activity on Quincannon and McGrain Streets. Is there any movement?"

"The horde is moving, sir. They're vacating, going southeast."

"Good. Let them. They're moving in on the Queen. Shoot any that move too far from the main group, but otherwise, let them move in. Get in touch with the Command Center in Alpena and give them the target coordinates." Bankowski climbed into one of the trucks, then snapped his fingers at the group. "Let's pull out. We don't want to be here when the party starts."

CHAPTER 30

Over the course of the next two hours, Air National Guard units monitored migrations traveling from Peanut Lake and the surrounding areas, to the farmland near Zolciak. Armored divisions surrounded the area, monitoring the Queen and the surrounding colony. During the time the military had to wait for the colony to gather, they had to fend off three attacks, in which artillery had to be used to drive the creatures back.

By nine p.m., the event made international news. The eyes of the world were fixed on Michigan. Talking heads on the news cycles were already circulating ideas of how many other invasive species lurked beneath the crevasses. Questions rose regarding how many passageways existed, as well as the threat of future invasions. Internet forums were overloaded with the scrambled texts of frightened civilians, demanding that every lake be investigated, and every crevasse be sealed.

****

"I've been to Lake Superior so many times in my life. I've been to the Great Lakes Aquarium. The Aerial Lift Bridge. The Two Harbors Lighthouse. I tell you, I've never seen the lake so dead in my life."

"Nor have I. I was at Lake Erie two weeks back, and there were boats all over the water. We just saw the images we've gotten. It's dead, even for this time of night."

"We've gotten reports from private locations all over the state. Crooked Lake Resort in Clare County reports two dozen cancellations and five early departures."

"I guess that leaves the question of where we go from here. Clearly, we can't risk another outbreak. The military barely managed to contain this one."

"It's clear, Carley, that this organization, N.E.C.T.O.R. will be put on the stand to address these concerns. My understanding is that they want to explore the world below. I don't think people will be so keen on having these expeditions take place. I think they'd rather keep the underground lake where it is—underground."

"There'll be a lot of discussion about this in the upcoming weeks. We still don't have an overall death toll yet. Reports are still coming in of places these things have taken over in the brief time they were ashore. There might be bodies under the crevasse that'll never turn up again."

"It's terrible. I don't understand how these things—what's that? To all of our viewers, we've just got confirmation that the National Guard is about to launch its strike against the Queen and colony. Do we have our aerial shot?"

"About time," Greg said. He leaned up in his hospital bed. The so-called cushion was the only thing worse than the pain in his leg. He heard the knock on his door. "Come in."

Hannah stepped into his room. She wore a fresh uniform, though her face and hair were as much of a mess as before.

"How are you feeling?" she said.

"I should probably be asking you that," Greg replied. "I can see the fun hasn't stopped since we got here."

She smirked. "Your leg okay?"

"Doesn't hurt as much now, thanks to the drugs. My head's feeling a tad better, now that the talking heads are done." Greg pointed at the monitor. "The National Guard's about to launch their strike."

The television showed aerial footage from a news helicopter. From high above, the creatures literally resembled ants in the way they moved about.

"There's not an inch of farmland that can be seen," Hannah said.

"God only knows how many are still in the underground lake," Greg replied. "Where's Wilkow?"

"In the ER with Joel."

"How's he doing?"

"Took a few bumps in the crash, but he'll be okay," Hannah replied.

"And Arnold?"

"Already back on the road. He'll be working all night. Still trying to do a head count of all the Troopers lost during the invasion. Something I'll be doing once I get out of here tonight."

They heard footsteps in the hall. The door swung open, making way for an enthusiastic Mike Wilkow. Immediately, he looked at the television.

"Oh, good. I didn't miss it."

"Thanks for knocking," Greg said. Joel followed him inside.

"Howdy. We're about to take off. Of course, the Doc wanted to watch the fireworks first," he said.

"Shh," Wilkow said. They could hear the intense sound of fighter jets. "Now, if the dumb reporters could keep their commentary to themselves, we might actually find out what's—oh, there it is!"

In the blink of an eye, the colony was consumed in a fiery explosion. A half-mile of farmland was reduced to a smoldering cinder. The mountain of mass that was the Queen was instantly flattened. More missiles and bombs pummeled the surrounding area, ensuring that all stragglers were eliminated in the strike.

"Good lord," Joel muttered.

"Well, at least we know what to do now in case they ever strike again," Hannah said.

Wilkow shook his head. "That's the worst part about it, actually. We were VERY lucky, all things considered. The only reason the Queen came up was because Major Sierra detonated the bombs in her nest. Otherwise, she simply would've sent wave after wave after wave of her warriors to the surface, until this area was completely taken over."

"So, if another colony of these things were to ever appear..."

"We wouldn't have the luxury of drawing them to their mother," Wilkow said.

Greg leaned back. His headache was already returning. "So, where do we go from here?"

"As Joel said, we're about to head back to Rodney. There's a lot of work that must be done." Wilkow offered his hand to Greg and Hannah, who shook it.

"The government will probably have you guys searching for new pathways, I imagine."

"They will, for sure. But that's only the tip of the iceberg."

"What are you planning on doing?" Hannah asked.

Wilkow smiled. "I'm planning on going down there. We keep losing the drone signals. The granite is too thick. Plus, there might be some electromagnetic interference. Whatever the case, we need physical bodies down there to study this world beneath the crevasse."

"You're gonna face public backlash," Greg said.

"Science always does," Wilkow replied. He shook their hands again. "Good luck around here, and good work. If you're ever in Clare County, hit us up."

"Good to meet you, Doc," Greg said. He then shook Joel's hand. "You going down there with him?"

"Ha!" Joel exclaimed. "After learning about these things? I'm not so sure."

"You said the same thing about joining N.E.C.T.O.R. and coming up here," Wilkow said as he stepped into the hallway. Joel rolled his eyes, then shook Hannah's hand.

"Take care."

"You too," Hannah said. Joel followed Wilkow out into the hallway, his voice echoing all the way into the room.

"Don't expect me to go down there."

"Oh, come on. Can't be any worse than when you parachuted into—"

"Another false age reference out of you, *you'll* be in the crevasse— without a submarine."

Greg and Hannah smiled. The Sheriff went for the door. "I'll check on you in the morning. If you need anything, just shoot me a text. Goodnight."

"Oh, wait! On that note…" Greg leaned up. "Before you go, there is something I really need."

Hannah stopped. "Yes?"

"For the love of God, I need a cup of coffee."

Hannah smiled. She could use one too. "Be right back."

The End

CHECK OUT OTHER GREAT DEEP SEA THRILLERS

THE BREACH
by Edward J. McFadden III

A Category 4 hurricane punched a quarter mile hole in Fire Island, exposing the Great South Bay to the ferocity of the Atlantic Ocean, and the current pulled something terrible through the new breach. A monstrosity of the past mixed with the present has been disturbed and it's found its way into the sheltered waters of Long Island's southern sea.

Nate Tanner lives in Stones Throw, Long Island. A disgraced SCPD detective lieutenant put out to pasture in the marine division because of his Navy background and experience with aquatic crime scenes, Tanner is assigned to hunt the creeper in the bay. But he and his team soon discover they're the ones being hunted.

INFESTATION
by William Meikle

It was supposed to be a simple mission. A suspected Russian spy boat is in trouble in Canadian waters. Investigate and report are the orders.

But when Captain John Banks and his squad arrive, it is to find an empty vessel, and a scene of bloody mayhem.

Soon they are in a fight for their lives, for there are things in the icy seas off Baffin Island, scuttling, hungry things with a taste for human flesh.

They are swarming. And they are growing.

"Scotland's best Horror writer" - Ginger Nuts of Horror

"The premier storyteller of our time." - Famous Monsters of Filmland

CHECK OUT OTHER GREAT DEEP SEA THRILLERS

SHARK: INFESTED WATERS
by P.K. Hawkins

For Simon, the trip was supposed to be a once in a lifetime gift: a journey to the Amazon River Basin, the land that he had dreamed about visiting since he was a child. His enthusiasm for the trip may be tempered by the poor conditions of the boat and their captain leading the tour, but most of the tourists think they can look the other way on it. Except things go wrong quickly. After a horrific accident, Simon and the other tourists find themselves trapped on a tiny island in the middle of the river. It's the rainy season, and the river is rising. The island is surrounded by hungry bull sharks that won't let them swim away. And worst of all, the sharks might not be the only blood-thirsty killers among them. It was supposed to be the trip of a lifetime. Instead, they'll be lucky if they make it out with their lives at all.

DARK WATERS
by Lucas Pederson

Jörmungandr is an ancient Norse sea monster. Thought to be purely a myth until a battleship is torn a part by one.

With his brother on that ship, former Navy Seal and deep-sea diver, Miles Raine, sets out on a personal vendetta against the creature and hopefully save his brother. Bringing with him his old Seal team, the Dagger Points, they embark on a mission that might very well be their last.

But what happens when the hunters become the hunted and the dark waters reveal more than a monster?

CHECK OUT OTHER GREAT
DEEP SEA THRILLERS

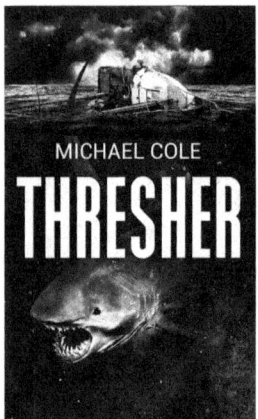

THRESHER
by Michael Cole

In the aftermath of a hurricane, a series of strange events plague the coastal waters off Florida. People go into the water and never return. Corpses of killer whales drift ashore, ravaged from enormous bite marks. A fishing trawler is found adrift, with a mysterious gash in its hull.

Transferred to the coastal town of Merit, police officer Leonard Riker uncovers the horrible reality of an enormous Thresher shark lurking off the coast. Forty feet in length, it has taken a territorial claim to the waters near the town harbor. Armed with three-inch teeth, a scythe-like caudal fin, and unmatched aggression, the beast seeks to kill anything sharing the waters.

THE GUILLOTINE
by Lucas Pederson

1,000 feet under the surface, Prehistoric Anthropologist, Ash Barrington, and his team are in the midst of a great archeological dig at the bottom of Lake Superior where they find a treasure trove of bones. Bones of dinosaurs that aren't supposed to be in this particular region. In their underwater facility, Infinity Moon, Ash and his team soon discover a series of underground tunnels. Upon exploring, they accidentally open an ice pocket, thawing the prehistoric creature trapped inside. Soon they are being attacked, the facility falling apart around them, by what Ash knows is a dunkleosteus and all those bones were from its prey. Now...Ash and his team are the prey and the creature will stop at nothing to get to them.

www.ingramcontent.com/pod-product-compliance
Lightning Source LLC
Chambersburg PA
CBHW071508170626
46811CB00007B/2772